What A Spinster Wants

Also by

Rebecca Connolly

The Arrangements:

An Arrangement of Sorts

Married to the Marquess

Secrets of a Spinster

The Dangers of Doing Good

The Burdens of a Bachelor

A Bride Worth Taking

A Wager Worth Making

A Gerrard Family Christmas

The Spinster Chronicles:

The Merry Lives of Spinsters

The Spinster and I

Spinster and Spice

My Fair Spinster

God Rest Ye Merry Spinster

Coming Soon

Spinster Ever After

What a Spinster Wants

REBECCA CONNOLLY

Phase Publishing, LLC
Seattle

Phase Publishing, LLC first paperback edition
May 2020

ISBN 978-1-952103-09-4
Library of Congress Control Number 2020906427

Cataloging-in-Publication Data on file.

Acknowledgements

To beloved Scotland in all her rich, wild beauties. I first fell in love with you over a decade ago, when the magic of your beauty bestowed itself in an almost heavenly fashion I will never forget. That love only deepens as time passes and my visits increase. Please adopt me. I will beg.

And to the Cheesecake Factory for being the site of this series' birth. Also because cheesecake rules. Seriously, though.

Want to hear about future releases and upcoming events for Rebecca Connolly?

Sign up for the monthly Wit and Whimsy at:

www.rebeccaconnolly.com

Prologue
London, 1818

"*A*re you sure about this, mistress?"

Lady Edith Leveson exhaled a painfully slow breath and turned from the dirty window of her drawing room, lowering the hand she had been waving. She pressed her tongue to the roof of her mouth, thinking hard before speaking her thoughts aloud.

"No. No, Owen, I am not sure. Not at all, in fact."

The burly man folded his arms, his common clothing doing nothing to establish his role as butler. Or footman. Or whatever position he had in her household.

What little could be considered hers in the household.

"Then why, mistress, would ye agree to receive them?" Owen demanded, his brogue somehow more pronounced than usual when he was irritated. "Ye've made yer wishes aboot living quietly known enough to us, an' if I'm understanding things aright…"

"You were listening to the conversation?" Edith queried with interest as she interrupted him.

Owen wasn't the slightest bit perturbed by the accusation. "I listen to every conversation that goes on here. Habit, and one I'm no' likely to abandon just yet."

Edith's smile faded as she nodded with reluctant understanding, memories of the last few years flashing and darting through her mind with breathtaking agony. She would have been lost if not for Owen, and his determination to come with her from Scotland for the wedding. When her family had insisted that he return with them to Inverness, he'd resigned his position with them to join Edith's new household.

However brief her marriage had been, Owen had never given her any indication that he wished to return to Scotland.

"Yer family gave you no reason to return to them," he'd once said. "Ye might as well remain while ye can."

And remain she had. They both had.

Owen had been more father and brother to her than her own father and brother had, and she wouldn't have considered him staff if he hadn't insisted on it. Something about having his pride and knowing his place.

If it would keep him listening to her conversations and protecting her from all possible harm, she'd let him have whatever position he wanted.

"So, you also ken what was said between myself and Lieutenant Henshaw," Edith said with a stern look.

Owen only nodded. "Aye. Seems a fair thing; I'd be obliged if ye'd agree to it."

Edith exhaled roughly, shaking her head. "I feel pitied, Owen. I didna come to London for its condescension, ye ken."

"I dinna think Miss Georgiana Allen or Miss Isabella Lambert are the pitying kind, mistress." Owen moved further into the room and glanced out the window, where the carriage could still be seen in the distance. "Nor the lieutenant, mind."

That might have been true, but offers of friendship and an almost adoptive sibling role seemed too fortuitous for a poor widow without connections in London. Whatever Lieutenant Henshaw had told her, the idea that her brother, Lachlan, had asked him to take care of her here was laughable.

Lachlan had no care for Edith. He'd proven that all too well.

"If ye feel so, mistress, I ask again: why receive them?"

Edith sank onto the divan near her, an embarrassing cloud of dust rising from it as she did. "I couldn't help it, Owen. It's been an age since I've had friends. I thought perhaps it might make my situation more bearable, and…"

She couldn't bear to finish the thought, not even to the person she trusted most on the earth.

And if things got worse, she did not want to endure it alone.

Chapter One
London, 1820

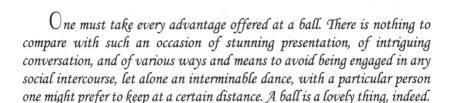

One must take every advantage offered at a ball. There is nothing to compare with such an occasion of stunning presentation, of intriguing conversation, and of various ways and means to avoid being engaged in any social intercourse, let alone an interminable dance, with a particular person one might prefer to keep at a certain distance. A ball is a lovely thing, indeed.

-The Spinster Chronicles, 15 August 1816

Lady Edith Leveson sat on the faded brocade of her couch, seething as she stared stonily out of the filthy windows of her London townhome. She couldn't tell if her face was devoid of color or shining with an excess of it, but she knew her complexion was currently altered, and not favorably. But when the alternative was to release her currently clenched fingers and let them give in to the impulse to scratch the eyes out of the man sitting in the straight-back chair next to her, an altered complexion would have to do. After all, the devil in the chair was holding her purse strings and insulting her in the same breath with which he propositioned her. It was not an unusual tactic for him, only the most blatant.

She flicked her eyes back to him, her stomach curling uncomfortably within her.

"Naturally, as you bear such an unfortunate label, I will not lower myself to the disastrous depths of marrying you," Sir Reginald was saying, his tight features pulling tighter still with an attempt at a placating smile. "However, I see no reason why this untoward tendency of mine to find such filthy Highland leftovers to be a delicacy of marvelously attractive prospects truly should not avail itself in less legally binding ways." He wet his lips once, then again, his narrowing eyes travelling the length of her.

Shapeless garment that her dress was, it apparently was not unappealing enough. All that work for nothing. Simms would be so disappointed.

Edith kept her expression, color changing as it might have been, free from further reaction.

"I do not think that would be wise, Sir Reginald."

A crease formed in his brow, then faded quickly as he folded his hands across his lap.

"I would be more than generous, Lady Edith, when we come to an arrangement in this regard. And you, as I am sure you are aware, are in no position to be particular, should you wish to have any place or position in Society. I control your future and reputation."

"I know," Edith murmured as a wave of nausea washed over her.

"You live on my stipend," he reminded her. "I own this house. I could cast you out in a moment, strip you of all your funds, and see to it that every door in Society would be barred to you. Would you really like to chance what you think would be wise against what I could offer? And what I can take away?"

"I know verra well the limitations of my finances, thank you, Sir Reginald," Edith snapped, her brogue rolling out, as it tended to with her temper. "And the power given you by the law and your cousin's inheritance. You do not, however, have authority over my free will."

"Yet." Sir Reginald smirked, not at all put off by her reaction. "But the time will come, my dear, when you will choose to do what I request, and that will be a day of great victory for me."

Edith sank her teeth into the flesh of her tongue, the sharp pain bringing tears to her eyes as she glared at her life's jailer, villain, and threat. If only the Almighty had endowed her with the power to take life at will, she could be free of her shackles at this moment.

Alas, she was not so blessed, and the druids in her family line had not transferred their abilities through the generations. No power from on high, no gifts from her heritage. Nothing but the wit in her mind and a law that crippled her freedom.

And the plan she would begin this evening, if this creature would only leave her in peace.

"I do hope that you will begin to show yourself in Society, Lady Edith," Sir Reginald told her as he pushed his wiry frame to his feet. "It would be a shame for you to be so confined as to be without friends or connections."

Edith found herself flinching at the edge to his tone, the sneer she could hear as well as see. She wasn't without friends or connections, but for her present situation, she might as well have been. Sir Reginald controlled everything in her life but her friends, and if he knew who her friends were or what their connections were, he would have found a way to intervene.

To ruin it all.

He had done it before.

She managed to contain her disgust long enough for Sir Reginald to bow and leave the tatty drawing room, not even waiting for her to rise and bid him farewell, as he usually expected her to do. When he had gone, Edith sank back against the couch and covered her face, her hands trembling slightly.

"I'd off him if ye'd let me, mistress."

Edith exhaled a laugh and glanced over at the large, hulking Scot in the doorway. "I'd let ye, if we wouldna have to flee from the law."

"We?" Owen raised a brow at her, folding his arms. "There'd be no need to include yerself in the affair, mistress. I'd desert my post at yer side and take matters into my own hands, leaving you innocent as a wee babe."

"Well, that would hardly do for me," Edith informed him, sitting forward with a sad smile. "I'd be lost without you, Owen, so this entire conversation is moot."

Owen grunted softly. "If only himself were moot."

Edith smirked at the wry comment. That undoubtedly would have cleared things up for her, if not several other people, as well.

Her late husband's cousin was the heir to all holdings, though the only one of real value was the estate in Hertfordshire. Reginald possessed all the same narcissism and arrogance that Archie had been

5

known for, but without any hope of the same charm, and he was hellbent on claiming every advantage the legacy had to offer. Including the wife of its last holder.

His desires had pushed her out of Haidh Park, just as she'd begun to make the place feel like home, and now he had followed her to London. Her already diminished finances, thanks to Archie's vice-like will and ruthless solicitors, were tightened further still by Reginald, which he loved throwing around her neck like a noose.

The house she lived in, ramshackle and rough as it was, belonged to him, every square inch; it was by his wishes that she wasn't out on the streets, as he frequently reminded her. He was quite content in the townhouse he'd had for years, and it suited him to have her in his debt.

Months of searching for available homes she could afford in London had proved to Edith just how pitiful her finances were.

She couldn't afford anything.

There was nothing of her dowry to be spoken of, her father hadn't made any provisions for her, and with virtually nothing to her own name, all that Edith could claim were a few dresses, her grandmother's pearl combs, and the thoughts in her head.

Everything that she had brought to her marriage was still everything she had. The only thing she had gained in her widowhood were her friends. And they knew nothing of this.

Yet.

Edith rubbed at her brow, sighing heavily. She would have to tell them soon. The secrets that had been her constant companions for the last few years would not be kept secret for long, now that Sir Reginald had come to London.

There was no telling how they would respond to the news. She had no fear of upsetting any of them, more a fear of them raining down chaos upon London itself.

Charlotte Wright alone could be horrifying.

It was one of the things that Edith loved most about her, and the rest of the Spinsters.

Although now that she thought of it, only Charlotte was truly a spinster now. The others had married, and some had started families. The Spinster Chronicles still circulated as regularly as they ever did, and with just as much popularity, but the unifying aspect of spinsterhood was waning fast.

Edith had never qualified in that way, being a widow instead of a spinster, but the others hadn't seen that as an impediment. Apparently, being married for the course of one day wasn't long enough to truly be considered wedded in their minds.

If they only knew.

She shook her head now, straightening and smoothing her skirts. She had nothing to lose anymore and worrying wouldn't solve anything. Bravery and boldness had never been the hallmark of Lady Edith MacDougal, especially when she'd married and become Lady Edith Leveson. Still, they would need to be her constant companions now. She would never survive her plan if she turned retreating and wilting, as she once had done.

She could never be that again.

"Mistress," Owen prodded from the doorway. "The time?"

"I know." Edith rose without grace or airs and faced Owen with resignation. "Am I daft to be getting on with this, Owen? Tell me truly."

Owen shrugged his burly shoulders, his expression not changing. "There's a verra fine line between daft and daring, mistress. Given what cards ye've been dealt, I'd say ye'd be daft to do otherwise."

There wasn't much hope or encouragement in his voice, but there was a certainty that steeled her spine and lifted her chin. "Verra true. I'll just go up and let Simms flick me out for the evening. If you would have word sent to Lord and Lady Ingram, they have offered to fetch me, so I would not have to use my own carriage."

"We don't have a carriage," Owen grunted.

A wry smile slid across Edith's lips.

"Rather a convenient offering, then, wouldn't you agree?"

She swept past him and made her way up the stairs, craning her neck back and forth, the strain of the interview with Sir Reginald making itself known in a profound way.

It would lend itself to a headache later, which could be a convenient excuse to leave the Martins' ball when it all became too much. Provided Grace and Aubrey could be convinced to quit the gathering. They were far and away more social than she would ever be, and this was widely rumored to be the last important gathering before the Season began. It would be the place to be for those fond of such affairs.

Grace and her husband also happened to be some of the most considerate and caring individuals Edith had ever known. She had passed the winter with them in Derbyshire after Christmas, which had been a lovely retreat from her cares, though the return to them afterwards had been all the more brutal for the respite.

The Ingrams wouldn't know that, though. All they knew was that Edith was attending this evening and that this Season would be different from the rest.

She was through with hiding from Society now.

She had to be.

"Nothing too ornate, Simms," Edith said with a sigh as she pulled her arms free of her drab gown, watching as her maid began to pull every outdated ensemble from the bureau. "Simple elegance."

Simms paused and gave her a bewildered look. "With my options, madam? I'll be fortunate to manage elegant, though simple is easy enough."

Edith frowned at the plump woman who had become both friend and advisor over the years. "I meant my hair."

"I'm sure you did, madam." Simms shook her head, pulling a familiar gown from the bureau.

Edith froze at the sight of it, her throat clenching. The boulder in her stomach rolled from end to end, and she swallowed as she stepped out of her dress. "That one."

Simms looked at her with wide eyes. "Madam... I was only moving it. I wasn't..."

"That one," Edith said again, more firmly. She cleared her throat and nodded. "It's the finest I have, and only the finest will do tonight."

Her maid looked at the gown, faded from what it had once been, but still elegant in its cut and color. "It's at least three years out of fashion, madam."

Edith blinked, her hands settling on her hips as she eyed it. "Will it be that noticeable?"

Simms pursed her lips in thought. "I could pull some tufts in the sleeves, and if we tighten your stays, your form might give you more of the shape that is fashionable…" She tilted her head from side to side. "If I set your hair aright, madam, it might be passable."

"I will take elegantly passable," Edith said with a wry smile. "If it can be done quickly. More permanent alterations will have to wait."

The pair of them got to work, and the tighter set of stays was uncomfortable enough that Edith's nerves vanished in the face of them. The yellowed cream of the gown appeared almost intentional due to the pristine condition of the fabric, and the black dots scattered along it had lost none of their luster. Black lace overlay on the sleeves and bodice, draping elegantly down to tufts at the hem, added to the evening elegance that had attracted her to the gown in the first place.

She hadn't known it would be her wedding gown. Black in her wedding gown should have warned her off the affair.

Not that she'd had any say in the matter.

"There's not time enough to do what I would wish to your hair, madam," Simms sighed as Edith sat before the looking glass. "I daren't even attempt curls…"

"Just plait and pin what you can," Edith insisted, smiling at her in the glass. "Plaits are always in fashion, no?"

Simms chuckled and undid the massive length of Edith's dark hair, her fingers flying through the tendrils as she worked it into a simple, sturdy, somehow still elegant updo. It would hardly be worth commenting on in any Society gossip sheets, nor would it get her any envious looks from other ladies, but it wouldn't scandalize any, either.

She would accept that gladly.

"The pearl combs, madam?" Simms asked with a satisfied exhale as she stepped back from her work.

Edith shook her head and rose quickly. "Not tonight. This will suffice." She turned to take the gloves from Simms, wincing slightly as a muscle in her side clenched against the stays. "Just my cross, please."

The delicate gold necklace was fastened around her neck, and Edith felt the weight of it pressing against her chest, comforting rather than weighing her down. She'd had it since she was twelve, and it was one of the few things from home that did not make her sad to see.

A knock at the door made Edith jump, and she turned, swallowing hard. "*Crivvens.* What am I about, Simms?"

"Trying to make the best of the abysmal, madam." Simms offered a sad smile. "Best be about it, lest you get cold feet."

Edith sighed and grabbed the cloak from her bed.

"I've no time for cold anything. Not anymore." She turned from the room and hurried down the stairs, nodding silently to Owen as she passed and receiving a silent nod in return.

The carriage was tastefully elaborate, but she barely blinked at it as she took the footman's hand and entered it, grinning at the others within.

"Good evening," she said.

"Lady Edith," Aubrey, Lord Ingram, greeted from one side of the carriage, inclining his head. He gestured to the seat opposite him with a warm smile. "I assumed you would wish to sit beside my wife for the duration of the ride."

"She is the fairer of the pair," Edith pointed out as she settled in beside Grace, Lady Ingram, and took her hand.

"No argument on my part." Aubrey tapped the ceiling, and the carriage jolted forward, the lump in Edith's throat mirroring it.

"You're both very amusing. Really." Grace snorted softly and patted the hand she held. "Nervous, Edith?"

Edith laughed through clenched teeth. "Is it obvious?"

Aubrey hissed. "The grimace gives it away, just a touch…"

That earned him a scolding look, which made him chuckle.

"I was never properly out, you know," Edith admitted. "Never been at ease with being on display, as it were, and tonight, I am displaying myself for all of London."

"If it is any consolation," Grace said, her dark eyes darker in the shadows of the carriage, "the Martins don't know all of London."

Edith laughed once. "I dinna ken if that helps me or no'. I have need of Society, yet I dinna wish to be among Society."

"Why the need, Edith?" Aubrey asked, his tone less teasing now. "You never have before."

"Aubrey…" Grace murmured with a shake of her head.

Edith swallowed once. "It is simply time. Much as I hate to admit it." She turned to Grace and changed the conversation to her recent article on the fading trend of fichus.

Not that she cared all that much about fichus, or any other kind of fashion, but she would ramble about anything rather than divulge her reasons at this moment.

Thankfully, the Martins did not live too far into the fashionable part of London. They had arrived and were being greeted by servants taking their cloaks before she could pretend to find one more interesting detail about something so minuscule.

Aubrey offered an arm to Edith, Grace on his other side. "Everyone is being announced, Edith. Now or never."

Her pulse lurched, and she clenched her free hand into a fist as though it would steady her. "Never isna much of an option, my lord."

"I've told you how I feel about you calling me that," he muttered with a slight nudge to her side that did more for her comfort than she could say.

Edith managed a smile for him, then caught Grace looking her over with a small furrow between her fair brows.

"Wrong?" she asked with a sigh, looking over herself.

"No, no," Grace replied hastily, reaching over to take her hand. "You look lovely. It's just a bit... worn."

"I know," Edith groaned, adjusting the skirt. "It was all I could think to wear, and I'm nervous enough as it is."

"It's not noticeable," Grace assured her with a smile. "I'm just overly observant."

"I'll say," Aubrey muttered good-naturedly, kissing Grace's cheek quickly. "Edith, you look lovely, don't let Grace make you anxious."

Edith smiled at him. "Thank you, Aubrey."

Grace grinned, even as she rapped her husband across the chest sharply. "No matter, Edith, you're perfect. Next time, we'll spruce you up a bit more, but for your first night, it's perfect."

Edith bit the inside of her cheek as Aubrey escorted them in, as it was not the time to tell Grace that this was the very best this gown would ever get, or that this was the best gown she owned.

"Lord and Lady Ingram," the majordomo intoned formally. "Lady Edith Leveson."

Edith received several stares as her name was announced, and the whispers and titters she'd always feared started. Her cheeks flamed, and Aubrey kept his hold on her firm.

"Easy, Edith," he murmured so only she and Grace could hear as they smiled for all. "You were going to make a splash no matter what. Just smile through the opening; we're making straight for the Sterlings."

She tucked her chin a bit in a discreet nod, and followed his directions, catching sight of a cluster of their friends, all of whom were watching with almost the same comical look of concern.

When they reached the group, Edith exhaled slowly. Camden Vale chuckled and leaned closer to her. "Bravo, Edith, that was grand enough."

"I shook the entire time," she muttered, taking the glass that he handed her.

"Nobody noticed," Charlotte Wright assured her with a smile, looking every inch the heiress that she was. "You're the topic of quite a few conversations, you know."

"So I heard," Edith replied, wincing a little.

Georgie Sterling gave her a shrewd look. "What was that for, Edith?"

Her husband was just as attentive, and suddenly, everyone in their group was looking at her expectantly.

Edith pursed her lips a bit and exhaled again. "I'm a widow recently out of mourning with diminished circumstances. What do you think they are talking about?"

Several of them winced at the thought, and Lieutenant Henshaw glowered. "Surely not, Lady Edith. Perhaps you misheard."

Edith gave him a look. "I misheard nothing, Henshaw, I can assure you."

He frowned slightly and huffed in exasperation. "I hate Society," he muttered to the rest of them.

Aubrey nodded once. "We'll fix it, Edith."

Edith wanted to tell him that was impossible, even for Lord Ingram, but then the music started up, and he looked at his wife for a long moment. "Contrary to custom, my love, I'm not going to open with you."

Grace smiled easily. "I thought you might not."

To her astonishment, Aubrey turned back to Edith. "Lady Edith, if I might have the pleasure?"

Her mouth dropped, and Camden plucked her drink from her hand, laughing softly. "What? After what I just told you people are saying? Sir, they will think that—"

He took her hand in his and steered her from the group. "They most certainly will not. My tempting wife aside, I am a complete monk, and everybody knows it. And don't 'sir' me, not after you've seen me in my nightshirt."

Edith bit back a laugh, the recent memory from their winter together diffusing her anxieties long enough to rid her of her refusal.

They proceeded with the dance. Edith had forgotten how she enjoyed dancing. It had been so long since she had felt such pleasure in something so simple, or since she had allowed herself to do so.

Since she had felt free to do so.

Chapter Two

There is a very short distance between opportunistic and desperate. Sometimes very short indeed.

-The Spinster Chronicles, 7 November 1815

Graham Hastings, Lord Radcliffe, found balls tiresome.

Not all the time, and certainly not in all circumstances, but as a general rule, he could be counted on to not particularly enjoy himself when forced to attend one. He wasn't exceptionally sociable, nor was he especially skilled as a dancer. The combination of dancing and socializing, therefore, was one he tended to avoid, and would likely have completely shunned had he the power to do so.

But responsibility, duty, and expectation kept him from his wishes more often than not, and so he would attend where he must with all due politeness, however he might long for the comforts of home and a good book.

He was a sixty-year-old man in the body of one much younger, his brother had always teased.

Matthew had been one of the few people in the world who had teased him, and the warmth with which he had done so had been merely an extension of his equally warm personality. It had been only fitting that his wife Penelope had been his perfect match, and that the pair of them had hosted some of the few parties that Graham had actually attended of his own free will. Everyone had adored Lord and Lady Radcliffe, and invitations to their events at Merrifield Park had been widely sought after.

Unfortunate, then, that the new Lord Radcliffe was practically a hermit, and that Merrifield had not seen a party or event in two years.

At least not an event of joy.

Graham would have refused the title if there had been an individual of value able to take it up. His closest relations with the abilities already had titles or bore responsibilities enough to make the title too much of a burden to take on.

He knew that for a fact; he'd checked.

So here he stood, Lord Radcliffe in all his glory, or lack thereof, in the ballroom of Mr. and Mrs. Martin, who claimed to be old friends of the family, though he couldn't remember seeing them more than twice in his life. He was growing used to people approaching him and claiming connections from the past, and he wondered what they truly intended by it. His fortune was impressive, but it was hardly the greatest in Society. He was a viscount, it was true, but there were higher-ranking titles in the room at any given moment.

He was unmarried; that, he feared, was the card that trumped them all.

His brother's death had left Graham one of the most eligible men in England, a hefty price to pay for something he had never, and could never, want. To lose his only brother and gain so much seemed cruel.

It *was* cruel.

And being here, though hardly comparable to all that, was rather cruel, too.

Trapped in conversation with someone whose name he couldn't recollect, and didn't care to, Graham focused on keeping his expression blank. He couldn't manage attentive, so he would have to hope that blank could be mistaken for polite listening.

A movement just beyond his conversational companion caught Graham's eye, and his attention flicked to it with almost comical desperation.

A woman in a cream gown covered with black overlay moved through the crowded room with determination, a furrow creasing the fair skin of her brow, accompanying lines etched at the edges of her presently thin lips. He recognized her from the entrance she'd made, and how the entire room had hushed and then begun to titter at the sight of her, but all he could remember was that she had entered with the Ingrams.

Despite his respect for Lord Ingram and his wife, it seemed a crime not to recollect their guest simply because it was easier to remember them.

She moved without care for her surroundings, which earned her some bumping and jostling, but she wasn't put off by it. She didn't speak to anyone, and every few paces, she would glance over her shoulder.

Strange. Fleeing an assignation or simply avoiding dancing with an intolerable partner?

Whichever it was, the beauty was doing the job admirably, and he hoped she managed to succeed in her efforts.

"Then, I met the Prince of Wales," the man before him continued to drone on, bringing Graham's focus reluctantly back to him.

"Before or after he became our King?" Graham queried with a tilt of his head.

The question seemed to catch his companion off guard, and he looked at Graham with mild alarm.

"It is, after all, only a few short months since King George III passed on," Graham continued, unable to help himself. "His Majesty at present, lately the Prince of Wales, can be called such no longer. His heir, as you know, is the Duke of York, who has not taken up the heir presumptive title of Prince of Wales, so could not be referred to as such. So, I must say, there is some confusion as to the identity of the man you met, and the timing of when you met him."

"I…" The man frowned and lowered his eyes to the floor, and Graham had to hide a smile.

Was this a case of a poor memory, or a story spun out of fiction instead of recollection? However boring the tale was, the outcome of this particular quandary was suddenly of great interest to him.

There was a sudden but insistent tapping at Graham's right shoulder then, eliciting a glower at having his current amusement interrupted. He glanced over his shoulder, raising one brow.

The fleeing beauty stood there, hands wringing together, eyes wide as she stared at him, the startling green of them striking something in his chest like the dinner gong might have done.

"I know it isna done, sir, and I know we are not acquainted, but if ye could please dance the next waltz with me, I should be most grateful."

Graham blinked, the rushed but musical Scottish brogue of the woman shifting his impression of her further in his mind. He ran over her words again, translating quickly before responding.

"You… are asking me to waltz?"

She nodded her dark head almost frantically. "Yes," she replied at once, her tone matching every other sign of panic he'd seen. "Please."

What in the world was this? The rules of politeness at a ball couldn't have changed all *that* much of late, and despite this woman's obvious beauty and captivating speech, he wasn't about to waltz on demand. Especially someone else's demand.

He snorted softly. "As you said, madam, it is not done, and I have no desire to refute that." He began to turn back, but the sleeve of his coat was suddenly seized, which was a feat, as it was perfectly tailored for his frame.

"Sir, I am no' being forward," the beauty insisted, clenching his sleeve with a tightness that he'd have been hard-pressed to break. "I am no' attempting to trick or trap you—"

"Madam, this is not personal," he interrupted firmly. "I have no desire to waltz with anyone this evening."

A bit of a whimper escaped her as she looked back over her shoulder, and Graham took the opportunity to attempt to shake her loose, but it was fruitless. She returned her attention to Graham and took a half step closer to him, the vibrancy of her eyes that much more stirring for being closer.

"I have no plans, sir," she told him, her voice tight, "and I have no designs on you or any man here. I hate to force you into something you clearly have no wish to do. But no one has claimed this dance, which was no' an issue until this moment, and I absolutely must dance with someone right now, and you were the closest man. I am out of time, so please will you haud yer wheesht an' take this waltz with me?"

Graham looked at her for a moment, searching the earnestness and tension in her fair face, his irritability fading despite his reluctance to do what she asked. Then, his eyes moved off her to a motion over her shoulder.

A thin, angular man in overdone finery was coming towards them, his eyes fixed on the back of the woman before Graham, and the expression on his face resembled one Graham had once seen on a weasel. The various pieces of the story fell into place without any context for verification, and he stiffened. His brow creased, and his eyes were back to the beauty, his decision made.

Exhaling softly, he covered her hand on his sleeve and turned towards the dance floor as the strains of the next waltz struck up.

"My dance, I believe," he announced, his tone somehow back to that of his normal one.

He heard the *whoosh* of her exhale as they moved and found himself leaning closer. "I take it you just told me to stop talking?"

"More or less," she forced out, seeming almost to stammer with it. "And less politely."

"I figured as much."

Her hand trembled in his hold, and he heard a noise resembling that of a sob coming from her, one of her gloved hands going to her throat.

"Steady," he murmured as he took her waist in hand, leading her into the first motions of the dance. "Nobody is that emotional to dance with me."

"Then this will be a first," she managed, forcing a smile. "You must accept that you are my hero tonight."

He grimaced as he turned her, his movements feeling easier than he remembered a waltz being. Perhaps not thinking about the waltz made it easier to dance the waltz.

"I am no hero, madam."

His partner glanced over his shoulder, then shivered and shook her head. "Yes," she said softly, "you are."

For agreeing to waltz with her? Hardly. He'd seen her pursuer, but what could he have been but an interminable annoyance on the dance floor, as he'd previously suspected her to be fleeing from? He gave her a strange look, then turned the pair of them so he could see where she had been looking.

The weasel was standing there, glaring at them both, a sneer fixed on his face, something superior and threatening in his stance and gaze.

Graham glared back, feeling the desire to pull the woman in his arms closer to him purely out of instinct.

"I don't like him," he informed her after a moment.

She looked up at him so quickly her head nearly hit his chin.

"You know him?" she whispered hoarsely.

"No," he said with a shrug, "but he looks too much like a weasel for my taste. And he forced me to waltz."

The woman bit her lip, a half-laugh escaping. "Which is worse, sir? The weasel or the waltz?"

Graham looked back down at her, noticing for the first time the intoxicating scent of lavender and pine rising from her, as if sprung into being from her fair skin. Her lips were no longer pulled tight, as when he had first seen her, but relaxed and full, somehow flushed from the recent pressure of her teeth upon them. The hint of a smile she was giving him now, the first he had seen her bear, created an unspeakable sensation in the back of his knees that raced into the base of his spine.

Waltzing had never done that for him before.

"I really cannot decide," he admitted, surprising himself with the answer.

Perhaps not the words themselves, as the weasel was undoubtedly the more evil of the two, but given his distaste for any kind of dancing and the unsettling nature of his reaction to it, he found himself unable to be entirely the gentleman in his response at the moment.

His partner grimaced. "I do apologize for that."

"You don't make the waltz an evil, madam," he assured her as gently as a man could gruffly do. "As I said before, it is not personal."

She nodded once, somehow managing the weakest of smiles. "As I said, if I had another alternative, I would have chosen it." Her eyes glanced over his shoulder once more, then darted to the buttons of his waistcoat, her hold on his hand clenching painfully.

There could be only one thing that rendered a woman bold enough to demand a dance with him into a trembling leaf, and that was fear. In this case, it could only be fear of the weasel. What hold did he have over her that enabled him to do this to her? He couldn't bear it. Somehow, he couldn't.

"As fine as my waistcoat is, madam," he said, attempting at the teasing that had come so easily to his brother, "my eyes are up here."

"Give me a moment, please," she whispered weakly, color fading from her cheeks, the trembling in her frame growing worse.

He sighed and dropped the hand he held, moving his hand to her back. "Come," he urged roughly, applying just enough pressure to urge her on, leading her from the floor.

"Where are we going?" she asked, resisting a little.

Graham took her hand in his, worried that the hand at her back wouldn't be enough to steady her. "You are suddenly unwell, and I am being gentlemanly and escorting you away," he said simply, once again keeping his tone and expression polite. "Put a hand to your head, sway a little, and tell me where to deposit you, if you would be so kind."

She did as he suggested and looked around, then indicated a group in a corner.

He could have laughed but thought it would be inappropriate in this moment. Still, there was something to be said for the irony of the situation.

Her friends happened to be some of the few members of Society he could tolerate.

Captain and Mrs. Sterling, Mr. and Mrs. Vale, Lord and Lady Ingram, and Miss Charlotte Wright all watched the pair of them approach warily, concern in each of their faces. They were joined by Mr. and Mrs. Morton, whom Graham knew by sight, though not especially intimately himself. Still, the gathering was one he could approve of, and if the looks forming on the faces of the gentlemen there were any indication, he need not have further concern for her safety.

He released her as they reached the group and bowed to them as a whole before turning to face her as she took the hand of Lady Ingram. "I am sorry our waltz was cut short, madam," he murmured, though he was not especially sorry to be done with dancing, beautiful though she was. "I hope you are feeling yourself soon."

20

He bowed once more, then turned and moved through the crowd with ease, which seemed unfair, given the trouble his mysterious dance partner had endured during her flight from danger. Graham's step faltered slightly as he realized with a jolt of guilt that he had not learned her name during the course of their dance together. He could blame the abruptness of their first meeting, and her unconventional method of finding dance partners, but the truth of the matter was that he'd had plenty of time to ask her name during the waltz and had failed to do so.

There wasn't much he could do about that now unless he wanted to ask around, but he wasn't one for gossip. There was enough undoubtedly said about him in certain circles that he did not want to know about, and if word got around that Lord Radcliffe was asking about a certain young woman, it would only harm them both. There would be no guarantee that the information he got would be accurate anyway. He did not have any close friends in Society, so there wasn't a chance he could trust anything he got by way of answer.

He could ask the Ingrams, he supposed, but he would not wish to raise questions or concerns on their part, either.

It was a bit of a mess, the politeness of Society. If he were more like Mr. Vale, he might have just come right out and asked, and to hell with the consequences of it. But Graham was not Mr. Vale, and he could not be. He was not carefree, nor was he able to do anything on a whim. Carefully organized, carefully constructed; that was what his life had been, and what he needed it to be again. The unknown had never been comfortable for him, and that had not changed with time or experience.

But what did any of this have to do with the identity of the woman he had danced with? What harm could there be in discovering her name? Why should anyone make something out of nothing?

Dancing with a woman without being introduced to her was not polite. Dancing with a woman whom he had not asked to dance was not polite. Making commentary on aspects of her life when he knew nothing about it was not polite. Inquiring about a woman's life without knowing her identity after dancing with her and learning more about her personal life would not be polite.

That would bring about comment.

And what of the weasel? Would Graham's intervention, or the questions he would hypothetically raise, bring more trouble where he was concerned?

Now situated against a wall across the room, Graham turned and took the opportunity to look back towards his dance partner, still facing her friends, her back to him.

The expressions on the faces of the group were unreadable, aside from the fact that none of them seemed particularly pleased.

What was she telling them about him? What did they know?

Why did he care?

He frowned to himself as he considered that question. Why *did* he care? He knew nothing about the woman except who she associated with, and that she had the weasel in her life in some capacity. Also, that she was Scottish, and her brogue was more pronounced when she was flustered.

A rather charming quirk of personality, though the circumstances surrounding it could hardly be less so.

He watched as she wiped at her face, as she leaned into Mr. Vale when he put an arm around her, and as she eventually made her way back out to the dance floor on the arm of Captain Sterling. She wasn't quite smiling, but it was close enough, he supposed.

Graham looked around the room, hoping to catch sight of the weasel to see if there was a similar reaction to the dance at present as there had been when Graham had danced with her.

Yet he could see no one particularly fixated on Captain Sterling and his partner. There were no scrawny men in overdone finery lurking at the edges of the onlookers, and there was nothing resembling a frown on the face of anyone present.

Had he left after the disappointment he had faced? Would he now make life more difficult for her?

"Radcliffe."

Graham blinked and looked up, surprised to see Lord Ingram there, his easy smile belying the tension evident in his frame. "Ingram."

Ingram gestured to the wall beside Graham. "May I?"

"Of course," he replied, though Ingram had already taken up position there and leaned against the wall with a show of casualness.

He said nothing, which made Graham more curious. The pair of them had never been close, though they moved in the same circles, and Graham would have been hard-pressed to call them friends. No one knowing Graham came to his side just for the sake of it.

No one.

"What can I do for you, Ingram?"

Lord Ingram exhaled a laugh and gave him a sidelong look. "I wondered how long it would take you to break the silence."

"Much as I respect you, sir," Graham said with forced ease, "we have never been close enough to keep company without words. Silence does not disturb me; only the reasoning behind it."

"Fair enough." Ingram indicated the dance now. "You see Captain Sterling there?"

Graham nodded, a slight smile forming as satisfaction hit him. "I do. Fine dancer, I must say."

Ingram snorted softly. "I'm sure he will appreciate the compliment, though I cannot vouch for his abilities myself. Now, look at the woman he is dancing with."

Oh, well, if Lord Ingram insisted.

He must say, looking at her now was far more enjoyable. She seemed more at ease, no doubt enjoying her freedom from the weasel. She was brighter, though he suspected there was still some lingering hesitancy there. What could that be? What kept her from enjoying herself here?

Why in the world did he care? And why did he keep coming back to that question?

"I see her," he grunted. "What of it?"

"You danced with her."

Graham scowled. "What of it?"

"You don't dance. Why?"

"Why don't I dance?"

Ingram practically growled beside him. "Why did you dance with *her*, when you do not dance?"

The question was an interesting one, considering Ingram's apparently close relationship with the woman. Surely, she ought to have given him some idea, if there was a question. Had he not seen the danger that Graham had seen? Did he not know about the weasel?

And if that were indeed the case, why should Graham be the one to betray secrets that were not his own?

"That, I'm afraid," Graham informed him with a sigh, "is between the lady and me."

"I don't accept that answer."

Graham slid him a wry look. "It is not my concern what you accept. That is the answer."

Ingram's frown deepened. "I have a significant interest in the well-being of that lady, Radcliffe."

"Congratulations," Graham replied without concern. "Is your wife aware?"

The jab was ignored, though Ingram's right hand formed a fist at his side. "My wife and I are both friends with the lady. I consider us family."

"That should make it easier to inquire of the lady as to what occurred during our dance." Graham smiled as politely as his temperament would allow at present, given the suspicion in Ingram's voice and the inquiry into his intentions.

He never took that sort of thing well.

"I want to know *your* reasons for the dance," Ingram demanded, apparently unwilling to let this go.

Graham straightened and turned to face him, grateful, for once, that his height was above the average. "The lady knows my reasons, Ingram, and if you do not know hers, you do not need to know mine. Good evening." He bowed and turned away, striding for the doors of the ballroom, having had quite enough of dancing and Society for one night.

Chapter Three

———— ⁓⁓ ————

A circle of friends is both a wondrous and dangerous thing. There are no secrets from one's true friends. Sooner or later, all secrets come to light under their influence, and heaven help you when they do.

-The Spinster Chronicles, 28 October 1816

The frequent gatherings of the Spinsters had never been something Edith had felt any apprehension about attending. Even in the early days, when she hadn't attended regularly, it hadn't been due to fear or reluctance, only her natural reserve and general mistrust of anyone and everyone. And attempting to hide herself from Sir Reginald's reach. Hiding in London was easier than one thought, as Edith knew full well. She'd been in London for three months before Lieutenant Henshaw, or the Spinsters, had known about her.

She bit her lip now, looking around her drawing room for a minute before starting her walk to Charlotte's home for the meeting, though there was very little structure to resemble an actual meeting in them.

"Mistress?" Owen called from the door.

Edith sighed and nodded, though Owen couldn't see her. "I ken, I'll be late if I dinna leave now."

"Nay, mistress. Ye've a visitor."

Owen's voice was closer now, and Edith turned to the entrance of the room, eyes wide, heart skipping several beats in sudden fear. "I've a what? Now?"

"You would prefer another time, perhaps?" a familiar voice asked in amusement from the corridor.

Edith swayed with overwhelming relief, one hand flailing for the back of the sofa near her as she attempted a swallow twice before succeeding.

Not Sir Reginald, then.

Anyone else, she could receive gladly, and the owner of that particular voice was always welcome.

The tall soldier appeared in the drawing room doorway with a rueful smile, dressed as any other gentleman in London would have been, and taking no notice of the state of her rooms.

He was very kind like that.

"Henshaw," Edith greeted with a quick bob of a curtsey. "I canna tell you how happy I am to see you."

"Really?" Henshaw grunted a laugh. "Seems to me you would rather I go so you can get on with matters most mischievous."

Edith put her hands on her hips. "Now, how did you know the Spinsters were meeting today?"

That earned her a genuine laugh, and Henshaw pushed into the room, coming over to bow before her and kiss her hand.

"How are you, Edith?"

"Well enough." She gestured to a nearby chair with a smile, and Henshaw moved to sit there.

"I'm not sure I like that," he told her with a frown as she also sat. "Well enough is not exactly glowing."

Edith shrugged a shoulder. "I rarely glow, as ye well ken. I've been worse, and I've been better."

Henshaw stared at her, the frown remaining. "Edith, what's going on?"

The somber note in his tone told her he knew more than he was letting on; the only question was how much did he know, and how much was he speculating?

She exhaled slowly and folded her hands in her lap. "Ye ken Archie's will didna leave me much to live on."

Henshaw nodded brusquely. "I do. Much as I have tried to argue that point, the solicitors have that locked at every bolt."

"Yer efforts have been most generous."

She smiled with real warmth at this goodhearted giant of a man that had taken her under his wing from the moment he had met her in London. He took such care of her, and she knew full well that had led to a great deal of speculation where the pair of them were concerned, yet he had never uttered a word of complaint about it.

"So…?" he prodded, and Edith shook herself from ruminating on his goodness.

"So," she swallowed once and forced a bland smile, "Archie's cousin, the heir, has come to London, and Sir Reginald… Well, he's rather cut from the same cloth, ye might say."

"How pleasant." Henshaw shook his head, exhaling roughly. "What does he want?"

Me.

Edith bit the response back and kept her strained smile where it was. "He's hemmed and hawed aboot, but it seems he's no' inclined to extend any generosity there. Which is as I expected, so I canna say I'm especially disappointed."

Owen watched her from the doorway, raising a brow at her. It was a very simplistic view of the situation, she knew, but there was nothing to be gained by going into the details of everything with someone who was powerless to change the situation.

"Yet you have decided to enter Society," Henshaw pointed out. "Officially. What changed? You were never so inclined before."

No, she hadn't been, and the truth of it was that she was not especially inclined now. She was only determined, and that changed everything.

Edith nodded once, swallowing again. "I ken that all too well," she murmured. "But I have decided that I've had enough of the men of the Leveson family dictating every move I make. I aim to change my situation by my own hand now, Henshaw, and I need Society to do that."

There. If that didn't make her plan clear to him, nothing would. She had just enough pride left to avoid stating anything more obvious, or more desperate, though she really was not above much anymore. Her finer associates might not understand that, which was why she would keep those details to herself.

But Henshaw nodded slowly to himself, his frown fading as his understanding sank in. "Edith, I'll say this once, and I hope you will take it as it is intended…"

She tilted her head in question.

"If it will do you any good at all, help in any way, I'll marry you."

The breath rushed out of her lungs at the offer, and her first thought was to adamantly insist against it, to laugh off his thoughtful nature, as she had so often done before. Henshaw had offered to marry Grace only last year, though he had been teasing, and she would not be surprised if he had offered the same to one of the other Spinsters at one time or another. He was the sort of man that knew the way of the world and the skewed nature of it. Yet, he would offer himself as a way to surmount such an obstacle, even if it were made in jest.

But there was no jest here, and it was that solemnity that kept her from reacting as that first thought called for.

Marrying Henshaw would solve everything. Absolutely everything. His offer was utterly genuine, without condescension or heroism, and made with what he thought a full understanding of her circumstances. There was no judgment, no prejudice, and no indication that he believed her anything less than capable of managing her problems on her own.

To alleviate her suffering, to give her peace of mind, this man would give up any of his own prospects for future happiness and marry her.

Her chest tightened, slowly clenching with emotion, and her eyes burned with the same. She smiled at him, beyond words for the time being, and wishing, faintly, that she could accept such an incomparable offer.

"Alas," she managed to choke out, "I dinna think I could allow that. It would break the heart of too many lasses, and for all my fondness for you, Hensh, I will insist that ye marry where your heart dictates, and no' your conscience."

"Not that many lasses, Edith," he assured her, smiling with more warmth than she deserved. "But thank you for giving me the courtesy of a moment's consideration. The offer will always stand, should anything change."

Edith nodded, swallowing hard. "Thank you."

The offer was a pointless one, for all its sweetness.

No matter what else changed, her decision in this never would.

"I hear that you danced with Lord Radcliffe at the Martins' ball last night," Henshaw said then, his tone and expression returning to his usual one. "I'm sorry I missed that."

"I didna mean to," Edith murmured, her cheeks coloring.

Henshaw chuckled. "How did you manage to get a dance with a man when you didn't mean to? I didn't know you were acquainted."

"We're not," she answered honestly, memories of the night before darting in and out of her mind at a rapid speed. "It was… a matter of chance. And he didn't want to."

Henshaw grunted, looking impressed. "Well, you can add your name to a very short list of women he has danced with."

That was curious, to be sure, and despite the distress she'd felt the night before, she could honestly say she was interested now.

"How short?"

He gave her a somber look. "Two others, that I know of."

Edith blinked at that, the answer settling on her heavily. How could a man who never danced give in to her demand for a waltz with relatively little fight? Granted, she had been quite determined, which was something that had once been a vibrant part of her nature, now long forgotten. She hadn't exactly given the man a chance to refuse her in earnest.

"Lord, did you say?" Edith murmured, wishing with some pain that she had tea at hand.

"You really don't know him, do you?" Henshaw chuckled and crossed one knee over the other. "Lord Radcliffe is a viscount. He inherited not long ago after a family tragedy. Everyone was devastated when we lost Lord and Lady Radcliffe like that. Merrifield will never be the same, that is certain."

Somehow, that seemed too much to hear, too much to think about. She had her own burdens to bear. The notion that her hero of the ball was also one to whom fate had not been kind weighed heavily on her heart.

Why could her desperate dance not have been with someone with the simplest of lives? She would never wonder about the life that sort of man led or feel sympathy that her actions might have added to whatever he bore.

"I dinna mean to inquire into his life." Edith shook her head, averting her eyes. "Poor man."

"You didn't. I offered it up, and it is common knowledge." He waited a moment, and when she made no answer or response, he spoke again. "Edith…"

She dragged her reluctant gaze back to Henshaw and found him smiling at her with some sympathy. "Yes?"

Henshaw's smile grew briefly. "Whatever you are thinking or planning, remember that you need only ask, and I will be happy to assist."

Edith found herself smiling back at him. "If I had any idea what I was thinking or planning, Hensh, I'd be pleased to include you."

He took her at her word, laughing again, then informed her of the food he'd had sent down to the kitchens, and invited her to accompany him to the theatre with their friends the following evening.

The theatre was not a ball, and there was no reason why Sir Reginald should attend the same night, especially with the other activities available to one during the Season.

She agreed, though her natural inclination was to remain at home and hide away from the world as she had so often done.

She could not do that now. More's the pity.

Henshaw left shortly after, and Edith stared after his carriage, her arms folded about her midsection in an almost protective fashion.

"I dinna ken why ye dinna jus' tell him, mistress," Owen remarked from somewhere behind her. "He's a right one."

"I ken he is," Edith murmured. "And tha's why I canna do it." She sniffed once and turned for the doors. "I'll be walkin' to Charlotte's now."

Owen grunted once. "I'll be some paces behind ye, as always."

She nodded in acknowledgement, then headed out into the damp London morning, her thoughts awhirl.

Lord Radcliffe. She hadn't meant to dance with a peer; she'd simply snagged the closest sleeve available to her and blurted out something desperate. The only thought in her head had been getting safely away from Sir Reginald in a manner that wouldn't earn her his wrath or punishment. He had been pursuing her for too long that night, her polite refusals meaning nothing to him, and the influence of too much of the evening's good wine had emboldened him. A dance with him could have ruined her before any plan had the chance to come to fruition.

Hence the desperation.

A desperation, which, unfortunately, surpassed any recollection of the actual person with whom she had danced. He was tall, he scowled, and he had dark hair. Beyond that, there was nothing in her mind to recollect Lord Radcliffe at all.

It seemed a shame to learn the name of the man from someone else, but to also doubt she would know him again should their paths cross once more. Hardly respectable, hardly polite.

So much for making a good impression with Society.

There wasn't much she could do about that, and there wasn't much she could say for herself. Her attendance at events would give her more opportunity to improve her abilities at names and faces when under impossible stress from Sir Reginald. However, she would seriously consider returning to Scotland if he began to appear at every event she attended.

The thought of her native land filled her with familiar pangs of longing, and she inhaled deeply, as if the stale London air could somehow match that of her beloved Highlands.

Home had ceased to be so for some time now, and her family would not welcome her back should she have appeared. Her mother alone, perhaps, and her younger sister if she were in the proper mood, but her father would turn her away at once. She had no fortune now that her husband was dead, and the family had wasted her dowry on a man who'd died before the ink dried on the contract.

Or so the latest letter from her father had said.

Her duty now was to find another husband and use whatever provisions Archie had left her to make the most of it. Edith didn't have the heart to tell her father that Archie had left her almost nothing and that she wouldn't be in a position to give her father the ties to Society he was seeking.

He might have told her to go along with Sir Reginald's schemes, for all she knew. He'd had no problem with selling his daughter to her first husband; having his daughter be mistress to a baronet might have been a capital idea to him. Provided she could benefit financially from the connection, and the family could, as well.

If only she had the means to return to Scotland without returning to her family. There would be so much freedom and joy in that. But freedom and joy were not in the cards for Edith at present, and perhaps not even in the future.

She would settle for security and self-respect. Maybe even security alone.

Edith shook her head and raised her chin as she approached Charlotte's home, knowing that her friend was rather inclined to looking out of the windows in anticipation of arrivals. She would never escape the meeting without interrogation if she were caught making anything less than a pleasant face.

She had a feeling there would be questions enough for her as it was.

Entering the grand house, Edith sighed to herself as she shrugged out of her worn cloak. The maids in the Wright household were well used to her tattered things and controlled their expressions accordingly. She never apologized for the state of her clothing, and they treated her as they did every other guest in the house.

It was a well-choreographed pantomime.

"If you'll follow me, Lady Edith," the friendly housekeeper said with a gesture towards the drawing rooms.

Edith refrained from reminding the woman that she knew full well where Charlotte's favorite drawing room was, having been to the house almost weekly for a year or so. She needed to keep all the good connections she could, even if they be servants in the grand houses. If Sir Reginald got his way, or if Edith had to resort to less respectable means of securing her future, these guardians of the entrance would be key to not losing every connection Edith had in the world.

The sound of at least a dozen doors slamming shut rang in her mind in the imagined scenario, and she shuddered at hearing it.

"Lady Edith Leveson, Miss Wright."

Edith blinked hard and forced a smile as the drawing room was suddenly before her.

"Thank you, Mrs. Evans," Charlotte chimed, rising from her seat within the drawing room and turning to face them with her usual grin, a dimple appearing in her left cheek. "Edie, I was worried you weren't coming."

"Edie?" Grace cried from her spot in a chair. "Wherever did that name come from?"

Edith snickered as she entered the room, watching as Charlotte rounded on Grace with an exasperated expression that spoke of a very entertaining conversation prior to her arrival.

"I was simply trying it out, Grace!" Charlotte insisted. "It could be an adorable shortening of her name that we use, as her friends."

Grace looked utterly bewildered and turned her attention to Edith. "Has anyone, in the whole course of your life, called you Edie?"

"Not since I was a wee thing," Edith said simply as she sat in the vacant seat on the sofa next to Prudence Vale, taking a cup of tea from her. "Thank you, lass. This is much needed."

"Of course," Prue murmured. She leaned closer and whispered, "They've been arguing the virtues of familiarity for a quarter of an hour. Heaven alone knows why."

Edith nodded as she blew softly on her steaming tea. "One can only hope Charlotte finds a point to come to very shortly."

Prue snickered a soft laugh, then groaned a little, one arm wrapping around her visibly swollen abdomen. "Merciful days..."

"The bairn?" Edith smiled gently, eyeing her friend's wince.

Prue nodded, biting her lip briefly. "I know I still have some time before my confinement, but this little one isn't behaving very well."

"That's because the child is Camden Vale's," Charlotte announced, interjecting herself into their conversation, as per usual. "You cannot expect an easy time of it."

Georgie Sterling snorted softly, bouncing her infant son on her lap. "That's so comforting, Charlotte. Really. Prue feels much better now."

"Well, it's her own fault," Charlotte insisted as she flopped herself inelegantly down in a chair. "Having your child in the middle of the Season. Really, Prue, you'll be off to your country estate in a matter of weeks, and then that will be it. Why could you not have arranged your confinement for the winter?"

"Arranged?" Izzy Morton laughed, setting her tea down to avoid disrupting it. "Charlotte, there is no scheduling something like this."

Charlotte huffed and shook her head. "I refuse to believe that. As adorable as the young Miss Vale will undoubtedly be, I shall take some time to forgive her for taking my friend away during the Season."

"Miss Vale?" Prue repeated with a small smile. "Cam would be delighted if that came to be."

"So would I," Georgie announced. She bounced her giggling son again, quirking her brows. "She has a suitor waiting."

Edith pursed her lips playfully. "The lass might have two Sterling suitors vying for her. Didna Janet and Lord Sterling have a strapping lad, as well?"

That earned her a scowl from Georgie. "How dare you! Thomas is far and away the better candidate for Miss Vale. Henry may be my son's cousin, but he is not suited for the match. Ask Elinor when she arrives next week, she will agree with me."

"Don't talk about that girl," Charlotte insisted, raising a hand. "I do not have it in me to call her Mrs. Sterling, and I may never accept her husband as I have the others. It is too monstrous."

Prue sighed heavily, rubbing at her belly. "Charlotte... Hugh Sterling has s-sent us all some very f-fine letters of apology, and he apologized again at the wedding breakfast. You've s-seen him yourself, and he was most p-pleasant."

Charlotte shook her head, her lips pulling down. "No, I cannot allow that. He has misled Elinor, and she is a fool for being so duped. The wedding was beautiful, and they were wise to keep it small, but that is one redemption I cannot see as valid."

"Then it is a mighty fine thing that you were not chosen to be the Almighty," Georgie snapped, smiling to soften the blow. "None of us would make it to heaven if you were. I like Hugh as he is now, and I will even go so far as to say he is good for Elinor."

"I am not hearing this." Charlotte covered her ears and pointedly looked out of the window.

Grace waved a dismissive hand. "It must be exhausting to have that much indignation about so many things. Are you all going to the theatre tomorrow? Henshaw asked Aubrey if we had a box, and we do, naturally, but…"

"I would love to attend," Kitty Morton chimed in, her soft voice ringing out clearly, surprising Edith.

A gentle beauty, Kitty was the shyest creature Edith had ever known, but in the last year, she had begun to come out of her timidity. Not entirely, but just enough that Izzy may wish to warn her husband, Kitty's brother, about the potential for an increase in suitors this Season.

The poor man would not take that well.

"Edith? Will you go?"

Edith inhaled sharply as she looked around, belatedly realizing the room's attention, including Charlotte's, was on her.

Wetting her lips, she answered carefully. "I would be delighted, provided I can find something suitable to wear."

Kitty's brow furrowed. "Why should that be an issue? You always look lovely."

Edith could have hugged the girl for her innocence, if not for her lack of understanding of fashion. "I took an inventory of my gowns this morning, and there isna much suitable for fine occasions. I can do well enough by visitations and outings, but for balls and parties, I should attract more attention for standing out in a poor way, no' a good one."

"What do you mean 'something suitable'?" Charlotte asked suddenly, giving her a look of scrutiny. "You have plenty of lovely things, you have always looked well."

This was not the direction this conversation should have gone, yet there was no escaping it. Not with that glint in Charlotte's eye and the mixture of interest and concern she saw on the other faces in the room.

She met Charlotte's eyes briefly. "I *had* lovely things. Once. I still have those lovely things, but it has been a few years since I've worn them, and they are out of fashion now. You have seen me wear what is appropriate for small gatherings and evenings with friends, no' the finery and elegance expected in Society."

"Can you not afford new things?" Grace asked as she set her teacup down, her eyes widening. "Your gown the other evening…"

Edith swallowed and shook her head without saying a word.

"What about updating the things you have?" Kitty suggested. "I know that Mrs. Forrester down on Bond Street can do some lovely things to old gowns."

Again, Edith shook her head, her cheeks beginning to warm. "I canna afford that, either."

All the ladies looked at each other, then back at her.

"Edith, how bad are things?" Georgie asked softly.

So long as the topic of discussion remained on her finances, and did not venture into other distantly related parts, she could bear the explanations she must give.

If things turned, however…

Edith bit her lip and felt tears start to rise as the strain of burden began to weigh more heavily on her. "I told you all from the beginning that I was in diminished circumstances. But the truth of the matter is that I have almost nothing, and it will only get worse. If I don't succeed this Season, I will be ruined beyond any hope of saving."

The silence in the room was complete, and somehow, her next swallow was the only thing to break the moment.

"Succeed how?" Izzy whispered.

"Ruined?" Prue repeated.

"Edith, I think you had better tell us everything," Grace said sharply, coming to sit beside her and take her hand. "All of it. From the beginning."

Edith nodded, though her mind spun as she quickly separated the complicated matters of her life into what she would share and what she would not.

Slowly, she told them about the loss of fortune with Archie's sudden death, the loss of Haidh Park, the sharply reduced number of servants, the condition of her house in London, her current finances, and Sir Reginald, but only insofar as to his forcing her out of York and now descending upon her in London. His offers, behaviors, and threats would remain unspoken, her secret shame, and were it not for her need to gain security in some manner, she would have left him out entirely.

Even so, shame filled her with every admission, until she was nearly ill with it.

"Why didn't you tell us?" Charlotte cried, looking a little shaken. "We could have done something!"

"There's nothing to be done," Edith assured her softly. "I've tried, both in York and discreetly since my arrival here. I cannot refuse Sir Reginald's coming to call; he could make so much more trouble. But he wields such power over my living."

"I can spare some additional servants," Grace said firmly. "And Aubrey will find you a bodyguard."

"Tony will *be* your bodyguard," Georgie ground out, looking murderous as she set her son on the rug to play. "Or call in his old company. Henshaw and Sebastian…"

"Sebastian will go," Kitty and Izzy said in almost an identical tone.

Edith laughed a watery laugh, shaking her head. "I have a servant that will do very well for that. You all know Owen, he has been with me for ages, and he is from home. He takes care of me as well as he can."

Grace nodded. "Good. But I will still send some servants."

"I cannot pay them," Edith reminded her.

She smiled with genuine warmth. "That's all right. I can."

Prue sat forward as much as she was able. "Cam might be able to help your situation, Edith. His brother-in-law, Mr. Chadwick, has some high connections and works closely with Mr. Andrews. They are very familiar with the law and have a great many connections. Will you permit me to ask them?"

Edith nodded, feeling as though she might cry. "But discreetly. I cannot have Sir Reginald suspecting that I am working against him. He has all the power now, and I have none."

Prue grinned a bit mischievously. "Oh, you have plenty of power, my dear. Between us and our husbands, who, by the way, are already quite protective of you, you will be quite powerful, indeed. Cam has already very passionately quashed some rumors and declared his loyalty and support of you, and I am delighted by it."

Edith grinned at her sudden energy, as well as her complete lack of stammer. She was most touched by Prue's words. "I hoped your husband might think of something, Prue."

"He will," she vowed, smiling at the mention of him. "He has a very intriguing view of the world and is quite brilliant. I think many would be shocked at how much he holds back. He will stand by you, Edith. He may even sleep on your doorstep to assure himself of your safety."

Edith laughed at the image of the tall and rascally Camden Vale sleeping outside her door.

What nonsense!

"I shall be grateful for his help, however he may apply it," Edith told Prue, taking her hand. She looked around at her friends, her heart tightening in her chest. "From any of you, and any of them." She exhaled a short breath, then ventured to admit one thing more. "The fact of the matter is that I must find some protection this Season. If that means marriage again, so be it. If I may only find protection by the law, that will suit, as well. But the more my circumstances are made known, the more dangerous the path will be."

A shudder rippled down her spine at the image of Sir Reginald from the morning before.

Charlotte and Grace looked at each other; then Charlotte smiled almost deviously at Edith. "Then, we have our mission."

"Do you?" Edith queried, more wary than worried.

Charlotte nodded once. "We have to find you some gowns. Mine are upstairs, and I feel sure the others have some they will donate to the cause, as well. We'll make a tour of our homes for the afternoon. Come with me now, and we'll get them fixed up so you may come to the theatre tomorrow and outshine us all."

Chapter Four

P roper attire is important in making the intended impression. It should be taken most seriously.

-The Spinster Chronicles, 24 September 1817

"Why?"

"Because I said so."

"That's a terrible answer."

"It's the truth."

"How can you be sure?"

"I'm your valet, my lord, not your chambermaid. I do believe I know what I am doing."

Graham scowled at the almost painfully thin man currently tying his cravat.

Morgan had been with him for years, and apart from the fact that it involved the death of Graham's brother, having this master inherit the title had been the greatest day of his valet's life. Ages of trying to get his master to dress with more style and finery rather than the country simplicity he doted upon, and now, finally, he could have his way.

He had not stopped being superior yet, and it was getting rather tiresome.

If he didn't trust Morgan to keep him from embarrassing himself in matters that Graham was completely ignorant of, he'd probably have thrown him out by now. His valet was also one of the few people in the world who hadn't shifted his treatment of Graham because of the change in his position. One could always count on Morgan to be steady, honest, and resoundingly himself.

"Fair enough," Graham grunted. "Just don't make me into a peacock, I beg you."

Morgan gave him a harsh look. "When have I ever done that to you, my lord?"

Graham tugged at the green waistcoat he was currently wearing. "It is entirely possible this will be the first time."

There was a quick flick of linen as the last fold in the cravat was made, then Morgan pinned it safely together. "A waistcoat of a distinct color beyond that of a neutral palette is not a feather in the cap of a dandy, my lord. The higher circles of Society have all manner of finery in their attire, and in varying shades, I might add. The cut of waistcoats most fashionable at present is far more daring and closely fitted. I am even told, my lord, that brocade and silks have started to become more prominent. I have no doubt you will barely be noticed."

"Where in the world did you hear all that?" Graham asked, craning his neck in discomfort against the noose of linen he now wore. "I don't take you out and about to various events, and I can't imagine you attending in disguise."

One corner of Morgan's mouth quirked as he brushed the coat Graham had worn earlier. "I read it in the Spinster Chronicles, sir. They wrote about it just last week."

Graham groaned and ran a hand through his once carefully combed hair. "You aren't serious."

"As the day is long, my lord." Morgan shrugged and returned the coat to the bureau.

"You dress me according to the opinions of spinsters?" He scoffed and moved to examine his appearance in the looking glass, grunting softly at the practical dandy he saw. "Who are they to have made their mark on the fashionable decisions of Society?"

Morgan barked a laugh. "You still haven't read them, have you, sir?"

No, he hadn't, and to be perfectly frank with himself, he really didn't see a need to. From what he understood, it was nothing more than a commentary on what was occurring in Society, and opinions on several topics by individuals who would otherwise have no bearing on anything of significance. He'd heard the articles were well written, even articulate, and that there was wit aplenty, which spoke well of the writers themselves. He had no reason to doubt they were ladies of the highest quality, but why should that render the reading of their column a requirement?

"My lord, you move in the same circles as the writers, and not all of them are spinsters now, you know."

"How fortunate," Graham commented blandly, trying to adjust his cravat just enough so he didn't feel so constricted by it. "This damned thing…"

"Don't touch it, my lord."

"It's fine. See?" He patted the fabric once and turned for his valet to see.

Morgan frowned with a sigh. "Yes, my lord, it appears you have not done too much damage."

"More's the pity," Graham grumbled. "What I wouldn't give for Merrifield and no schedule."

A knock at the door prevented whatever answer Morgan was going to give.

"Come," Graham called, turning in anticipation.

His tall and stately butler appeared, somber expression fixed on his thin face. "My lord, you have a guest in the drawing room. Mr. Tyrone Demaris. He has agreed to wait upon your convenience."

Graham nodded once. "Excellent." He turned to Morgan. "Have you trussed me up sufficiently?"

Morgan grinned unreservedly and shrugged. "Well enough, my lord. You shall not be found wanting."

"Oh, good." He tugged at his ridiculously colored waistcoat and nodded at himself in the looking glass one more time. "Thank you, Wilson, I will see him directly."

Wilson nodded and turned from the room without waiting for Graham to follow, despite the fact that he did so. Graham smiled to himself at that. Wilson had served a proud line of Lord Radcliffes in his time, and Graham was never supposed to become one of them. Oh, he would serve Graham well, there was no question there, but he made no secret of the fact that Graham was not, and likely would never be, his favorite, or even his preferred Lord Radcliffe.

Graham didn't particularly care about such things, so it made no difference.

Most of the time.

Silently, they made their way down the corridor of family rooms, then down the moderately grand staircase, which was, thankfully, nearly adjacent to the drawing room in which Tyrone had been installed.

Wilson left them as soon as he'd announced Graham.

Graham shook his head and stepped forward to shake hands with his friend. "Sorry about that."

Tyrone Demaris, tall, dark, and tanned, only raised a brow. "Something off with your butler's supper, or does he always look so pleased to see you?"

"That is, unfortunately, his usual expression." Graham sighed and shook his head. "I'm not the Lord Radcliffe he wants."

"Ah." Tyrone clasped his hands behind his back with a wince. "None too pleased with the spare on the throne, is he?"

Graham smirked at his friend, raising a sardonic brow. "I'm none too pleased to be here, myself. I rather enjoyed being the second son. The relatively unfortunate one. But there is nothing for it, is there? No matter how much any of us wishes Matthew alive and well and fully in possession of the title, it cannot be."

"True enough," Tyrone grunted, rocking on his heels. "Only glad my brother James is engrossed in his role as Lord Eden and already has his heir. I find myself content to be relegated to the background and ignored. I shall endeavor to make the most of it for us both."

"Thank you," Graham replied dryly. "Most kind. Really." He exhaled and fidgeted with his cravat once more. "Shall we go? The sooner we get there, the sooner it can all be over."

Tyrone chuckled in his deep, low way and clapped a hand on his shoulder. "Hastings, you sound like a cantankerous hermit of seventy rather than a strapping man of nearly thirty. Shall I warn your valet that your cravat may double as a noose in the hallowed halls of the theatre?"

Graham scowled as they turned from the room and headed out to the carriage. "Don't tempt me. And I don't think you can call me

Hastings now."

"Someone has to remind you who you are beneath the title. Might as well be me."

Fair enough.

They loaded into the coach and were soon rattling off towards Covent Garden, and Tyrone distracted Graham from his foreboding thoughts, stupid though they were. It was only a night at the theatre, and he was not exactly being swarmed by desperate misses and their more desperate mamas to be matched up. He wasn't surrounded by fools and peacocks vying to appear part of his circle either.

Additionally, he wouldn't have to converse at all once the play began. He could safely admit that the theatre was a good deal better than a ball. If he could survive the more social aspects of the evening, the rest of it would be simple. Perhaps even enjoyable.

Not likely, but perhaps.

It wasn't far to the theatre itself, but the line of carriages once they were there was abysmal. Yet another reason Graham rarely ventured there, or to any great Society gathering.

Rather, why he'd *previously* rarely ventured.

The title needed to be taken seriously now that the mourning was over, and the self-imposed tutoring of his responsibilities was at an end. Part of honoring and upholding the title was sustaining worthy connections and crafting new ones, none of which were things with which Graham could say he was comfortable.

Why shouldn't he have become a hermit of sorts? Stayed away from London and Society as a whole? He could write letters and missives to all who might need them, acquaintances and connections, matters of business, as well as those of a more social nature. He was excellent at letter composition and would do the job creditably.

Was his presence really necessary when he was not inclined towards engagement?

"You can't run away," Tyrone murmured. "They have rules for that."

"Did Eden tell you that?" Graham asked with as much mildness as a man strangled by his own cravat can.

"He might have mentioned it. Once or twice. Every family gathering."

Graham sniffed a laugh as their carriage finally reached the entrance to the theatre. "You enjoy giving him grief over it, then?"

Tyrone flashed a rare grin in his direction. "Thrive on it, mate. I pride myself on preparing the best barbs in advance and seeing just what I can raise in him."

It was astonishing that the pair of them were friends at times, though they both shared a reserved, more serious nature. Graham would never have poked and prodded at Matthew over his title, though he had played a trick or two on him over the years. Graham was more droll than witty, while Tyrone possessed an abundance of wit, even if he also possessed reluctance to share it.

"So, this is why your father wishes you to find an occupation," Graham mused aloud as he followed Tyrone out of the coach.

His friend gave him a dark look. "That will be the end of your opinion on the subject, thank you very much."

Graham held up his hands in surrender. "Understood." He looked up at the theatre with a reluctant sigh. "Gads. Why are we doing this?"

"Because we're gentlemen," his friend replied without any enthusiasm or pride, "and someone at some time decided that gentlemen go to the theatre."

"Not well done, there."

"Not at all."

Nearly as one, they strode forward and moved into the theatre itself, their hats and cloaks being taken by the staff as they were directed to the elaborately furnished corridors where every other patron was currently milling about.

Graham fought to ignore the rise of perspiration forming on his brow the further within the bowels of Society's cradle he ventured.

It was fine. This was fine. People were fine.

Fine. Fine. Fine.

"I am well aware that you are just as reticent as I, Hastings," Tyrone said quietly, his mouth quirking as though he would smile, "but is it necessary to look so murderous? People will start to comment."

"Smiling is unnatural under such circumstances," Graham grunted by way of reply.

Tyrone made a low sound of amusement. "Did I say smile? If you will see, I neither smile nor frown. I simply exist. Yet, no one would fear me."

"Congratulations." Graham almost shook his head. His friend was not only just as reserved as he was, but he was oftentimes less prone to attending social events than Graham. How could he possibly have any commentary on Graham's expression, activity, or behavior in public?

The whole thing was ridiculous.

Why were they even here?

"What miraculous act has brought my cousin to the theatre?" a feminine voice said near them.

Graham felt himself smirking as Janet, Lady Sterling, crossed their path, her dark eyes flicking between the two men, her lips quirking in a smile.

"Lady Sterling, what a pleasant surprise."

"Pleasant is a matter of taste," Tyrone muttered, grimacing in the presence of his lovely cousin. "Shouldn't you be at home with the baby? Surely, it is too soon for you to reappear in Society."

Janet smiled pleasantly as though her cousin's surly nature amused her. "I am feeling quite well, thank you, Tyrone." She turned the smile up to Graham. "Good evening, Lord Radcliffe. Would you be so good as to explain the proper manners of a gentleman to my cousin? He seems confused on the subject."

Tyrone blustered beside him. "Janet, for pity's sake. Where is your husband?"

"Likely hiding from your thunderclouds, dear. They are really quite ugly this evening."

Graham bit back a snort of laughter at the bickering between the cousins, knowing full well that the Demaris family, extensive as it was, had some very strong bonds of affection. His own family was a small bunch, even all branches together, and their ties were not especially strong.

The fact that he and Matthew had maintained their connection as well as they had was something of a family anomaly.

And now that, too, was gone.

"Won't you join us in our box?" Lady Sterling offered with a faint gesture in the direction before them. "Francis isn't thrilled to be here, so the three of you can keep each other company while I enjoy myself."

"Why should tonight be any different?" Tyrone offered a heavy sigh and extended his arm to his cousin. "Lead the way, cousin."

Janet looped her arm through his, lifting a brow. "So gallant. Really. Quite touching."

Graham fell into step behind the pair as they continued their dry bantering while maneuvering through the crowds mingling on the outskirts of the theatre seats. They made their way to the box, and Janet paused just prior to entering, her attention drawn to something just beyond their box.

She hissed softly under her breath. "'Tisn't right."

"What isn't?" Tyrone asked, following her gaze.

Graham followed as well and saw, to his surprise, the woman he had waltzed with the other night at the Martins' ball. She was on the arm of Lieutenant Henshaw, a distant acquaintance of Graham's, but known well enough by sight, and neither the lady nor the gentleman looked particularly at ease presently.

"Henshaw's companion?" Tyrone suggested, sounding surprised. "What about her? She's lovely. Why should you disapprove?"

Janet's fan rapped her cousin's hand sharply. "Ty, I don't disapprove of her! She is just as lovely a person as she is a figure. That is Lady Edith Leveson, and she's finally coming out into Society in earnest."

Graham stilled, his attention now rapt on the lady, who was lovelier than his hazy waltzing memory had attested. There was a pucker between her brows that should not be there, for it marred her otherwise fair face, and the hold she had on Henshaw was clutching. Out of sheer instinct, Graham looked around them for the weasel, yet saw no sign of him.

Curious.

"She doesn't look particularly pleased about it," Tyrone observed, losing his previously light air.

"Do you see how the others stare?" Janet murmured quietly. "Look. Listen. She has somehow become an outcast without having been cast out. It's despicable."

Once Graham's attention had been called to it, the reaction from those in Lady Edith's presence could not go unnoticed. Wide eyes and whispers followed her; blatant stares and shameless gaping were her fanfare. Yet somehow, she held her chin high, though the tension there was just as visible as her beauty.

Tyrone grunted once. "What is her supposed crime, then?"

Janet shook her head, her glower potent indeed. "Marrying the wrong man, may he rot in torment. The rest is all speculation, but it does quite enough. At least she isn't without friends."

Graham nodded at her words, watching as Lady Edith and Lieutenant Henshaw were greeted by the Ingrams and the Vales, and Mr. Vale left no onlooker in any doubt how he felt about their behavior. Only then did he see any sign of weakness from Lady Edith. Her chin quivered, and her cheeks flushed, then she was escorted into their box by Lady Ingram and a clearly pregnant Mrs. Vale.

The men stood outside the box for a moment, conversing quietly, and Graham felt his interest pique as Lord Sterling, Janet's husband, joined that group, his expression as serious as the rest.

"Not in the box, then, Janet," Tyrone said unnecessarily, elbowing his cousin. "You were mistaken."

"I don't track my husband as if on a hunt," Janet protested. "Honestly, why should my being mistaken matter?"

"Your being wrong on occasion always bears additional emphasis, I can assure you."

Janet rolled her eyes and turned to Graham. "May I go in on your arm, my lord? I am currently seeking a replacement cousin."

Graham felt himself chuckle almost reluctantly, laughter in public not being his usual habit. "If it would please you, my lady."

"It would please *me* to have the arm of my wife for a change," Francis, Lord Sterling, announced as he reached them. He grinned easily at Tyrone and shook his hand, then turned to Graham and sobered only just. "Lord Radcliffe, good to see you."

Graham inclined his head in an almost bow. "I do believe the right to bear this arm lies with you, sir," he said to Lord Sterling, holding out Janet's hand.

Lord Sterling took it, bowed, and brought the hand to his lips.

"And what a right it is!"

"Suffocating," Tyrone groaned. "Please go in, I beg you."

Lord Sterling and his wife laughed, moving into the box. Tyrone gave Graham a longsuffering look before following them. Graham cast his eyes back towards the box where Lady Edith had vanished, his mind turning over what he had seen and heard.

Would he be able to see her from where he was? The exact layout of the boxes in this theatre escaped him, and he wasn't entirely sure why he was curious about seeing her. It was clear she had protection, if not interest, and despite his waltzing with her, apparently saving her somehow, he didn't have any ties to involve him in whatever her situation was.

Nor did he wish to be involved with something that created whispers and gossip.

He shook his head and entered the box, pushing aside the curtains and moving to a vacant chair. He sat and crossed one leg over the other, his attention on the stage as the Sterlings and Tyrone chatted together.

The hum of conversations surrounding him wafted in and out of Graham's ears, almost lulling him to sleep with the sound, despite his not being the least bit fatigued. How would it affect his reputation if he actually did doze for the duration of the play? At least the first act, anyway. He could scoot his chair back into a corner of the box, out of sight, and have quite a nice rest of it. See what they made of the new Lord Radcliffe then!

A crooked smirk inched its way across his lips, and he aimlessly scanned the theatre, looking without seeing. Then, the box next to his came into view, and with it, Lady Edith Leveson in plain sight.

His eyes rested there, one hand situating itself at his mouth in a gesture of consideration, his attention fully in focus.

She smiled at something one of her friends said, and something in the arch of Graham's left foot twitched at the sight of it.

So much for dozing.

Chapter Five

Not all theatrics are confined to a stage.

-The Spinster Chronicles, 16 August 1815

Was anyone in the theatre actually watching the stage?

Edith could feel every inch of her skin crawling as she sat in the box between Grace and Prue, her eyes fixed on the actors without seeing a single one of them. The whispers had been difficult to hear, but nothing she hadn't heard before. The stares, however, were new.

Well, new for London. She'd gotten plenty of stares in York.

A familiar cold shiver ran up her spine as the memories of those stares flashed across her mind, and she suddenly felt small.

If only she were small. If only she could hide from all of this and still accomplish her designs.

How had she so completely underestimated Archie's influence? Or the impact his death would have had on Society. If not Society, then at least her standing in it. A lesser-known widow of a man who moved in certain circles, however disreputable, and the rumors that would follow that widow.

Define that widow.

What had she been thinking? London had been the worst possible choice in location, the center of Society, why in the world had she come? Why had she chosen it? In theory, it was a place where one could get lost in plain sight, yet she had stayed in the ratty townhouse that belonged to Sir Archibald's family. She had kept herself in the path of Sir Reginald and any other Leveson relation that might have come along to torment her.

This was her fault.

She could have truly hidden deep in the London darkness, were it not for her pride. She hadn't thought that existed anymore. More the fool was she.

Gòrach…

Her father's low, gravelly voice sounded in her mind, ricocheting off every surface, calling her foolish yet again. That had been his only response to her refusals to marry Archie.

Foolish.

And those foolish refusals had been flatly ignored. Her wishes had meant nothing, and her will had been crushed. There was no pride left in her from the day she'd first set foot in England, nor as she was dragged down the aisle of the church, nor as she watched her family abandon her to the care of her new husband.

Archie's death had been a beacon of hope. An opportunity for freedom. She hadn't realized then that it would only lead to more shackles.

Perhaps that was where her pride had snuck in. She couldn't afford it anymore; it had to go.

Edith exhaled slowly, praying they would soon reach intermission. She needed to walk, to stretch her legs, to clear her mind, to get out of sight of so many who were only speculating about her.

Breathe, *mo nighean*. Breathe.

On command, Edith inhaled a carefully controlled breath, finding with it the refreshment hearing her grandmother's voice always brought her.

"Are you all right, Edith?" Prue whispered softly beside her, placing one small hand over Edith's tightly laced fingers in her lap.

"Aye," Edith replied on an almost controlled exhale. "I believe I will slip out for a wee moment, though." She nodded and rose only so far as a crouch, slipping around her chair and between the gentlemen seated behind them.

"Edith?"

She waved Aubrey, Lord Ingram, back into his seat. "I shall only be a moment; stay as you are."

His expression told her how he felt about the suggestion, but she didn't linger to see or hear any further response.

Out in the corridor, Edith's breath came faster and with more aggression. Her lungs squeezed and released with agonizing pain, and it was all she could do to attempt to control them.

Inhale... exhale... inhale... exhale...

Music from the stage wafted out into the corridor, and something about the strains, faint as they were, soothed her. The frantic pace of her mind settled, the air in her lungs entered and exited with more ease, and the pounding in her head began to recede. Walking became easier, and slowly, Edith continued to move, keeping her breathing as steady as she could and letting the music continue to calm her.

Despite the comments and stares of people, the course before her was the right one. The only one, really. She alone had made the choices in her life, and there was no point in regretting them. She had done the best she could under horrific circumstances, and no one would judge her for that if they knew the truth of the situation.

Which no one did.

Edith sighed heavily and paused near a column, leaning her back against it as she thought back to Scotland, its beauty and majesty, its wildness and energy, and the perfect purity in every breath of air one took in. Scotland would always be home, even if she never set foot on her soil again.

The thought sent a sharp pang into her heart, and a rare wash of tears began to form.

"Ah, Lady Edith," sneered a chilling voice at her ear, a hand settling on her hip.

Edith sprang back, the column scraping the buttons of her gown as she slid along its surface. She glared up at Sir Reginald as he loomed over her, the hand once at her hip now gripping her skirts.

"Don't touch me," she spat, eyes still burning.

He grabbed at her arm, leering maliciously. "Come now, Lady Edith, be a good lass and greet your cousin properly."

Before Edith could tug free of his grasp, Sir Reginald yanked her to him and kissed her hard on the mouth. Edith squirmed against the pressure, sealing her lips tightly together as she desperately tried to tug away. She shoved at his chest, nausea rising within her at the taste of him, but he only chuckled and pulled harder on her arm, sending jolts of pain shooting into her shoulder.

He finally lifted his mouth away, licking his lips and exhaling with satisfaction.

"You'll make a scene, Edith," he whispered with a cruel laugh. "And the intermission is upon us. You wouldn't want to do that with so many witnesses, would you?"

Edith clamped her lips together, swallowing the wash of bile there and whimpering at the pressure still pulsing in her shoulder. Tremors began to course through her as she still struggled against him.

"Still," he mused, his hold on her firm, "suggestion is more powerful for its subtlety. Therefore…" He released his grip on her skirt and reached up to tug at her hair, disheveling it with his fingers and tousling it quickly, her pins falling to the floor below. Then he grabbed at her sleeve, pulling the gown off one shoulder, ripping the fabric in the process.

Edith immediately went to adjust her sleeve when Sir Reginald slapped her hard across the face, drawing a gasp from her. She immediately cradled her face with her free hand, turning away from him as much as possible, though his hold on her was still secure. She tasted blood, her cheek throbbing, and the shaking in her legs intensified.

"There," he said, running a cold finger along her jaw. "That should do." He yanked on her arm again and leaned in for another kiss.

Edith restrained a cry and stomped on his foot, jerking out of his hold as Sir Reginald hissed in pain. Backing away, Edith looked about her, unable to run, as it would draw attention to the guests who would be emerging from the theatre at any moment if the applause within the theatre was any indication.

Sir Reginald chuckled and raked a lascivious look along the course of her body that renewed the nauseousness in her, shudders accompanying the sensation.

"A delight as always, Lady Edith." He bowed mockingly, and left her at last, still laughing.

A dry sob escaped Edith, and she covered her mouth, whether to hide the cry or prevent the rising sick feeling, she couldn't admit.

Either. Both. Anything.

The heat of shame flooded her cheeks, and she inhaled shakily through her nose before focusing on the attempt to adjust her gown however she could. A whispered curse escaped her quivering lips as she found the effort fruitless; the tear was too great, and the dress hung askew on her, just as Sir Reginald had wanted. She bent to the floor to retrieve her hairpins, casting her eyes about for any stray ones.

The chatter of people met her ears as the intermission began, and Edith jerked up to a straightened position, creeping closer to the column, hoping to remain unobserved. She had not stopped particularly close to the main part of the theatre, but any hope she had of truly restoring her hair would require a looking glass, and she would have to venture further into the people in attendance to see to that. Her only hope was to wait for intermission to end and restore herself to rights then. Or attempt to manage something far less refined as she was, and she was already poorly refined in the eyes of Society.

Her eyes flooded with tears of anger and shame, a few crawling down her still burning cheek. She reached back to twist a long, mangled tendril of her dark hair back into the rest, pinning it in the hopes it would look respectable, at least.

Respectable.

As if she could ever be considered respectable now.

She longed to tell everyone and anyone what a horrid man Sir Reginald was, how he had wronged her, how terribly he was abusing her. But in her present situation, and in Society, she could not do so without ruining herself and all hopes of her future in the process. She might be ruined in many respects now, but there was a shred of dignity still, somehow, and the hope of a better future. Without that, she would have been ruined indeed.

"Come with me," a deep voice murmured near her.

Edith jerked away again, one hand rising to strike, fearing he was another man like Sir Reginald. But to her surprise, it was Lord Radcliffe, looking even more massive than she recalled from their waltz. Faintly, it occurred to her to wonder what had possessed her to dance with such an imposing man.

His dark eyes took in her cheek, and his strong jaw tightened. He took her arm in a surprisingly gentle hold and tilted his head. "Come."

"What are you doing?" she whispered. "How did you know—?"

"I saw you leave the box," Lord Radcliffe murmured, "and then I caught sight of your weasel friend just now. He looked too smug; I didn't like it. And from the looks of things, my instincts were correct." He shook his head and peered around the column. "If we go now, I can take you back to your friends with hardly anyone seeing you."

"Hardly," Edith murmured, reaching back to try fixing another lock of hair, "but I will be seen."

The pressure at her elbow increased with a firm comfort. "Just stay close to me, all right? No one will notice you."

She snorted in derision as she allowed him to lead her from her hiding space, staying almost improperly close to him out of instinct. "Not likely, my lord."

He gave her a look, then pulled her closer, setting his arm around her waist and tucking her into his side as others started to approach. "I can be a peacock if I need to be."

It took Edith a moment to realize it, but by his pulling her closer as he did, he ensured that the side of her face that had been struck remained hidden against his side. Further, in keeping her in conversation with him, he also ensured that she would not meet the eyes of anyone else.

Quite clever, she would freely admit.

She had to smile at him for that, though it pained her face to do so.

"I cannot see you being a peacock, sir."

He grunted an almost laugh, his mouth quirking.

"Use your imagination, madam. It does not happen often, but it is quite the sight when it does."

Edith giggled and covered her mouth with a hand, unintentionally turning her face more against him.

"That's better," he said gruffly. "No one looks so upset at the theatre, besides myself, unless Madame LeFonte is singing. Now you blend perfectly well."

Pressing her tongue to the back of her teeth, Edith shook her head gently. "I forgot to thank you, my lord, for saving me at the ball." She swallowed hard. "And as for tonight…"

"It's nothing," he said simply, steering her out of the way of some others.

"If you ken my situation, my lord, ye'd not think it to be nothing at all," Edith managed hoarsely. "And for me to force you into a waltz when you do not care for dancing…"

Lord Radcliffe gave her a hard look. "You did not force me, Lady Edith," he said firmly, his dark eyes suddenly darker. "I had every choice I needed at that time. I do not need to know your situation, nor do you need to bear guilt. I do hate to dance, but not as much as I hate troublemakers like the weasel. Who is he?"

Edith shivered, and his hold on her tightened in response.

"My nightmare," she murmured.

He was going to ask more, she could see, but they had returned to the box, and Lieutenant Henshaw, Camden, and Aubrey were outside of it.

"There you are!" Cam said, his relief evident. Then his eyes took her in.

"Edith…"

"Lady Edith will need to be tended to discreetly, and perhaps taken home before the show is ended." Lord Radcliffe spoke in low tones, his voice calm.

Aubrey nodded once, his eyes on Edith.

"I'm going to venture a guess, Edith, if you will confirm it. Sir Reginald?" he asked in clipped tones.

Edith nodded, her tears starting to well up again as she swayed a little into Lord Radcliffe.

He bolstered her up at once even as Lieutenant Henshaw swore, and started away.

"Not here," Edith begged, grabbing his sleeve. "Not now."

He looked at her for a long moment. "Very well, Edith. But soon."

There was no questioning him, so Edith only nodded once more.

"Lady Edith, perhaps now formally I should introduce you to

Lord Radcliffe? As it appears he is now caught up in this, as well." Aubrey gestured to him. "Radcliffe, Lady Edith Leveson."

Lord Radcliffe looked at Edith, and there was a small hint of a smile on his face.

"Charmed," he said in a droll tone, giving her a nod.

"You're a hero, Lord Radcliffe," she told him, bobbing a makeshift curtsey. "Twice now."

He removed his hand from her waist and took her hand in his. "I told you before, madam, I am no hero." He pressed a polite kiss to her glove, though the sensation of it raced up her arm as if to soothe the pain Sir Reginald had caused there. "But a third time may change my mind."

"I know how you hate heroics, so I shall venture not to require you." She tried for a cheeky smile, praying he would take the show of levity for what it was.

His eyes showed a bit of amusement, though his face did not. "I would be most appreciative." He bowed, and made eye contact with Aubrey, apparently communicating some message as both men nodded. Then, with a final nod to Edith, he left the group.

Without another word, Edith was ushered into the box, and seated out of sight of any other guests of the theatre while Grace and Prue descended upon her.

"Darling, what happened?" Grace pleaded, her fingers tracing the damage of her gown.

"Edith, a-are y-you q-q-q…?" Prue's distress returned her stammer to its former notoriety, and she bit her lip to keep herself from stammering further as she took Edith's hand in her own.

"*Dinna fash*," Edith soothed as much as she was able, though she felt her body tremble in earnest now that she was fully removed from the situation. "I'm well enough."

Grace's fair brow creased at that. "But what…?"

"My love," Aubrey said firmly, cutting her off as he settled a hand on his wife's shoulder. "Now is not the time, and this is not the place."

"No, indeed," Cam agreed as he gestured for his wife to come to him.

She did so, and he rubbed soothing circles on her back,

whispering to her, no doubt to calm her anxieties and set her to rights. He was so good at that, and just what Prue needed.

If only someone could set Edith and her life to rights. That would solve everything.

"But," Aubrey went on, his tone very serious indeed, "may I suggest that we leave before the second act has concluded, and that we continue this conversation at our home immediately after our departure? I don't think we can waste another moment, quite frankly; nor do I think we ought to."

"Agreed," Lieutenant Henshaw intoned gravely, one hand resting on the scabbard he still wore at his side, not nearly as decorative as the rest of his regimental uniform.

Edith swallowed hard. She couldn't bear this, couldn't tell them, couldn't reveal...

"Edith?"

Grace's soft, kind, loving voice broke through her resistance, and Edith felt herself slump in her chair, her head lowering as the tears once more began to fall.

"Aye," she whispered, the words barely audible. "Aye, I'll tell ye all of it."

Chapter Six

A little investment can get a body in a great deal of trouble. One ought to take care to only take an interest in matters that concern them, and in which they will not mind devoting their attention. Once you are in, it is very, very difficult to get back out again.

-The Spinster Chronicles, 17 February 1817

This was a mistake.

Graham wasn't sure how he knew that, but know it, he did. How else could he explain the overwhelming feeling of dread encompassing him in the carriage as he rattled his way towards the Ingrams' home? His stomach clenched in apprehension, wondering faintly if he shouldn't have remained at the theatre with Tyrone and the Sterlings.

But if he had, he wouldn't know what was going on in the life of Lady Edith Leveson.

Coming to the aid of Lady Edith hadn't been part of his plans that night, nor had he intended the action to bring him into her confidence, or that of anyone else in her circle. But he would not deny that he was growing more and more intrigued with the woman, and equally concerned with the weasel that seemed incapable of leaving her alone.

When he'd found her at the theatre, tucked away just around a column, he'd been torn between pursuing the weasel and seeing to her aid. As he had no context for the situation, he'd opted to stay with her, and the combination of strength and weakness within her was startling. Whatever had occurred between the weasel and Lady Edith, it had worn on her, made her quiver and retreat, and one look in her eyes had shown Graham just how tired the woman was from whatever her life was doing to her.

Yet behind and beneath all that, there seemed to be a will of iron and a spine of steel within her. The grip she'd had on him as they'd walked back had been strong, and something about the set of her jaw made him want to smile. She wasn't the weak and retreating type, he suspected, and his finding her in such a distressed state was likely something she would feel ashamed of upon recollection.

No matter what he said to dismiss such feelings, she would have them. Pride would dictate this for her, and it would be all she could do even to meet his gaze in the future.

He could understand that. He didn't agree with it, in her case, but he understood it. He'd have felt the same way, were the roles reversed.

Strangely, he didn't mind that he had come to the aid of Lady Edith twice now, in her estimation. She was smart, witty, fascinating, and beautiful; she wasn't the silly type who would make something out of nothing, and he had yet to see anything regarding dramatics from her. There was something about the brogue he'd been hearing from her that made him want to keep her talking.

For someone who frequently wished people would do anything other than talk with him, this was new and untrodden territory.

Graham glanced out of the window as the coach rolled on, and he exhaled slowly. He hadn't meant to get roped into the fallout from his role in the situation. He was only supposed to deposit Lady Edith into her friends' care and return to his evening, dull as it had been. Yet when exchanging looks with Lord Ingram, Graham had seen the silent invitation there and agreed to it.

A note delivered to him during the second act confirmed the invitation, as well as gave him a time and destination. Which was why he was where he was now, and he hadn't even begun to think about the possibilities that would render such a meeting to take place so suddenly.

He was tied into things now, like it or not, and even the weasel would know it, or soon would. He had seen them waltzing, even if he hadn't seen them tonight.

Whatever the third incident would be, should there be a third, Graham could hardly expect to remain anonymous after it. Somehow, he knew there would be a third. If not a fourth, fifth, and sixth. Why else would they be cutting their evening short and inviting him to the Ingrams'? Something was happening, or about to happen, and he was now involved.

But was he part of the problem or part of the solution? Or was he simply a bystander being permitted further information?

Time alone would tell.

He'd already chosen his side, he supposed. Made a judgment based on observations. Knew his course of action, come what may. All he lacked was the context behind that course, the meaning behind those observations, and the risks of being on the side he had chosen.

What was Lady Edith involved in, and how had she gotten there?

Quickly, Graham ran through what he knew about her, which wasn't much at all. Lady Edith Leveson wasn't notorious or infamous, wasn't even popular, let alone well known. Her late husband, however, had done little to keep his name out of scandal sheets or gaming halls, and he frequently seemed to keep his name there intentionally. Sir Archibald Leveson had been familiar with each of the seven deadly sins, though gluttony for excesses he reserved for the other sins rather than in food.

Everyone had been surprised that Sir Archibald had married, as no well-bred family would wish to link their daughter to him, no matter how vast his fortune was reputed to be. His status was certainly not as enviable as some, being merely a knight, and his fluctuating financial situation would be too great a risk to take on.

How in the world had Lady Edith's family agreed to the match?

Sir Archibald hadn't been in the match long, dying after a drunken ride on his horse shortly after his wedding. The details of the thing weren't all that clear to the public, and he suspected only Lady Edith and the local magistrate in York knew the full truth. In many respects, life should have improved for Lady Edith with her new bridegroom gone.

By present accounts, however, that was not the case.

This was going to be complicated, and it would, undoubtedly, be a mistake.

The carriage pulled to a stop in front of the London home of the Ingrams, prompting a rough exhale from Graham as he eyed the façade.

Too late now.

He rose and pushed out of the carriage, not bothering to pause before striding up the few steps to the door. He rapped his knuckles on the surface twice and was let in before he could go for a third.

Clearly, he was expected.

Graham nodded at the butler as he handed his cloak and gloves to a footman nearby. "Am I the last to arrive?"

"You are, sir," the older man confirmed. "Word has been sent to some others, but I understand they are not expected this evening."

Interesting. Unless Graham was mistaken, nothing Lady Edith had suffered at the hands of the weasel would require a meeting of such urgency that others would need to be roused from their beds. But perhaps whatever evils that were afoot had been going on for such a length of time that enough was enough.

One instance would have been enough, surely.

But he was not here to judge; he was here to learn.

Silently, he was led down the corridor by the butler, taking fleeting notice of the details of the Ingram home. Nothing overly ostentatious, but perhaps more embellishments to the simple structure of the place than Graham would have made. Tastefully done, though, and fairly refined.

He would chalk that up to the tastes of Lady Ingram and think all the better of her for it. She was from one of the more prominent families in Society, though hardly the wealthiest, and in Graham's limited experience, the more prominent families had peculiar, if exorbitant, tendencies. He hadn't known much of Lady Ingram before her marriage to Lord Ingram, so he couldn't have said prior to this if she followed suit.

It seemed the Ingrams were not of that sort.

A soft clearing of the throat brought Graham's attention up, and he felt a faint level of heat enter his cheeks. It was rare that he was caught gaping at anyone or anything, but to do so at this moment seemed somehow worst of all. He knew that some butlers doubled as spies for their masters, and the inference that Graham was somehow in awe of the Ingrams was not something he would be pleased to have spread about.

The butler moved to a nearby doorway and stood at attention. "Lord Radcliffe."

Graham raised a brow. Formality? At this time of night? He mentally shook his head as he strode forward and bowed to the general room without pausing to look at anyone within.

"What's he doing here?" Lady Edith cried, her rich Scottish brogue ringing out prominently. "Aubrey!"

"Thank you, Locke," Ingram replied mildly, unruffled by the protests to Graham's presence. "Radcliffe, please come in."

Graham nodded once, finally looking around as he stepped into the room. The same individuals from their group at the theatre were present now, and, but for the pale look of sheer horror on the face of Lady Edith, all appeared the same as before. Interestingly, he did note that all held small plates in their laps or near them, bearing parts or crumbs of an evening repast.

Perhaps they should have met in a dining room, instead.

"Would you care for some refreshment, my lord?" Lady Ingram asked, gesturing to the spread atop the sideboard in the room.

Not really, no, but if everyone else was…

"Thank you," he murmured as he nodded to her, moving to the food.

"I ask again, wha' in the devil's wee pockets is he doing here?" Lady Edith demanded.

"I don't recall hearing that one the first time," Mr. Vale mused aloud, shifting his weight as he stood behind the couch his wife sat upon. "I think I would have remembered it."

Mrs. Vale reached up to cover his hand on her shoulder with a slender hand of her own, no doubt silently shushing him.

Graham hid a smile as he saw the look Lady Edith gave Vale for his comment, and it was clear that Mrs. Vale's gentle warning wouldn't help the situation.

"I ken you're no idiot, Cam, so dinna patronize me," she snapped.

"Not patronizing," he shot back, somehow avoiding injecting any irritation into his tone. "Just trying to make light."

Graham made quick work of gathering bits of food, not particularly paying attention to what he was grabbing, and caring even less. The interaction among this group was fascinating, and if he took nothing else away from this night, increased exposure would be worth it.

Unless he would be expected to participate.

He nearly choked on a bite of warm bread at the thought. Social interaction made him break out into a rash of sorts, and that was with preparation. Impulsive and unforeseen conversation would be worse than pulling teeth or being bled. He'd never had a tooth pulled, but he had been bled a time or two, and he took great pains to avoid it.

"Radcliffe," Ingram began, leaning back on the couch where he sat and draping an arm casually around his wife's shoulder, "are you acquainted with all present?"

Graham swallowed his bread quickly. "Indirectly," he grunted, "and not well."

"Thought not." Ingram made quick reintroductions before loosening his cravat, making Graham instantly envious, his own linen noose still troubling him.

"Now that we've dallied around with names," Lady Edith huffed, her fingers clenching together in her lap, "will ye kindly explain yerself, Aubrey?"

Ingram raised a brow. "About what, lass?"

Lady Edith rolled her eyes and gave Lady Ingram a look of pure exasperation. "How the devil do ye bear him, Grace?"

Lady Ingram smiled, patting her husband on the knee. "He has his moments." She followed this up with a scolding look to the man beside her. "For pity's sake, Aubrey, she's all wrung out."

Ingram instantly softened and looked at Lady Edith with something akin to tenderness. "I have no intention of embarrassing you, Edith, nor of making this more uncomfortable than it needs to be. Lord Radcliffe has had run-ins with you twice in a short period of time under unusual circumstances. Knowing him to be a man of good character and sound judgment, I saw no reason to exclude him from a conversation that he is becoming increasingly involved in."

Well, well. That was a flattering take on a strange situation if he ever heard one. Graham wasn't entirely certain he could have said the same of Ingram purely due to his own reserve and wary nature where others were concerned. It was oddly humbling, and he dipped his chin in acknowledgment of the praise.

"He deserves to know," Lieutenant Henshaw murmured, standing against a wall nearby, looking nearly as fatigued as Lady Edith. "As much as the rest of us."

"If you are comfortable with that, Edith," Vale insisted from his place behind his wife. "It is your decision."

Impossibly, Lady Edith turned her attention to Graham, the conflict within her evident in her luminous eyes. She wasn't an indecisive creature, he knew that much, but she seemed to be looking for instruction here, and he had none to give. Vale was right; Lady Edith ought to have the final word, though she might not have wished for this in the first place.

Graham met her eyes steadily, not daring to blink. He couldn't think of words to say that might comfort her or encourage her. He could barely think at all under the circumstances. He hardly knew her. Knew nothing beyond what he could see. Had no authority or connection to call upon.

What could he say?

Something exchanged between them in their silent observance of each other, standing as they were on the precipice of the unknown, and Graham felt himself exhale slowly. He would swear he saw her do the same, and a thin thread of trust extended from him to her. Or from her to him. From one to the other. Thin, trembling with newness, but firmly in place.

Whatever this was, he was in. And she accepted that.

Why did he suddenly want to smile?

"I'm here! I'm here!" a new voice shouted from the corridor, accompanied by the pattering of slippered feet against the floor. "I hope you haven't said anything important yet; I'm here!"

"You canna be serious," Lady Edith said in alarm, breaking the connection between her and Graham as she looked to the doorway, wide-eyed.

A young woman in a plain but clean sprigged muslin gown

dashed into the room, her long, dark hair loosely plaited and dancing around with the motion. Her cheeks were flushed, and she panted shamelessly for a moment or two.

"Miss Wright, my lord," Locke intoned belatedly, his voice stiff with displeasure, his expression resigned.

"So I see," Ingram replied with a faint smile. "You may commence with listening at the door as you were, Locke."

"Thank you, my lord."

Graham stared as the butler left them again, wondering if Ingram were teasing or the butler truly was prone to eavesdropping.

"Charlotte, do you have any idea what time it is?" Lady Ingram inquired with the same expression Lady Edith wore.

"Quite." Miss Wright looked around and saw Graham, then bobbed a hasty curtsey. "Good evening, Lord Radcliffe. Or does one say 'good night' at this hour? I've always thought that a farewell or an incantation for bedtime, neither of which this is. Either way, greetings and so on."

Graham was intrigued and amused, he would freely admit. He knew Miss Wright well enough, as anyone in Society did, but their personal interactions had been limited.

Still, he was in possession of some wit.

"The same to you, I believe," he replied with a half bow.

Someone in the vicinity of Mr. Vale snorted, and Graham was instantly more comfortable with his surroundings.

"Ch-Charlotte," Mrs. Vale stammered, her throat working with the effort. "Wh-wh-what… are you…?"

Graham's attention flicked to the woman with mild concern, though no one else in the room seemed to have noticed anything out of the ordinary. The hand Mr. Vale had on his wife's shoulder suddenly shifted higher, his fingers brushing against her cheek and neck in an almost absent manner.

"I got Aubrey's message, of course." Miss Wright sniffed and sat herself in an open chair as though this were nothing more than an afternoon tea with friends. "I came straight away."

"From your bed?" Lieutenant Henshaw suggested, a rueful smile appearing.

Miss Wright speared him with the sort of look she might have given a troublesome brother. "Vulgar question, Hensh, but yes, as it happens. My servants are under strict instructions to bring me all messages forthwith upon their arrival, no matter the time. I was not asleep, and this seemed important." She tossed her long, thick braid over a shoulder and looked around at the room, daring anyone else to have an opinion on the subject.

No one did.

"Right, then," Ingram murmured, drawing out the words. He shifted his attention to Lady Edith, as did the rest. "Edith, whenever you're ready."

Lady Edith looked at Ingram for a long moment. "Tha' would be three weeks on the long side of never. But I suppose I dinna have much of a choice." She swallowed and looked down at her hands, exhaling slowly. "It will surprise none of ye to hear that I am almost entirely wi'out means of my own. Archie... Sir Archibald, didna make adjustments to include me in his will before he passed, and there's no way of knowing if he would have changed it had he lived. When his will became known, it was made verra plain to me that I had no funds and no claim to my dowry, though I had been married one day."

Graham's brows shot up at that. One day? He'd heard stories, of course, but he'd thought every one of them an exaggeration.

"How can your dowry not be returned to your family if the will had not been adjusted?" Mr. Vale interrupted without tact. "That seems..."

"The will did not include *me*," Lady Edith corrected, overriding the man. "That adjustment had not been made. But there was plenty in the document about the funds brought into a marriage despite having nothing to say on the woman to whom he entered marriage with." She gave him a soft, bitter smile. "I was permitted to remain in the house in York until the heir to Archie's fortune and title could be found. It was a glorious time while it lasted."

Glorious? To be abandoned in an estate one hardly knew, away from family, and with plans all thrown into upheaval? None of it made sense to Graham, but he could not bring himself to question her, or to ask the others present if they were just as ignorant to the meaning of all this as he seemed to be.

Lady Edith cleared her throat and lifted her chin, something in her neck tightening as she did so. "I became acquainted with Sir Reginald some three months after Archie's death. Much as I disliked my husband, Sir Reginald is far and away the worse of the two. He refused to make reparations to his cousin's widow, or to permit a portion of my dowry to be returned to my family, given the lack of advantage that would be had from its investment now."

Graham frowned at the use of the word investment. A dowry was designed to be an inducement to a prospective suitor, it was true, but it was intended to be used in maintaining the lifestyle worthy of a gentleman's daughter when she left his house for that of her husband. Some fathers even put aside additional portions specifically for their daughter's use, though it wasn't particularly common.

It certainly wasn't meant to be a wager or a bribe, or something used to value a woman.

"There wasn't much to the dowry to begin with," Lady Edith muttered then, a harsher edge coming through the words. "Nothing about my marriage to Archie ever made sense to me, and those who arranged it refused to tell me a thing."

Those who…

He stared at Lady Edith openly, his head spinning. What the hell had happened to her prior to her marriage that had brought her into all of this, anyway? Who had sold her off to a worthless husband? What sort of deal had been struck if Sir Archibald hadn't been a fortune hunter? Unless the man had only been looking for breeding in his bride, he could see nothing beneficial in a match that was so far from one of love.

Lady Edith stopped speaking, her gaze on the small table before her, eyes unfocused. The color had yet to return to her cheeks, though she didn't seem to be near to swooning or ill. Simply lost.

So very lost.

A small corner of his heart cracked at seeing it, and he shoved a bite of food into his mouth to get over the surprising pang in his chest. He was growing sentimental over a stranger's story, and without pertinent facts to fill the tale out properly. A scheming man had taken advantage of a young woman without influence. It was the same sad story heard in ballrooms all over England.

Nothing unusual, distasteful though it was.

"Edith," Henshaw prodded more gently than Graham would have managed. "Sir Reginald."

She blinked and looked up, not at Henshaw, but at Graham, and he felt that pang in his chest streak down the backs of his legs, sending bolts of lightning into his heels.

"Sir Reginald has taken a personal interest in his cousin's widow," she told the group. "Very personal."

The flatness of her tone left no room for misinterpretation and brought with it a severity that had Graham setting his plate aside as the fire of indignation began to curl in his fingers.

"No!" Miss Wright gasped, eyes wide.

Lady Edith gave no indication she heard her friend. "He has no interest in wedding me, only bedding me. He calls weekly to remind me of his offer and to make his point clear. Accept him, and I will be free from my poverty and the suspicion of Society. Refuse, and he will make everything far worse."

"Vague threat," Vale growled, something in his hand cracking as it formed a fist to one side. "Sounds ominous but has no teeth. What can he do beyond what you currently suffer?"

This brought Lady Edith's eyes flicking to him. "I willna repeat the details he has shared with me on this topic, Cam, given there are ladies present. Think of the devil, and then do a quick jig further into hell, and ye might find a fair enough idea of the thing."

"Let's not," Lady Ingram protested weakly, one hand at her stomach, her cheeks somehow paler than her friend's. "Could he cast you out, for example?"

"He could," Lady Edith confirmed with a nod. "And he most certainly would, without the meager pin money I am allotted. He claims to have more influence in Society than I can possibly imagine, though I have no way of confirming such a thing." She shook her head, and her fingers began to wring together again, almost frantic in their agitation despite the apparent calm the rest of her held. "He will ruin me, of that there is no doubt. In his mind, agreeing to give myself to him is the only option."

Mrs. Vale whimpered and turned her face into her husband's hand, still lingering near her ear. Vale bent and kissed her head, whispering softly to her, before straightening. "So, you thought you'd take Society by storm first, eh?"

"Aye. If I could find myself protection, some kind of connection or security, I might find a way out of his clutches." Lady Edith bit her full bottom lip, her fingers stilling. "I fear I am powerless. By law and by funds. I have no claim, no stake, and verra few options."

"But you do have friends," Ingram chimed in, his voice hard, his expression harder. "And I'll be damned if anyone will treat a woman this way, closely connected with me or otherwise."

"Amen," Henshaw snarled. "Edith, why didn't you tell me?"

Idiot, Graham hissed in his mind, skewering the man with a glare. Now was not the time for recriminations or guilt, especially with everything else the woman had to contend with. Surely, his pride would recover faster than her situation.

But Lady Edith was kinder than the man deserved and only smiled, though tears seemed to be hovering at the corners of her eyes. "How could I, Hensh? I can barely speak of it now. After all of this, I dinna trust easily, especially with this."

No, she wouldn't have. She couldn't have. No one could.

And yet...

"Well, we can certainly do something about this," Ingram insisted almost too strongly, thumping the couch he sat upon. "What if Edith moves into a home with someone else, eh?"

"Who do you know in the law, Hensh? We'll need an expert."

"We need a *husband* is what we need."

"No, Charlotte," Cam warned.

"Yes! Trust me; I know what I am saying."

Graham watched Lady Edith for a moment while the others in the room began to throw ideas between each other as one might have done with a ball, discussing Lady Edith without involving Lady Edith or addressing her. She could be silent now, and she seemed relieved by the fact.

She settled into the couch further, peering at the tips of her fingers, though her eyes barely moved. Color slowly seeped back into her face, and her breathing grew more even. While the others talked around her, she sat quietly, taking it all in, offering nothing by way of opinion or idea.

They would all go on with their lives tonight, still trying to concoct ways to help her, while she would return to the darkness no different than when she had left it.

How did she trust anyone at all?

As if she had heard him, her eyes rose to his, a raw openness there, and he exhaled silently, meeting the surprising steadiness without looking away.

The thread between them seemed to expand, coiling around and around itself, weaving itself into a cord that tugged at his spine. He knew he could trust her, that had been a given fact almost from their first meeting, but she could trust him, which he wouldn't have said as quickly. He was never invested enough to be particularly trusted one way or the other, not particularly caring for such a responsibility or effort. His integrity was never in question, nor would he ever be accused of not being trustworthy; he simply never took it on. But in this, with her, it was different. Everything was.

He was.

And she knew that.

Her lips curved in just a hint of a smile, and Graham felt himself nod quite decisively, if discreetly, in response. Those lips quirked further still, then the almost-smile faded altogether, the eyes lowering again.

What exactly Graham had agreed to, he couldn't have put to words. He only knew he had.

Fully and freely.

Chapter Seven

———————— ❧ ❧ ————————

One can always depend on the ladies to present creative solutions to problematic situations. While the gentlemen circle around blustering the point, the ladies will quietly and efficiently resolve matters in such a way that never entered into the mind of any man. Whether this solution ends for good or ill, this author will own, may not be so clearly predicted.

-The Spinster Chronicles, 24 September 1818

"You cannot be serious."

"Of course, we're serious. Why wouldn't we be serious?"

"Charlotte," Edith said, "you canna invite a young woman of high standing and good breeding to be my companion."

Charlotte had the good sense to look a trifle startled at the accusation. "Who said she would be your companion?"

Edith raised a brow in lieu of sending steam spewing from her ears. "What else do you call a young woman who stays with an older woman purely for the sake of keeping her company?"

"A houseguest," Elinor Sterling, formerly Elinor Asheley, answered without blinking an eyelash. "You needn't make yourself sound so decrepit, Edith. You're hardly headed for the grave."

"Age is relative, and experience a better measure," Edith shot back. "In that regard, lass, I am positively ancient by comparison to whomever you choose."

Izzy Morton cleared her throat softly. "She would not be a paid companion, Edith. It is not that sort of arrangement. We were only thinking more of a friend to come and stay."

"Yes!" Grace nodded vigorously at this description. "Rather the way you came to stay with Aubrey and me this winter."

Edith did her best not to roll her eyes as she shifted her attention to Grace. "We are friends, Grace. I canna expect a young lass of Society to pretend to be so and endure such poor living as what I can offer, especially given the situation with Sir Reginald."

"Who said anything about pretending?" Georgie inquired without the heated note someone else might have. "You don't even know who we thought of."

"Thought of?" Edith shot to her feet, looking around at them all as though they had hidden the poor girl in their midst. "You've already decided?"

The ladies in the room looked around at each other, their hesitation palpable.

"Yes…" Charlotte finally admitted, drawing out the word slowly.

Edith sat back down hard, stunned that not only had they decided on a course for her, but had followed through with it. All without asking her.

Her mind spun, emotions shrieking in five different directions.

These were her friends, she reminded herself. Her dearest friends. They were not like the other people who had made decisions for her without her knowledge, and their motivations were entirely different. This hadn't been done maliciously, but with love.

And they had no idea how she felt about such things. She'd never told them. How many secrets would she keep? How long could she keep them?

She looked at her fingers, and the grit under her nails from the life she lived away from all of this. So many secrets. So much away from the finery her friends lived in. So many memories that had haunted her, had shaped her, had led her to this mess.

She had no choice. She'd never had a choice.

Her friends were not her family. Her friends were not her father or her brother. Her friends were not Archie.

She was fine. She was safe. She had a voice.

This time, she had a voice.

"Who?" Edith asked them softly, gritting her teeth against the emotions within her.

Georgie straightened in her seat, staring at Edith carefully. "Edith, we haven't asked her to do anything yet."

Edith blinked, her lungs releasing tension just a bit. "No?"

"No." Georgie shook her head in confirmation, her green eyes seeming to see more than Edith wanted to reveal. "We have, however, asked her to join us today. It will be up to you what she is told and if she will suit."

There was that, at least.

"I h-hope that m-makes you m-m-more comfortable," Prue offered, trying for a smile as she absently massaged her abdomen.

Edith gave her sweet, timid friend a look. "If only the thing made you comfortable, Prue."

Prue's smile turned more genuine. "N-nothing makes me c-comfortable lately. At all."

The quip did more to settle Edith than anything thus far, if for no other reason than because it was still refreshing to have Prue verbally spar along with the rest of them. Once, she wouldn't have done so, but her husband had brought confidence into her life along with his love, and the change had been extraordinary.

Edith could only pray for a similar change in her life. Not to give her confidence, or to settle her nerves, but to change her for the better. To improve her situation enough to remove her fears.

But a husband she'd had, and there hadn't been anything helpful in that.

"It is better than being force-fed a companion," Edith admitted reluctantly, her thumbnail clicking underneath that of her index finger in a nervous tick. She sighed heavily and sniffed. "I so dislike having no control or say in my own matters."

"So do I," Charlotte moaned in sympathy, putting a hand to her brow. "Only yesterday, Mama approved the final details of my new ballgown without consulting me and having no idea what I wanted. It's too late now, so I can only pray she made the right choice."

Grace looked at Charlotte with wide, disbelieving eyes, and Edith dropped her head with a soft snort of amusement. "How in the world is that the same thing, Charlotte?" Grace demanded.

"Why do you need to ask?" Izzy answered before Charlotte

could. "It's Charlotte."

The room laughed, Charlotte included, and Edith's haunting memories and fears faded from her mind.

For the moment.

"That's better," Charlotte announced with a smile at Edith. "It's been an age since I've seen a genuine smile from you."

Edith managed to smile back. "It seems an age since I've been able to wear one."

Steps in the corridor drew their attention, and Edith felt her pulse skitter at the sound.

"Miss Perry to see you, Miss Wright."

Charlotte didn't even bother to thank or dismiss her butler as she rose and dashed to the door. "Amelia! I'm so glad you could come!"

If she hadn't been announced, Edith would never have guessed the young woman entering was Amelia Perry. The girl she remembered was a robust, lively, healthy woman with a glow of good nature about her at all times. She would never be the most beautiful woman in the room, but anyone would admit that, when taken altogether, she was resoundingly pretty.

This lass was pale, somber, and thinner than Edith had ever seen her, though she was not yet sickly in appearance.

The contrast was stark and nearly horrifying.

"Thank you for inviting me," Amelia replied with a flimsy smile, her voice almost the same as it had been before. She looked around at the room timidly. "I've always wanted to come to a meeting of the Spinsters."

"Well, here we are!" Elinor gestured grandly before giggling and shrugging her shoulders. "Not nearly as impressive as we ought to be, but there it is."

Charlotte propped her hands on her hips, huffing playfully. "I beg your pardon. I am *very* impressive."

Something about Elinor and Charlotte's behavior pricked at Edith's thoughts, and she leaned closer to Prue to ask, "Am I imagining things, or are the two of them exaggerating enthusiasm?"

"They are," Prue whispered, her brow furrowing in concern as she looked at Amelia. "Amelia has not been well for some weeks and has been brought so low. I think they are trying to get her out of her melancholy."

"By being silly?" Edith shook her head but smiled with real fondness. The effort was plain to see, yet it was sweet in its observation. Neither Charlotte nor Elinor were especially jubilant people by nature, although they were undoubtedly full of enough passion, and here they were exerting all efforts to brighten the countenance of a young lady.

This was why Edith had joined with them despite wishing to maintain a low-profile life in London; this genuine concern for others and willingness to act on that concern. Prue was probably the closest of them all to Amelia in friendship, but that didn't matter. They could all adopt the girl and attempt to lighten whatever burdens she bore.

"What's wrong with her?" Edith murmured with a sigh as Amelia tried for a laugh at something Charlotte said.

"Who can say? She's not ill, nor has she been, but anyone can see she is not as she should be." Prue smiled sadly and looked at Edith. "It was o-one of the reasons I th-thought she might like to come and stay with you."

Edith's brows rose in surprise. "She was your idea?"

Prue's smile turned almost sheepish. "She was. Charlotte and Grace thought having a companion in your home might help you and keep certain things at bay, and I thought Amelia could do with being away from her usual surroundings for a time. Especially when she could have such a sympathetic friend to stay with." She reached out and took Edith's hand, squeezing gently. "Do you mind?"

"Not in the least," Edith assured her. "Had I known you meant Amelia... Well, I only wish I had thought of it. But do you think she will wish to?"

Unlike some of the others might have done, Prue watched Amelia for a moment, giving the question some serious consideration and thought. "I don't know, Edith. I hope she does."

"Stop monopolizing her!" Grace protested loudly, gesturing for Amelia to come over to the rest. "We wish to visit with her, as well!"

It was a perfect interruption, and Amelia blushed with a smile as she moved away from Charlotte and Elinor to join the rest. "I apologize, I should greet everyone."

"Nonsense," Izzy protested, waving her hands dismissively.

"We're not going to take offense. Did you have a nice Christmas?"

Amelia sat and talked aimlessly of the Perry family Christmas as well as the winter, and none of it was particularly entertaining to hear. It ought to have been, but the note of enthusiasm was missing from the retelling, and they all knew it.

Even Amelia.

"Forgive me," Amelia said suddenly, her shoulders slumping. "I'm not myself. It really was lovely, I promise."

"Nobody had a Christmas as lovely as Elinor; it's safe to say," Izzy pointed out, throwing a teasing smile towards the newest bride of the bunch.

Elinor flamed as the others chuckled, and her smile was one of the most charming things Edith had ever seen. Despite the shock of it, the marriage between Elinor Asheley and Hugh Sterling was a love match if there ever was one. She rarely spoke of it, but there was no denying the joy Elinor exuded at any given moment since then.

A love match with a reformed villain. How was that possible?

Yet it was.

"Hugh surprised me," Elinor managed, averting her eyes and tucking a lock of hair behind her ear. "But Christmas itself was as chaotic as it ever was. Shocking number of engagements, though."

"Perhaps I should go to your estate next Christmas," Amelia said with a laugh, though Edith caught the tension in her voice as she said so.

She hadn't thought Amelia Perry was particularly searching for a husband, though it did seem to be on the mind of every other young woman in Society. Perhaps Amelia's melancholy was a broken heart, but who would have done such a thing? There had never been any indication of a suitor for her, as far as Edith knew, unless she had missed something during her time away in Derbyshire.

"Amelia," Georgie suddenly began, lacing her fingers across her lap, "Edith has a question to ask of you, which is why we asked you here."

Amelia's eyes widened, and she looked at Edith expectantly. "Yes, my lady?"

Edith smiled at the girl, shaking her head. "Lass, don't 'my lady' me. Edith is fine."

"Edith," she corrected with a quick smile, "if you insist."

"I do," Edith replied with a wink and a smile, "especially if you come to stay with me."

Amelia's smile froze, and she blinked once. "I beg your pardon?"

"I would like to have you stay at my home with me," Edith replied. "I am there alone but for my servants, and it would be best for all concerned if I had some company for a time."

Again, Amelia blinked, her mouth beginning to gape open.

Poor thing, this was such a strange request, and possibly harmful to a reputation, given Edith's situation. Why would she agree to stay with her? She had a perfectly lovely home in London, far nicer and more elegant than Edith's home could ever be, let alone actually being in a livable condition. She barely knew Edith, and...

"When can I come?" Amelia suddenly said, looking brighter and more like her old self than she had yet. "I would love to stay with you; are you certain?"

That was certainly unexpected.

Edith blinked unsteadily, her heart stopping in shock. "I am if you are, but are you sure, lass? Ye've no' seen the state of my house, and..."

Amelia shook her head firmly, cutting Edith off. "If you can live there, Edith, I can live there, I vow. I'm not nearly as fine as I look, and I am desperate to be away from home."

"Well, that's simple enough," Charlotte commented with a laugh. "I'll go see about a tea tray." She rose and exited without another word.

Edith bit her lip, staring at Amelia with some concern. "Do you need to check with your parents, Amelia? I live in Cheapside, and the situation is not... I dinna ken why I'm asking. The more I consider the idea, the worse it gets!" She pushed up from her seat and began to pace. "I canna do this to you, or to anyone. It's too horrid, too much. I dinna ken why I agreed..."

"Edith!"

She stopped as Grace stepped directly into her path and grabbed her arms. She met her friend's eyes helplessly, panic and regret welling within her.

"I canna ask her to do this, Grace. It's not right."

"None of this is right, Edith," Grace insisted, her voice as firm as her expression. "None of it. It's not right that you are in it, either. You have Owen at the house. Bringing Amelia in may make things more bearable until we find a more permanent solution for you."

Edith shook her head slightly, tears welling. "I have to tell her everything. She has to know what she is risking."

Grace gave her a firm nod. "All right. Then tell her everything." She took Edith's arm and led her to the seat beside Amelia, then gestured for the rest of them to follow her out of the room.

Without a word, they did so, leaving Edith and Amelia alone in the drawing room together.

"This is a little worrisome," Amelia murmured as she turned towards Edith. "Are you all right?"

Edith exhaled slowly, blinking away the tears of her panic and trying for a smile. "Well enough. It's just… Amelia, my late husband's cousin wants me to be his mistress. He calls frequently to renew his addresses, and while he has yet to make advances towards me there, he has made advances elsewhere. He controls my finances, as well. I do not live in finery, and my continuing to refuse him may make my situation worse. I dinna want to bring you into this unawares."

There was no change to Amelia's expression, then she reached for Edith's hand and squeezed tightly. "If you can live in it, I can live in it, Edith. You shouldn't have to face it alone, and if I can help in any way, I will." She finally smiled, albeit ruefully. "I don't mind telling you, but I've had a disappointment, far beyond what I thought I would. My mother, sweet though she is, will not leave me in peace, and the reliving of it all makes everything hurt more."

"I can imagine," Edith said softly, her mind racing back to her more innocent days in Scotland when she had romantic dreams and imagined beaus. Had she ever fancied a lad enough to find her heart broken in that way?

The only heartbreak she could recall was that of being betrayed by her family and forced down an aisle she would have fled from.

A cold shiver raced down her spine, and she shoved the dark memories away.

"Perhaps," Amelia continued, "in staying with you, I will find the healing I need, and in helping you, distract myself from it all." She smiled further still, looking bright again. "It sounds as though we are both suffering in some way. We might as well suffer together."

Warmth spread from Edith's chest out into the tips of her fingers, and she felt hope for the first time in ages. "I will confess to ye, lass; it will be lovely to have a friend in my home."

Amelia nodded, her eyes bright. "And it will be lovely to me to be of use again. Shall I come tomorrow?"

Edith laughed once. "Aye, if ye please! I'll have a room ready for you."

"Finally," Charlotte announced, entering with a tea tray in her hands, the others trailing behind her. "I've been hovering out there waiting for you both to agree to it. Now, can we please discuss the articles this week? Amelia, would you like to write as a guest? Sterling ladies, perhaps you might consider working together on something? Anything, really."

Chapter Eight

———— ⌾∞∞⌾ ————

A meeting of men is shrouded in mystery from ladies such as we. One can only imagine what is discussed in such goings-on, and whether it really should be such a mystery at all.

-*The Spinster Chronicles, 16 June 1819*

"It's not that bad."

"It is."

"Tony, it's not."

"Cam, it is."

"I can assure you, it's not."

"It *is*," Tony Sterling insisted, flicking the ends of his cravat for emphasis. "It's the most ridiculous bit of frippery I've ever seen. What was wrong with how I wore it before?"

Camden Vale exhaled heavily, turning the glass in his hand against the surface of the table. "I don't care. It doesn't matter. Is your wife pleased with it?"

"Yes…" came the reluctant response.

"Then shut up and wear the damned thing."

Graham watched their exchange from a nearby table at the club, his own drink in hand. He hadn't intended to interact with any of Lady Edith's friends and associates today, having spent far too much time with the lot of them lately, but their paths did seem to cross inordinately frequently. And he was sitting alone for the present, Tyrone clearly having forgotten the time or the location of their meeting this afternoon.

No matter. His friend would likely have a decent enough excuse, and it wasn't as though Graham had pressing engagements today.

He wished he did; a life of idleness and pleasure-seeking had never been one he wished for himself. The country was far more his taste. No one minded there if he worked alongside his tenants or just for the sake of it. No one cared if he didn't dress finely or ride his horse across the lands for hours on end. No one expected him to be on display or to be aimlessly social.

Merrifield was his responsibility and where all his energies ought to be focused. Had he gained just Merrifield with his brother's death, he would have had no reason to leave it. But the title required more from him, so here he was, sitting alone at a table in London.

Marvelous.

"Care for some company, Radcliffe?"

Graham glanced up to see Lieutenant Henshaw pausing at his table, his eyes fixed on him. "Wasn't looking for any in particular, but I won't refuse some if it's offered."

Henshaw raised a brow at him. "Which is a long-winded way to say that you wouldn't mind it. Hell's hounds, man, why not just say so? Come on." He clapped Graham on the back and gestured for him to follow.

Barely restraining a face, Graham pushed himself up and did so, nodding at Sterling and Vale as he joined them. "Gentlemen."

"Radcliffe." Vale nodded in return and indicated Sterling. "You know Captain Sterling?"

"I do," Graham acknowledged. "How are you, Captain?"

Tony Sterling made a face and yet again flicked his cravat. "Dressed like a peacock but surviving nonetheless." He rolled his eyes. "And for pity's sake, call me Sterling. Or Tony. My commission is a mere formality at this point."

"Oh, disregarding formality, are we?" announced Lord Ingram as he approached the table. "Excellent, that is my favorite thing." He took an open seat and sat inelegantly, looking just as at home here as he did in his own residence, somehow. "First time anybody says 'my lord' to me, I'll put my fist to his jaw."

"That's harsh," Vale said with a smirk. "Show some respect, and you get a bruise? You're clearly spending too much time with me."

Ingram nodded and took a tankard from a nearby servant, then clinked it against Vale's. "Woe is me. I feel so poorly influenced." He craned his neck from side to side and gave Tony a wry look. "Your cousin is part of the Spinsters contingent. Are we to expect him today?"

Graham frowned, looking between the men in confusion. Whose cousin? What spinsters? It would do him no good to sit and listen to conversations he could not follow or understand.

"No, Hugh is still mending fences with Francis and Alice, though we've told him time and again it's all forgotten." Tony widened his eyes in exasperation, but smiled, then caught Graham's abject confusion. "We've lost you, haven't we, Radcliffe?"

"From the beginning," Graham admitted without shame. "Apologies."

Ingram snorted a laugh. "Don't apologize, Radcliffe. We practically speak our own language, and it's devilishly hard to follow." He pointed at Tony. "His cousin, once a villain and now less so than Cam here, married the hoyden of the Spinsters, Elinor Asheley, and now is one of our little husbands' club. Though he has yet to attend a gathering with us."

"Husbands' club? How quaint." Graham shook his head with a soft laugh.

"It's adorable, isn't it?" Henshaw agreed, grunting from his seat. "They moan and complain about their wives, then go home and live in incomparable bliss, and I get to hear all about it." He patted Graham's arm once. "Glad to have you here to endure it with me."

Graham gave him a sardonic look. "Charmed." He returned his attention to the others. "And the spinsters you speak of?"

"Oh, not another one," Cam moaned. "Must we always do this?"

"Do what?" Graham asked, looking around. "What have I missed?"

"Unfortunately, the truth doesn't make all that much sense now," Cam admitted, his face screwing up. "There aren't many actual spinsters left in the Spinsters."

Tony shook his head in agreement. "Not really, no. Just Charlotte. Well, and Edith."

Graham's interest was piqued at this. "Edith?" he repeated before he could stop himself. "What's she got to do with spinsters?"

"Don't ask, Radcliffe," Henshaw warned with a shake of his head. "Don't…"

"Ever read the Spinster Chronicles, Radcliffe?" Cam asked as he rubbed his hands together, almost eagerly.

Graham flicked a quick gesture with his fingers. "Only recently, and not extensively."

Cam mimicked his gesture a bit more grandly to encompass the table. "We are the fortunate husbands of the writers. Well, not Henshaw, he's that irritating younger brother no one quite knows what to do with."

"Speak for yourself," Henshaw grunted, then sipped his drink.

"But the rest of us," Cam went on smoothly, "married the actual spinsters from the Spinster Chronicles, and were thus lumped together by association. So, put your intellect to work, and conclude that…"

"Miss Wright and Lady Edith are also writers of the Spinster Chronicles," Graham finished without any difficulty whatsoever. "You'll find my surprise at a minimum. I see I must become a more avid reader while in London."

The other men stared at him for a long moment, and he stared back, unsure what they were waiting for.

"That's it?" Ingram finally asked, sounding disappointed. "That's all the reaction we're going to get?"

Graham lifted a brow. "I'm not generally prone to dramatics. I know little of Miss Wright, but she is outspoken, which suits the tone I have found in the Chronicles as I've read them. Lady Edith possesses spirit and wit, such as can be found there, as well. I confess to having more difficulties imagining Mrs. Vale and Mrs. Morton taking part, but it's certainly not outside the realm of possibility." He sat back against his chair and restrained a smile. "Any other surprises?"

Ingram made a face, shaking his head. "Having a friend who is a patron of the field of logic takes the enjoyment out of everything. No, there are no other surprises, devil take you."

"This is the most entertainment I've had in ages," Henshaw

proclaimed with a wide grin. "Quick, think of something else."

That wasn't likely; Graham was not one to make a habit of light or ridiculous banter, even among his friends. Despite the treatment and statements of those at the table, he couldn't count these men among them.

Not yet.

"Speaking of Edith," Tony commented, deftly changing the subject, "have any decisions been made? Georgie didn't say."

"That's a first," came a muffled muttering from Cam's general vicinity.

Was it? Interesting.

"She's having Amelia Perry stay with her," Henshaw informed them. "I believe she arrived yesterday."

"I can't believe the Perrys agreed to that." Cam shook his head. "I like Amelia a great deal, but this is just putting another woman in harm's way. Do her parents have the details?"

Henshaw shrugged. "All I've been told is that they know what they need to. Amelia is very determined."

Graham shook his head firmly. "I've heard of widows of a young age hiring a companion for themselves, and even of sponsoring younger ladies for a Season. But this? It's certainly not… orthodox." He winced at the word, wondering if his opinion would be taken as passing judgment when it was never intended as such.

But it only led to a round of chuckles. "Welcome to life with the Spinsters, Radcliffe. With a capital S, mind."

"Noted." He looked around at them again. "Is this really the best option?"

"Of course not," Tony replied without missing a beat. "It's only the easiest."

Now that was most certainly not true, and he took no pains to adjust his facial expression to claim otherwise. "Surely, it would be easier to install Lady Edith into someone else's home," he said flatly. "She would undoubtedly be safer, and no one else would be put into a potentially harmful situation."

"Sir Reginald would find that suspect," Henshaw told him. "Edith hasn't made a point of staying with anybody else since her arrival in London."

"So, take her out of London." Really, was it so difficult to put these pieces together? "Surely, not everyone in this group thrives upon being in London for the Season."

Tony's mouth curved in an almost smile. "You forget one thing, Radcliffe."

Graham turned his attention to the smug captain. "Do I?"

"Edith is looking for security and protection among Society. She is making concentrated efforts to increase her social appearances and take up more engagements." He shrugged his broad shoulders, seeming amused by something Graham did not understand. "Taking her out of London defeats that purpose quite soundly."

"She joined Grace and me in Derbyshire after Christmas," Ingram pointed out. "I've never seen her happier. She joined us in the evenings, regaled us with stories from Scotland, walked the estate despite the cold, painted daily. She even snuck down to the kitchens in the middle of the night."

Cam coughed in surprise. "How the blazes do you know that, Aubrey?"

Ingram grinned without shame. "I was doing the same. Bit awkward to be seen in my nightshirt and dressing gown by a guest in my home, but we had a laugh over it. She would get out of London in an instant if she could; she belongs out in the country in a quiet estate. The fact that she is remaining in London and going out in Society is proof enough of her commitment."

The image of Lady Edith Leveson sneaking around a country estate in her nightclothes was not one that would leave Graham's mind any time soon. He swallowed and shifted in his seat, trying to do so as unobtrusively as possible.

Did Edith wander about with her hair down or plaited?

Graham shook his head slightly, forcing the impertinent thought back. There was no point in dwelling on that question, though the idea of her dark, treacle-colored tresses waving down her back in loose curls did have a certain appeal.

Curses...

"The point is," Ingram went on, blessedly taking Graham out of a deadly whirlpool of imaginings, "we can't take her out of London, and she would refuse to move into one of our houses purely to spare us Sir Reginald."

"Let him come to my house," Cam growled, sounding like the man prone to fighting he was reputed to be.

Suddenly, Graham saw the man in a whole new light and made a note never to anger him.

Graham was a man of above-average height and an athletic build, but he would be no match for Camden Vale.

Tony sighed, ignoring Cam's dark invitation. "At least with Amelia staying with her, Edith will be sure to garner a few more invitations than she might have done on her own. Amelia is very popular, and the Perrys well-respected; once word gets out of the friendship, Edith will be invited absolutely everywhere."

"Good." Henshaw nodded, taking a long drink from his glass. "Rumors already fly about her, so we will need to see that she is seen in the right company and under favorable circumstances. Sir Reginald will likely object to all of it and start his own rumors about her. That won't help Edith make connections."

Graham glanced at the man in surprise. "So, we are trying to get her a husband? I thought Miss Wright's idea was vetoed."

"We?" Tony repeated with raised brows. "You're joining in?"

Apparently so. It had been clear to Graham the moment he'd exchanged nods with Edith, but he hadn't admitted such until this moment. He was committed now. He lifted a shoulder in a shrug.

"Ingram brought me in, and I feel honor-bound to see this through."

"Good man." Henshaw thumped his back once. "And no, not getting her a husband. We're not going to force anything, but if Edith happens to form a connection with a gentleman of whom we approve…"

Graham rolled his eyes and rested his elbows on the table. "Surely, there's another way to keep her protected. Or why not just marry her yourself, Henshaw? You seem close enough to her already; it would be a comfortable match."

As soon as the words left his mouth, he hated the idea. It was the simplest of all the ideas yet, but it was undoubtedly the most distasteful one.

Funny, that.

Henshaw grunted once. "I offered already."

"You did?" at least three of them asked.

He nodded. "Before I knew the situation in its entirety. I call on her once a week, you know, to check on things and make sure she wants for nothing. I know how comfortable the match would be, and likely it would be exceptional. But she refused, and it is for the best."

"Is it?" Tony asked with more interest than Graham would have thought. "I would have sworn the two of you were destined. Georgie and I have wagered on it."

Henshaw glowered at his friend. "What have I told you about making matches for me? I respect Edith immensely. It would be a good marriage, but it is not to be, and both of us are happier that it is so."

"I bet you are," Ingram murmured under his breath, smiling at something Graham didn't catch, and Cam snickered alongside him.

Tony, it seemed, was just as clueless. "What was that?" he asked.

Ingram waved it off. "Nothing. So, we're not getting Henshaw down the aisle, and Edith will be out and about, which could also give Sir Reginald more chances to make trouble. How do we account for that?"

"Ensure one of us is present at each event?" Tony suggested. "We can keep an eye on Edith and intervene where and when it is necessary."

"Which works well, if one of us is invited to the same thing," Cam pointed out. "I don't know about the rest of you, but I don't move in particularly exalted circles, no matter how beloved my wife is."

Henshaw nodded slowly, his dark brow wrinkled with thought. "The Spinsters are fairly good at intervening at the events where there would be mostly ladies, but as for the rest..." He looked over at Tony, one brow lifting. "What about Miranda?"

Tony, Cam, and Ingram all crossed themselves in a strange motion of unison.

"Who's Miranda?" Graham felt the need to ask, if for no other reason than for explanation of their actions.

"My stepmother," Tony murmured with a weak smile. "I love her dearly." He sounded as if he would say more on the subject, but just left the statement there, which made the others laugh knowingly.

Graham was just as confused as before. "And she would be helpful?"

Four sets of eyes stared at him in disbelief. "I forget how removed you have been, Radcliffe," Ingram said on a sigh. "Miranda has the ability to move in the highest circles effortlessly and could be employed as an operative for the Home or Foreign Office. She is conniving, she is mischievous, and she has absolutely no shame. I've never been more terrified of any person, male or female, in my entire life."

"I find this difficult to imagine," Graham admitted with some hesitation, seeing the effect the woman's name had on the others. At their matching sly grins, he hastily added, "But I'll take your word for it."

"Wise notion," Henshaw grunted, shaking his head.

"Miranda could help in the right circumstances," Tony confirmed, taking them back to the topic. "What other measures are we putting in place?"

Henshaw straightened in his seat. "Edith is having word sent to me whenever Sir Reginald calls on her. I don't have many calls upon my person at present, so in theory, I should be free to come if needed. Her footman, Owen, is everything a Highlander is expected to be, so I do not fear for much while he is there."

"Good," Graham murmured, his eyes staring off at nothing for the moment. "But why can we not do something about Sir Reginald himself?"

"Cam?" Tony asked with some invitation.

Cam heaved a disgruntled note. "My sister's husband has some dealings with the law, and with some powers behind the law, none of which I know anything about. I am meeting with him this evening to beg for his assistance. And I hate begging."

Ingram patted his back twice. "There, there."

Graham snorted once. "But surely, for Lady Edith, we will all be making sacrifices."

The table grew silent, all eyes on him.

That was unnerving, to say the least.

Was he wrong? He was willing to sacrifice for her, and he barely knew her. Why wouldn't these men, who knew her better, do the same and more?

"I like you, Radcliffe," Cam stated as though revelation had come to him.

Tony hissed in apparent pain. "So sorry, Radcliffe. Nobody deserves that."

"No, indeed," Ingram agreed.

"Lads, behave," Henshaw suggested lazily. "The man only knows Lord Sterling. It's not his fault we've got Tony instead."

"Hey!"

Graham chuckled at that. "I trust Lord Sterling is also involved?"

"He will be," Tony muttered with a dark look at his friend, "and anybody else we can trust."

"Is that a long list?" Graham asked, lifting a brow.

The men looked at each other, faces wreathed in confusion.

"No," Henshaw said slowly. "No, it isn't."

Chapter Nine

An unexpected guest is rarely a pleasant thing.

-The Spinster Chronicles, 4 September 1819

"A letter for you, Miss Perry."

"Thank you, Owen! I cannot imagine who would wish to send me a letter here; I saw my mother only yesterday, and she had nothing of great importance to say at all. There is no reason for my brother to send me anything, either. He is far too busy gaming at present. Do you know anything of gaming, Owen? Apparently, James is rather skilled, but I have no idea what that means."

Owen blinked at the barrage of words, and Edith bit her lip to restrain a laugh. Amelia had been staying with her for a week now, and there was a distinct change about the house since her arrival. Everything was brighter and more filled with cheer, and though Amelia was still not quite herself, she was an improvement on the place.

Even if she did talk a good deal more than Edith ever did.

"I dinna gamble much, miss," Owen admitted after a heavy pause. "An' ne'er well, when I do. But I'd be willin' to teach ye if ye've a mind to learn it."

Now it was Edith who stared, her mouth gaping. Owen rarely offered to do anything that did not involve physical violence, and there was nothing he detested so much as company. Yet here he was, offering to instruct Amelia in gaming, of all things.

"Would you?" Amelia squealed and beamed up at Owen as though he were her oldest friend. "That would be so wonderful, Owen. I would be ever so grateful. I do feel quite the dunce at times, you know. No one ever teaches young ladies the practical things in life."

"Gaming is no' verra practical, miss," Owen told her with a wry smile Edith couldn't believe she was seeing. "But I see yer point right enough. When next ye've an evening free, I can teach ye. Mistress, too, if she's of a mind."

Edith raised a brow at her manservant, catching his mischievous glint. "Should I be of a mind?" she inquired mildly. "I've nothing to gamble *with*, Owen, and ye ken it well."

"Offer still stands." Owen bowed to them both and left the room, leaving Edith to shake her head.

"I have never seen him so accommodating," Edith said to no one in particular. "Clearly, you are a reforming influence, Amelia."

There was no response from the girl, prompting Edith to glance over at her, another teasing remark on her tongue.

She bit that back the moment she caught Amelia's face, devoid of warmth and pleasure, reading over the letter in her hand.

"Amelia?" Edith prodded as gently as she could. "What is it?"

Amelia's eyes raised to hers, a sheen of tears visible. Her teeth grazed her full bottom lip in a clear sign of hesitation.

"I have..." She swallowed and cleared her throat. "I have, for the last year, been engaging in a rather unconventional sort of courtship. It was slow, but it was fervent. I did not know how much so until we had to start corresponding rather than meeting. Then, for no reason at all, his letters stopped." She looked down at the letter in her hand, her fingers trembling as a tear rolled down her cheek.

"Oh, lass..." Edith reached out a hand, then drew it back when Amelia didn't take it. "Is that not a letter from him there?"

"No." Amelia swiped a hand across her face. "It is my letter to him returned to me." She held it up briefly, a sad smile crossing her face. "He never received it."

Edith sighed, shaking her head. "Is there not some consolation in that? He never received it, so ye canna know how it would be received. This isna jilting, if he's not seeing your letters."

"Isn't it?" Amelia whispered, the letter crinkling in her lap now. "If he isn't receiving them, where is he? Why am I not having letters from him? What purpose is there in corresponding with someone who, for all intents and purposes, no longer exists to me?" She clamped down on her lips hard, turning away. "I'm not a woman with an impenetrable heart, Edith, and I do not always wear the countenance of sunlight, as everybody thinks. I have a vulnerable heart, and it is breaking in pieces, but nobody will know that, because he refused to court me for the world to see."

This was unbearable. How was Edith supposed to comfort the lass when there were no answers to be had? When Edith knew nothing of love herself, only the dream of it? How could she soothe a broken heart when her own had not been whole for years?

And who was this man that had broken Amelia so?

"Refused?" Edith repeated, though she likely should not have done. "How…?"

Amelia shook her head. "He said it was not possible but could not say further than that. I didn't mind; I only wished to be with him in my own small way. Now, even that is gone."

Edith reached out again, this time taking Amelia's hand without hesitation. "This is your disappointment? Lass, this is heartbreaking, even in hearing. What can I do?"

"You're doing it." Amelia turned to her and smiled through her tears. "Being here with you, away from my mother's questions and efforts, away from my home, is a cure beyond anything." She wiped at her cheeks again, sniffling. "I'm sorry, I didn't mean to turn watering pot on you. I think I'll go to my room for a time to collect myself. When I'm better company, I'll come back down."

"No rush, lass," Edith insisted. "And you needn't go up; I'm no' fit company much of the time. But if ye need some privacy, I understand."

Amelia rose and slid the letter between her fingers absently. "I believe there are more tears yet to cry, Edith. I freely admit to feeling guilty for crying them in front of you, given all that you're contending with at present."

"Pain is pain, Amelia. It needn't be compared."

"And you've got more of it than me," Amelia told her with a

serious look. "I'll recover from mine, but we're all trying to find a solution to yours. Once I've cried my tears, I'll be better suited to helping you, and that will cure my disappointment, as well." She smiled once more and left the drawing room, leaving Edith to her thoughts.

There were no words for the girl's offer, and Edith would not pretend there were. How could she expect to forget her heartache just to give Edith some aid? Her situation was dire, it was true, but it did not, could not, negate the pain of anyone else. Especially something as tender as a lost love, or, at the very least, a disappointed one.

She and Amelia had been mere acquaintances before this, hardly close enough to engender this kind of loyalty or effort on her part. Or that of the others who were moving heaven and earth to help her. Her friends in the Spinsters, perhaps, but their husbands? Henshaw? Lord Radcliffe?

How did someone repay such a debt of kindness when it was so little deserved?

"What happened to yer curious friend?"

Edith looked towards the doorway to the drawing room, sighing a bit at Owen's furrowed expression. "She went up to her room for some rest. She's... well, she's got some private pain, and needed a moment."

Owen shook his head, surprising her. "Poor wee lass. What kind of a man would injure a bonny thing like that?"

"I dinna ken," Edith murmured. "She willna say, and I dare not ask it of her."

"I'll ask. He deserves a solid thrashing."

Edith gave him a look. "Really, Owen, ye canna thrash a man wi'out knowing the truth of it all. He may be just as keen on Amelia as she is on him."

Owen scowled. "If that be the case, he's no' worth the tears she's shedding, abandoning her like this."

A pounding at the door saved Edith from having to explain any laughter, as Owen turned from the room to answer it, but she gave in to the impulse the moment he was gone. Her burly manservant, a rough and gruff Highlander, was a romantic? Took personal offense at the pains of Amelia Perry after only a week of knowing her? It was far more a surprise than anything else Owen had ever said or done, and it could hardly have been expected or anticipated. What in the world would he say or do next?

Shouts sounded in the corridor from the front of the house, effectively eliminating any laughter Edith was prone to.

Owen almost never raised his voice, being much more prone to using his size for intimidation than to engage in actual fighting. Who in the world could stir him into such a fury?

The question was answered moments later when Owen appeared in the doorway yet again, his face tense, his jaw twitching.

"Yer mangy brother, mistress."

Edith's jaw dropped in amazement. "My *what?*"

"Mangy?" echoed an outraged voice that stopped Edith in her tracks. "I ken yer eyes are weak, Owen, but if ye'd open them a bit wider, ye'd observe this is the cleanest I've been in years."

It couldn't be... There was only one voice in the world filled with that particular blend of gravel, cynicism, and charm, and he couldn't be here.

He couldn't.

But then he rounded into the room, and no amount of blinking cleared him from her sight.

"Well, Edie, are ye no' going to kiss me in greeting?" Lachlan asked with a grin, spreading his arms out as though she would run into his arms.

Edith stared at him, from the unfashionable length of his dark hair, to the scar down the left side of his face, to the kilt he currently wore.

Nothing about the sight made her want to run to him. Not a thing.

"No," she snapped at last, her jaw clenching as her mouth closed.

Her brother looked confused by her tone. "Edie... *Tha an teaghlach as cudromaiche.*"

Edith barely restrained a snarl. Family was most important? He would claim that? To *her?*

"No, Lachlan," she ground out. "No. *Tha fuil a 'ciallachadh dad, dìreach dìlseachd.*"

The widening of his eyes told Edith her brother understood more than she thought. That blood didn't make them family without loyalty. That his actions had broken their family for her. That they were not family now.

They couldn't be.

Taking advantage of his silence, Edith went on. "The last I saw ye, *mo bhràthair*, I was dragged into Father's study to meet the man ye sold my hand to. Ye gave me to him, Lachlan, as though I were yours to give! An' for what?"

"Don't you think I know what I've done?" he cried, truly sounding upset. Lachlan exhaled slowly, his eyes steady, the shade so similar to hers. Then, he swallowed and scratched the back of his head. "Will ye have grace enough to let me explain afore ye rightfully set me out on my arse?"

Edith eyed her brother as though she'd never seen him before, and he certainly did not appear as himself. He was haggard and drawn; his eyes held shadows that she had never seen in him, and it was clear he had lost some weight. He had never appeared thus, not even when he was insensibly drunk.

"By all means." She gestured limply to the drawing room, strangely satisfied that it was sparse, mismatched, and poorly kept.

Let Lachlan see what he, and their father, had brought her to.

She sat on the tattered divan and waited for him to take a seat. He did, choosing the wingback chair that Sir Reginald favored.

There was an irony in that.

Lachlan surprised her by leaning forward and rubbing his hands over his face. "I ken what I am," he told her in a low voice, "and I ken what I have done. I never meant tae trap ye like that. I ken my actions were selfish an' that ye were the one tae suffer for it. I couldna face ye on yer wedding day, knowing what I'd done. Sir Archibald was a blackguard, and I ken tha' from the moment our hands were dealt. He made it verra plain he had fortune aplenty but no nobility tae enforce his position. I thought when Da discovered the truth, he would call it off. But then he moved the wedding up, and Da insisted so forcibly. Faye never told him, and—"

"Don't you dare blame Mama!" Edith scolded at once.

"I'm not," he said, raising his hands. "I'm not. I am the villain here, and I own to it. It surprised me how eagerly he wanted ye," Lachlan admitted, sounding far away as he rose and began to pace before her. "I think he may have cheated the final hand for ye alone. I got myself right and truly soused oot the head wi' drink tha' night. 'Twas the only way I could bring him tae Da and tae ye." He looked at Edith then, his expression raw. "I ken the depth of my sins, Edie. I ken verra well what Da would say and do. But I didna care enough to intervene. Tae take my debt like a man. I went back tae my regiment, and I did my best tae forget ye, and him, and all of it. Believe me, I never thought he would use you so. If I had… if I had…"

Edith folded her arms and gave him a look. "You would have been less of a villain?"

He gave Edith a ghost of a smile. "Perhaps only half of one. I heard about the wedding, and your husband's death, and I felt I should have ridden into the church and rescued you from it all. What sort of a brother lets his sister be sold off to the devil? I should be as dead as Archibald. I'd be better to the family for it."

"Oh, stop that," Edith said, relaxing at last. Taking his hand, she forced him to sit down next to her. "We may despise you at times, but none of us want you dead."

"I cannot pretend that I will be a good man," he said, squeezing her hand. "I cannot change my spots that much. But I would like to be a better one. I want to make amends."

"You did send Henshaw," Edith reminded him. "He has been a great friend."

"I know. You are perhaps the only person I have ever done good for. I knew Henshaw would treat you better than I could have at the time. The most honorable man I've ever met, and one with many sisters. I thought, there is a man who kens how tae be a brother. I ken I wasna fit, but I wanted someone tae look in on ye when I heard ye'd come to London."

"Henshaw was no replacement for you, Lachlan," Edith murmured softly. "There's only one of you, *mo bhràthair*."

"I'd hoped tha…" He smiled very weakly, his hands rubbing together between his knees. "I'd hoped he'd take ye tae wife in yer widowhood. Make up for my mistakes."

"He offered," Edith admitted, matching his smile. "I refused."

"Why?"

"He's in love with a lass, though I doubt either of them have admitted so." Edith sighed and began to look on her brother with pity, and even some grudging affection, somehow. "Why are ye here, Lachlan?"

His smile faded, and his look grew intense. "I'm no' a saint, Edie, but I'm no' the same sinner who betrayed ye. I've come to make amends and better myself. I've come to be yer brother again, if ye've a mind tae have me."

A lump formed in Edith's throat, a sharp pang of longing accompanying it. "The rest of the family doesna want me back," she whispered harshly. "Da willna let me return, and I canna…"

"I ken, lassie," her brother interrupted, turning towards her. "I dinna care. I didna serve ye well before, but I'll be damned if I dinna serve ye well now." He reached out and brushed his thumb fondly along her left temple, tucking a tendril behind her ear with the motion. "*Piuthar mo ghràidh… Tha mi duilich.*"

His apology sent warmth out from her heart to the ends of the fingers he held, the warmth increasing with every beat. Tears slowly rolled down her cheeks, and the stiffness in her spine melted away, leaving her to sag and let the tears helplessly fall.

Lachlan pulled her hard against his chest, his large arms wrapping around her better than any blanket or wrap she'd ever known and twice as snug. "I'm so verra sorry, Edie," he said against her shoulder. "Ye canna ken how much."

"*Tapadh leat,*" she murmured through her tears. "That's all I ever wanted."

"I should have said it then," he admitted, pulling back to give her a sad smile. "I couldna bear the shame of it."

Edith shook her head and took his hand. "It's done wi' now, and Archie's been dead for years. It could have been worse."

"Doesna have tae be worse to be *uamhasach,*" he told her. He cleared his throat and sat back, looking more like the brother she remembered and had once adored. "Now tha's oot the way, do ye have any food, Edie?"

She laughed merrily in surprise at that. This, at last, was her brother restored to her in all his maddening glory. She supplied him with a light repast, which he found insufficient, and refused to serve him any strong drink, which he was almost indignant about.

"I hold my whiskey better'n anyone else ye know," he insisted. "I can manage a wee snifter."

"I don't have whiskey," Edith laughed, "and no money to purchase any, if ye were about to ask."

He raised a brow. "I wasna, but whiskey is cheap, is it no?"

Edith huffed playfully and gestured to her surroundings. "Does it look as though I have money to hand out, Lachlan?"

He finally looked around, then gave her a strange look. "Bide a wee moment," he said as he rose, ran out of the room, and charged up the stairs, leaving Edith to stare after him in horror.

When the first door slammed, she winced. When the second, third, and fourth proceeded to do so, she rose and began to pace the room. The upper rooms were much worse than the main floor, as no one ever saw them, and they had no funds for a proper staff to keep them up. What if he discovered Amelia hiding there? That would help no one at all, least of all Amelia.

It did not take long for Lachlan to thunder down the stairs once more and return to the drawing room, his expression hooded. "The house is awful, Edith."

She snorted, despite her fingers knitting. "Yes, I know. If I had money, I would make repairs."

"Ye'd be better served burning it down," he said, looking around with a wrinkled nose.

"Then where would I live?" she asked him, wondering how stupid her brother really was.

He shrugged. "One of yer other estates. Forget London. Ye're too good for this."

She was flattered by his thinking so but amused that he knew so little of her situation. "Lachlan, do you pay any attention to family matters at all?"

Again, he shrugged, and it was accompanied by a grin. "Why should I? I have no interest in most of them, and Greer is going tae save us all with her triumphant marriage tae someone important, if the rumors be true." He waved his hand dismissively.

Edith sighed and rubbed at her head. "Lachlan, I have no money.

At all. No other estates, no income, and nothing to live on."

His eyes went wide, and he gaped openly. "But... yer husband... He was rich."

She gave him a sad smile. "Aye. *He* was. I am not. His cousin has taken control of everything, quite literally. I have five regular gowns, four nicer ones, and a few accouterments. In the house, I have Owen as a footman, butler, and bodyguard, Simms as a maid, and Cook in the kitchen."

Lachlan frowned. "Tha's not right."

Edith sighed and shrugged. "No, but I canna do anything about the law."

"So, what are you doing?" he asked, looking concerned.

"Trying to find protection somewhere," she answered truthfully. "Anywhere, really."

He grinned too wickedly. "Going to be a mistress, Edith?"

"No," she said forcefully, giving him a glare, which he laughed at.

"I didna mean it!" he chuckled. "Ye know I would pummel a man for taking that sort of advantage of you. I'd run a man through for ye, if ye needed, but ye dinna."

"That's because you like to fight," she reminded him.

He grinned at Edith warmly. "True, but it sounds better if I say it's for yer honor."

The bell rang, and Edith froze, looking with wide eyes at Owen, who had appeared in the doorway. They were not expecting callers, which was a clear indication that it could be Sir Reginald.

Owen peered out, then returned and gave her a slow nod.

She closed her eyes and tried to find calm. "Send for Hensh," she told him softly.

"Edith? Do I need to go?" Lachlan asked, looking between the two of them. "Why do ye need Hensh?"

For a moment, she'd forgotten her brother had been sitting there, and now looked at him with new interest, which made him suspicious.

"How much is your family loyalty worth today?" she demanded.

"What?" he asked, clambering to his feet and looking disconcerted that she did so as well. "Why?"

"I need you to be my overprotective relation," she told him, though Owen was shaking his head. "This man is the one who is taking everything from me."

Lachlan's jaw tightened, and he gave her a look. "Why is he here?"

"He... he wants me to be his mistress," she murmured, looking away. "He's threatening to ruin me if I continue to refuse."

Lachlan swore viciously, which shocked Edith, but he turned around and nodded to Owen, who moved back to the door.

"Stay behind me," Lachlan told Edith, taking her hand and carefully shielding her behind him.

The door opened, and Sir Reginald came in without invitation, as usual. "My Lady Edith," he called in his oily voice.

He stopped suddenly as he rounded the drawing room and saw Lachlan glowering at him. His eyes flicked to Edith's hand in Lachlan's hold, then took in their positions.

"What is this?" he demanded, trying to look around Lachlan's bulk to see her.

Lachlan would not let him. "Who the hell are ye?" Lachlan barked, making Sir Reginald jump.

"Sir Reginald Leveson," he replied with a stiff nod of his head. "I am Sir Archibald's cousin."

Lachlan defied propriety by not responding with a nod or a bow, or any sort of introduction. "Sir Archibald is dead. And we were not expecting ye. Get out."

Sir Reginald drew himself up as tall as he could, though he still could not reach Lachlan's chin. "I will do no such thing; I have every right to be here."

Lachlan actually snarled at him, and started forward, still holding Edith's hand. "The only right ye have is tae exit on yer own terms or tae exit on mine. Three... two... one..."

Sir Reginald's eyes went round, and he scurried out of the room, fumbling for his walking stick and slamming the front door behind him.

Edith stood there for a moment in stunned silence.

Then, Lachlan turned to her, looking almost bored.

"Will that do?" he asked simply.

She laughed out loud and wrapped her arms around his broad chest. "You are the most wonderful person in the world!"

He snorted and patted her back. "Dinna get carried away, Edith. Several hundred people are burrowing in their graves at this moment."

"Mangy cur or no', I'm right pleased ye were here," Owen admitted as he returned to the room, his hand extended towards Lachlan, who shook it without hesitation.

Lachlan gave him a stern look. "Next time that *cnap de todhar eich* appears, ye will send for me as well as the lieutenant, aye? I dinna ken wha' the law says, if he is permitted tae enter or no', but it will be o'er my cold, dead corpse tha' he gets wi'in ten feet of her."

"Aye, sir," Owen replied with a shocking amount of respect. "I ken yer meaning exactly."

"Edith? Edith, what's happened?" Amelia's voice called from the stairs.

Lachlan looked down at Edith in surprise. "Now, who is that?"

Edith patted his chest with a sigh. "She's my friend, and no, ye canna have her."

"I didna ask."

"Ye will ask. And the answer is no."

Chapter Ten

————— ❧❧ —————

This author has heard some debate as to whether or not a gentleman truly enjoys a ball. This is undoubtedly why gaming rooms became fashionable accessories of the host's location. But this is no kindness to the ladies, as such an accessory removes potential partners from the ballroom. And why else would one attend a ball but to dance?

-The Spinster Chronicles, 20 August 1818

"Do you know how many years I have spent avoiding the Wintermere spring ball, Radcliffe? All of them. Every single year that I have been eligible to attend, I have avoided it. Why? Because Annabelle Wintermere is a desperate cat and wants me for her husband. I cannot believe I let you talk me into this. What was I thinking? And what is this abysmal theme they are attempting? It fails, whatever it is. Why aren't you saying anything?"

Graham glanced at Tyrone as the two of them proceeded into the ballroom, thankfully without having to endure an official introduction from a stuffy majordomo.

"You seem to be carrying on a conversation well enough on your own. I saw no need to intervene." He returned his attention forward, scanning the guests already in attendance. "Besides, I cannot abide whining."

Tyrone gave him a dark look. "Whining?"

"What else would you call incessant complaining? You had a choice about attending, and you chose to attend. There is nothing to complain about."

"I beg your pardon; there is a great deal to complain about."

Graham smiled to himself, shaking his head. "Then do us both a kindness and confine the complaints to your head."

"That is hardly as satisfying," Tyrone grunted. "Did you convince Francis to come?"

"Didn't have to," Graham informed him, frowning at the lack of familiar faces. "I believe his wife took care of that, though I don't see either of them here yet."

Tyrone smirked and swiped a drink from a stoic footman. "It's early in the evening for them. Or for anyone important, for that matter."

"You're here."

"As I said, too early for anyone important." He flashed a quick grin, then looked about the room himself. "Gads, this will get stuffy, though. Already twelve couples on the floor and barely room enough to maneuver. The Wintermeres must be feeling particularly ambitious this year."

Graham looked at his friend again, ignoring the scratch of his over-starched cravat. "How would you know? You just said you never attend. This might be normal for them."

Tyrone's cheeks flushed, and he looked away quickly. "I've heard. The Spinster Chronicles have detailed the event every year."

"I'm sure that's it." Graham nodded sagely, trying not to smile. Despite Tyrone's comments, his friend hadn't been overly difficult to convince to attend tonight. He'd made more noise after the fact than he had before it, and he was perfectly free to leave whenever he chose.

He wouldn't do so, however. Tyrone's pattern was fairly well established. He would dance a few times, never with a lady he had a particular interest in, then take himself off to the gaming room for a few hours, only to return to the ballroom for a few more dances with ladies of whom he approved. Any and all young ladies wishing for the attentions of Tyrone Demaris in truth would watch for his return from the gaming room, hoping for a dance.

Those chosen prior to his departure thence were usually sensible enough not to care either way, which was likely why they were chosen.

Graham had no such elaborate plans dictating his behaviors at balls and assemblies. He did as he wished, and only as he wished, and rarely thought through his actions of the night prior to his arrival.

Only once had he acted differently from his wishes, and it had taken a stubborn Scottish beauty to change that for him.

On instinct, he looked around again, this time with more intensity. He was only here because the others had said they would attend, as Lady Edith and Miss Perry had been granted invitations and intended to come. He barely knew the Wintermeres, but he had been repeatedly assured that everyone who was anyone attended if invited, so attending had seemed the thing to do.

Every young lady he saw seemed to be dressed in her very finest, on her very best behavior, and every gentleman was far more attentive than he might have been at another ball in London. Graham couldn't understand why, as it was the same sort of Society they engaged with at every other event, if not on a daily basis. What made this place and this event better than any other?

The Wintermeres were not nobility, though they had ties to it, and they had wealth, though not the most extensive fortune in London. Yet their ballroom was full to the brim, and more guests were entering every minute.

This was not the sort of event that Graham would enjoy. Too many people, too many expectations. He might spend his time in the gaming room tonight, as well.

After at least one dance, that is.

Just one.

If he could find her.

In this crowd, that might be more difficult than he had previously anticipated.

"I heard a little something about your Scottish beauty, you know."

Graham jerked and looked at his friend with wide eyes. "What?"

Tyrone chuckled, shaking his head. "You're a terrible liar, my friend, and you hide things even worse." He looked over at him with a smile. "Your interest in Lady Edith Leveson isn't exactly a secret."

"I'm helping to protect her," Graham reminded him, his pulse racing at an almost panicked pace. "She's having significant difficulties; you know that."

"All I said was an interest," Tyrone said, holding up his hands in surrender, though his smile said a great deal more. "Nothing more, nothing less."

Graham scowled at the unspoken implication, and at his own reaction to it. That would tell far more than he would wish, if it hadn't already done so.

"What have you learned, then?" he grumbled, wishing he had taken a drink earlier, as well.

Tyrone moved a step closer to him, sipping his beverage slowly. "A man was seen exiting her house the other day after having spent a considerable amount of time within."

Graham rolled his eyes. "Sir Reginald calls on her at will, and Henshaw calls on a regular basis. That means nothing."

"Would I have said anything if it was Henshaw or Sir Reginald?" Tyrone shot back. "This was no mere visit. The man entered before Sir Reginald visited, and was there after he left. I've been told he's a rugged Highlander who comes with his very own kilt."

Something sharp lanced through Graham's chest, and his jaw tightened. There were several rumors surrounding Edith at any given time, and there was no guarantee that any could be believed. Why should this one be any more true than any of the others? Yet, if Tyrone was mentioning it, there had to be something in it.

"Who saw the man?" Graham asked in a low voice, fighting for ambivalence.

"Sir Reginald, of course." Tyrone snorted softly. "He's making it known that Lady Edith is entertaining a single man alone for an extended period of time. It wouldn't be condoned if it weren't for the fact that Lady Edith's neighbor confirmed the arrival of a dashing kilted warrior."

Graham felt his teeth grind together, and he only nodded. "She did say she was seeking protection. Perhaps she has found it."

"So, you wouldn't care if Lady Edith had taken a lover?"

"Why should I care?" Graham inquired in as mild a tone as he could manage. "She is an independent woman who should take her freedom as and where she may. She has so little of it elsewhere."

Tyrone hummed under his breath. "Noble sentiment, I am sure. Does it change your intentions?"

Graham turned to face his friend more directly, giving him a hard look. "My intentions," he ground out, "remain the same as they were before. To help Lady Edith find a way through her present troubles into something better. That is all I have been aiming for."

"Is it, indeed?" Tyrone murmured. One side of his mouth curved in an almost bemused manner. "Intriguing sort of interest, but to each his own."

"Dance with Lady Edith tonight," Graham instructed as his attention moved to a corner of the room where a small group had gathered and was now dispersing into the ballroom. One face in particular caught his attention, and the sight of it sent a boulder dropping into the center of his chest.

Loveliness itself, Edith moved through the other guests with minimal difficulty, her complexion rosy, her smile bright. Her dark hair was curled and twisted into something elegant, ribbons and flowers entwining within the luxurious locks. The color of her dress wasn't immediately obvious to him, but he didn't care.

Seeing her was enough.

"Dance with her?" Tyrone echoed behind him, his voice somehow seeming far off. "Why?"

Graham felt his lip twitch in amusement. That was a stupid question; there was no doubt of it. Who wouldn't want to dance with the most beautiful woman in the room, and the cleverest, the wittiest, the bravest...

"Just do it, will you?" Graham clapped his friend on the shoulder and moved away, his eyes on Edith still, his attention fixed. He'd promised himself he would look after her, had told the others that he was with them in their protection of her, had roped himself into a mission of sorts that he didn't fully understand, but he was committed, nonetheless.

Who wouldn't be, after the interactions he'd had with her?

Even Tyrone, the skeptic that he was, would have devoted himself to the cause.

Graham smiled as he watched Edith, seeing her with all the brightness he'd thought she was capable of and more, which she had worn so little in his previous encounters with her. This was as she should have been, mingling with others and full of life. She did not deserve the harshness her life had brought, nor to wear the reserved expression she so often had.

So, you wouldn't care if Lady Edith had taken a lover?

Tyrone's question echoed in Graham's mind, and he felt his smile fade as his chest tightened at it.

He *would* care. He *did* care.

But it changed nothing. Not a thing.

A movement behind Edith distracted Graham momentarily, then with real interest as the cause of the movement revealed itself.

The weasel was approaching her, and she had no idea.

Graham moved at once, though the crowd had thickened considerably, and his pace was slow.

His eyes flew back to Edith, hissing to himself.

He wasn't going to make it in time.

It seemed that Edith had learned a great deal about moving in Society, if tonight were any indication. Or perhaps it was that Amelia was so very in demand. At any rate, the pair of them had made so many calls and had made the acquaintance of several gentlemen, though most they had no interest in maintaining.

Edith had found two potential candidates for protection in the future, and both had vowed to come this evening. Mr. Copeland had five thousand a year, an estate in Yorkshire, and was quite a striking fellow. So tall and with the sort of face one would see on a Grecian statue, and the fine coloring to match. But one would never think that he was also remarkably intelligent, spoke eloquently, and acted almost as if he had no idea just how attractive he was. Additionally, according to Grace, he was one of the finest horsemen in England.

There was no way for Edith to be entirely certain if that should endear him to her or not, as she had also heard that an Englishman could not ride half so well as a Highlander.

The other gentleman of interest was a Mr. Tomkins, who was a bit older, nearly forty, but still possessed the looks and vigor of a younger man. He would age well, for he had very few lines, and what lines he did have were very well situated. He prided himself on being a great sportsman, but also bore a keen interest in the new industrial works, if one could believe it.

A man of fortune who wished to work? Unfathomable.

Neither of them had professed any serious intentions, but Edith would feel quite comfortable in encouraging either of them, should they wish to. Aubrey assured her that both were universally well respected and men of excellent character. What could she want more?

But as she had seen neither gentleman yet this evening, she was left to meander about the room in the hopes of finding another agreeable gentleman to converse with, if not dance with. Amelia had insisted that Edith put her best foot, and face, forward, dressing her in a silk gown of the palest pink and instructing Simms in a new style of hair. While Edith could not say either were particularly comfortable, as she seemed to be standing out a bit more, she could admit to feeling rather prettier than she usually did.

Whatever that meant.

The ball was very well attended, too well for her taste, as it was quite a crush. Her toes had been trampled three times already just in moving about the room and moving now was considerably awkward. She'd already enjoyed dances with Henshaw, Tony, and Cam, for something they called "a good impression".

No doubt they meant to show the gathering what influence surrounded her, though how anyone could see anything in this ever-increasing mass of people was a mystery.

A pair of hands suddenly ran up the full length of her torso, settling just aside her chest. "Lady Edith, you have been avoiding me," a chilling voice whispered at her ear.

Edith stiffened in Sir Reginald's hold, gasping. She tried to flail, but he pinned her arms behind her back. To anyone seeing them, she might have been standing politely, and he simply a man standing behind her. Truly, it was the most innocuous sort of position. She saw no less than four others watching the dance who looked exactly the same.

The difference was that she was in danger, and they were not.

"I am pleased that your Scottish bull has abandoned you for the moment, for there was something I needed to tell you," he whispered, his hands now toying along the buttons of her dress.

She tried to stomp his foot, but he twisted his leg with hers, effectively trapping her. And then he pulled her along, moving between people, so they were no longer in front to see the dancing, and thus were more hidden from view.

"Stop struggling," he hissed, gripping her arms more tightly, smiling for the effect of those around them, though very few were paying attention. "I could compromise you so easily right here, in front of all of these people. And then your plans for finding a new husband would be quite ruined."

Edith swallowed and obeyed, forcing her face to relax as much as she could.

"Better," he purred, his hands gliding around to the front of her bodice. "Now, if you keep avoiding me, Edith, I will make things most unpleasant for you."

"How's that?" she asked, clenching her teeth. "They are already far from pleasant."

"Tart lassie," he said with a laugh, mocking her accent. "Have you forgotten that the house you live in belongs to me?"

She had not forgotten, could not forget, but refused to reply, lifting her chin.

"You agree to be at my disposal, entirely, in every way," he murmured, one hand sliding up the front of her bodice and tracing up her neck, "and I will let you remain in the house. If you do not, I will take the house from you, and you will be cast out."

"You wouldn't dare," she replied, feeling her cheeks grow cold even as her heart began to race desperately.

She could not return to Scotland, not like that, and not without some assurance of being taken care of in some way. Lachlan was returned to her, but how could she rely on him for anything so early in their rekindled relationship? Her friends could take her in, but at what cost to their own lives and reputations?

"Try me," Sir Reginald said, his hands wandering over her body and lingering where they ought not. "I have told you I want you, that I would be generous with you, and that your heritage will not deter me in this. It is your only option."

"Hardly," growled a deep voice that Edith had come to know well.

The pressure at her back vanished, as did the wandering hands, and suddenly Edith was flung forward into a pillar. She turned to find Lord Radcliffe setting Sir Reginald into the hands of Tony and Cam, both of whom looked positively murderous. They escorted Sir Reginald from the room immediately, and with such discretion that no one would have thought anything amiss by it.

Sir Reginald glared over his shoulder at her with such venom that Edith trembled from head to foot. She couldn't even feel relief at her deliverance, knowing what such a look would mean for her. Before, she had only thought Sir Reginald would ruin her, which was bad enough, but now could see what a naïve thought that was. She had earned his hatred by spurning him, and there was no telling what he might do when in such a rage or in seeking vengeance.

Lord Radcliffe was back to her at once, and he took her shoulders in hand, giving her a very serious look.

"Are you all right?" he asked softly, his eyes hard.

Edith tried to nod, but her emotions were too close to the surface, and her trembling increased.

He took pity on her and ushered her to a small alcove just off the ballroom, hidden from view. He directed her to sit in the chair within, while he sank to his haunches before her and took her hands.

"Edith, did he hurt you?" His voice was rough, but surprisingly gentle, particularly for such a large man who seemed to have equally rough manners.

She shook her head, swallowing back her tears. "No, he did not hurt me."

Lord Radcliffe raised a disbelieving brow but said nothing.

Edith sighed and tried to tug her hands free, but he held them fast. "He... he touched me," she admitted, disgust and shame rising within her. "More boldly than he usually does. I tried to get away, but he trapped me, and I knew if I screamed, I would be ruined. I couldn't move, I couldn't—"

"I know," he overrode, squeezing her hands tightly. "I know, I saw you try. And I heard what he said to you, there is no need to relive it."

A tear broke free of her eyes, and she hated herself for it. Smiling despite it, she quipped, "There's your third time, my lord. You've attained hero status."

His lips quirked, and he shook his head as he quickly wiped that tear away. "Are you always going to make light of your situation?" he asked.

Edith shrugged one shoulder. "What else can I do? I must laugh, or I must cry, and I look a fright when I cry."

He grunted and muttered something that sounded suspiciously like "I doubt that", but his expression softened into a sincere look. "I am sorry I could not get to you sooner."

"No." Edith immediately shook her head. "You could not have known, sir. I didna even know he was here until he had me. The whole thing happened so quickly."

"Yes, but I saw," he said, sliding his hands from hers and rising to his feet. "I saw him there, and I did not come as quickly as I ought."

"Are you... watching me, Lord Radcliffe?" Edith asked, her heart oddly fluttering at the thought.

His eyes were suddenly so intense that breathing was difficult, her chest clenching. "You might say that I have developed an interest."

Edith had to swallow and clear her throat, then rose herself, though he was still very much taller than her. "Oh?" was the most brilliant reply she managed to make.

Pathetic.

He nodded once, then almost smiled again. "I've never been a hero in my life, and yours is the only opportunity I may have."

The tightness in Edith's chest eased, and she smiled up at him, delighted that he would tease her. "Well, I verra much hope I shall not have to be always in distress simply to bolster your ego," she replied, lifting a brow so he would know that she meant it in jest.

He tilted his head for a moment. "We do always meet like this, don't we?"

Edith shrugged a little and ducked her chin, cheeks flaming. "You must think me a helpless creature indeed."

A gentle hand reached under her chin and tilted her face up to see a somber expression.

And what a powerful look he had!

Edith was speechless, breathless, and quite captivated, though he was not standing particularly close, and there was very little warmth in his eyes.

"Do not presume to tell me what I think, Lady Edith," he murmured, his fingers warmer than his expression. "My thoughts at present just might surprise the both of us. Understood?"

She nodded, and he dropped his hand with a nod in return.

"So, what do we do?" she asked, somehow finding her voice. "I think I may have angered him beyond anything just now, and he will find a way to get me alone, despite our efforts."

Lord Radcliffe made a low humming noise as he looked at her. "I have an idea, but I must discuss it with the others first." He took her arm gently and peered out of the alcove, and then led her out and directly onto the dance floor.

Edith looked up at him in surprise. "A dance, my lord?"

"I do occasionally dance, Lady Edith," he said with a shrug.

She laughed outright. "You do not. I might have been trying to bathe a cat last time for all I tried to get you to."

He quirked a brow as he bowed to her. "Not bathing a cat now, are you?"

No, indeed, she was not.

It so happened that Lord Radcliffe was quite a good dancer, for all his apparent dislike of it.

She would have to remember that.

Chapter Eleven

On occasion, one must take a stand, even if it is unfashionable. But only on occasion.

-*The Spinster Chronicles, 27 March 1819*

It was an utterly ridiculous idea. Foolhardy, reckless, and very likely improper, considering the circumstances. But it was the only idea he had.

And it wasn't going away.

Graham shook his head as he ambled rather aimlessly about Mayfair on this fine spring day, wishing he had a better suggestion for Henshaw and the rest. At this rate, he wouldn't even be able to get the words out, let alone go into any great detail about it.

Why in the world would anyone want to give up the Season and come to Merrifield for a lengthy stay? Who would want to venture thus when the host was the most boring man on the planet, especially compared to his predecessor? The thrill of such an invitation had vanished entirely with Matthew's death, and there would be no entertainment to speak of.

He could see it all now. Guests would wander the halls and the gardens with wistful nostalgia of what the place had once been and would never be again. All talk would be of the difference between the brothers, and what a disappointment it was to have this particular Lord Radcliffe rather than the other.

Edith wouldn't know the difference, but he would have to invite others in order to have Edith come, and she would hear what they had to say.

The pretense of inviting anyone to Merrifield in order to invite Edith seemed utterly insane, but it would do. Merrifield could be a worthy retreat for her, and he could ensure the weasel never came near enough to be a bother.

The others would have to consent, however, and Edith would have to wish to venture there.

What if she hated the idea? Why did that matter?

So many questions and very few answers. Graham's least favorite combination.

"Radcliffe!"

Turning quickly, Graham fixed his usual polite smile on his face in anticipation of whoever had called to him. The smile eased into something less forced as he saw Francis, Lord Sterling, approaching with an elegant woman some years his senior on his arm, and, of all things, a large bloodhound on a lead before them.

"Sterling. Good morning." He bowed to them both, taking quick stock of the woman, ignoring the dog.

While it was clear she was older than Francis, she could not be considered old in the truest sense. Still lovely, still attractive, and still full of life and energy. And, if the twinkle in her eye was any indication, some mischief.

Francis bowed in return. "Radcliffe, this is Tony's stepmother, Miranda, Mrs. Sterling. And that's Rufus. He's done for." That earned the peer a sharp look from his companion.

"He is not! And you could just call me your aunt."

"You always tell me not to," Francis protested, eyes wide, but smiling wryly. "You say it's unflattering."

Mrs. Sterling rolled her eyes without any delicacy and looked at Graham frankly. "How very ungallant he is, my lord. I don't know what to make of him."

Graham almost grinned, surprising himself. "I believe that is a commonly held understanding, Mrs. Sterling, if Tyrone Demaris is to be believed."

"I always believe Tyrone, no matter what he says," Mrs. Sterling admitted at once, lips curving.

"Well, there's your first mistake," Francis muttered. "Miranda, this is Lord Radcliffe."

"Yes, thank you." Mrs. Sterling widened her eyes in exasperation. "How I managed to be coerced to walk out with you, of all people, Francis, I will never understand."

Francis looked up to the cloudless sky and seemed to be silently praying.

Graham chuckled, strangely loving this dynamic between relations. "It *is* a fine day, Mrs. Sterling. I cannot blame you for wishing to partake in a walk, no matter whose arm you are on."

"Call me Miranda, my dear," Mrs. Sterling told him at once, her smile turning almost matronly. "I know formalities and politeness mean well, but I prefer to tear down the barriers preventing me from forging true connections with my friends."

No doubt sensing this conversation would not be a passing one, Rufus groaned and flopped himself down to the ground, apparently comfortable enough to wait them out.

"Radcliffe isn't much for familiarity, Miranda," Francis warned, eyeing Graham with a warning in his expression, though what precisely the warning was for remained less clear.

Graham raised a brow at the statement. "Am I not? How interesting."

Miranda tossed her head back with a throaty laugh, then surveyed Graham through her crystal blue eyes. "Brava, Radcliffe. So droll, I approve."

He gave the woman a half-bow of acknowledgement. "Thank you, Miranda."

"Spare me," Francis groaned, pinching the bridge of his nose.

"If only we could, my love," Miranda quipped without sympathy. Her eyes narrowed slightly. "Radcliffe, you recently inherited, yes?"

Graham stiffened but did his best to hide it. "I did."

Miranda's chin dipped just a touch. "Then, it was your brother before you."

A swallow trapped itself in Graham's throat. "It was."

"I didn't know him," Miranda murmured, stepping closer and resting a hand on his arm, "but I knew his wife. Lovely woman. Very charming. Very popular."

"She was, yes."

There was nothing else to say. Penelope had been universally adored, and even Graham had thought her the best of all women. Had he been given a sister by birth, she could not have been so close in his affections as Penelope. In losing her, he had not simply lost his brother's wife, but a sister as well.

Twice the loss.

But how to admit just how much their relationship had meant to him without it being taken as holding a passion for her? He hadn't done, couldn't have. He would freely admit she had been beautiful and enchanting, but their feelings for each other had always been safely platonic. She had been his brother's perfect match but could not have been Graham's.

Who could fully comprehend that?

"A terrible loss for you, I'm sure, to lose them both. You have my deepest sympathies."

Graham came back to the conversation at hand and saw understanding in Miranda's countenance.

"Thank you," he told her, stunned by the sincerity in his words.

"I am of the opinion," Miranda continued in a much lighter tone, stepping back, "that family ties can be much closer, much more binding than we are generally willing to admit. Myself, I would be nearly as devastated if Mr. Johnston died as if his wife, my sister, did. But I understand that not all families are as fond of each other as mine." She smiled as though she had been indulging her own feelings in her words, though Graham knew better.

Somehow, this new acquaintance had seen beyond his reserve and into his heart within moments.

He wasn't sure if it was unnerving or consoling, but he liked Miranda better for it. That, he could freely admit to.

Miranda suddenly cocked her head. "Correct me if I am wrong, but did they not have a child?"

"Miranda…" Francis warned at once, sounding severe for the first time.

"Hush, Francis," she replied, holding up a hand to him. "I have a reason for prying. Radcliffe?"

Graham hesitated. This was not universally known, though

Matthew and Penelope hadn't taken particular pains to hide the fact. Were they in full public, he would refuse to discuss it. As they had no other listeners, he exhaled shortly and gave a brief nod.

"They did."

Miranda did not react to the revelation. "And the child is…?"

"At Merrifield," Graham told her, unwilling to give the specific details Miranda was undoubtedly looking for. "Under my guardianship."

"So, you have inherited the role of parent as well as a title."

That took him by surprise, and he shook his head. "Well, I…"

Miranda frowned at him. "Call it what it is, my dear, the challenges are the same. Do you have help with the child?"

"Of course," he nearly stammered, the statement settling in uncomfortably. "A nanny, and my aunt…"

Miranda's gasp made him jump. "Don't tell me Eloise is also at Merrifield!"

His jaw dropped. "You know her?"

"Adore her, my boy. Utterly adore." Miranda laughed again and clasped her hands together. "That settles it. I must come to Merrifield. Invite me, won't you? I'm sure you can find a reason soon enough, or else I can invent one." She turned to Francis in her excitement. "You should see the estate, Francis. Utter perfection out there in Berkshire. Glorious landscape and gardens, and Merrifield itself is one of the loveliest houses ever constructed. I am quite in raptures over it."

Francis raised his brow. "So I gathered. You invited yourself to it, after all."

"Oh, tosh," Miranda sputtered with a dismissive wave of her hand. "Radcliffe will invite me, won't you, Radcliffe?"

"I…"

"What a lovely way to reopen the place!" Miranda exclaimed, whirling as though she could see the estate beside them. "A house party, Radcliffe! It would be so inviting, and I know exactly who we could invite to keep things intimate yet polite, tasteful, and respectable." She gestured wide at the imaginary house. "The ivy would be such a lovely color, and those wildflowers would be of such a shade…"

Graham glanced at Miranda's vision, not impressed with the reality of the row of plain townhomes standing there. "I don't see it."

Francis snorted a loud laugh before coughing into his fist to cover it.

Miranda scowled at Graham. "I said droll was approved, not cynicism."

"I knew I had crossed a line somewhere," he relented before he could stop himself. "Not quite sure which time, though."

Francis shook harder with his laughter, making Graham smirk.

"Ugh!" Miranda groaned, tossing her hands in the air. "Men!" She leveled a finger at Graham, and his smirk faded. "I am not giving up on this, Radcliffe. I know a very capable artist, and once I describe Merrifield to her, you will completely comprehend the vision I have."

"I've seen Merrifield in the spring, Miranda," Graham assured her. "I simply don't understand the need for others to."

"Don't you?" Miranda asked, folding her arms to glare at him properly.

Graham stared back, his mind spinning. He had just been considering an invitation to Merrifield, but he hadn't spoken the idea aloud to anyone. Hadn't been convinced he would do so. Or could do so.

Now someone was demanding he follow through with the idea, unaware it was already a possibility?

Perhaps he didn't like Miranda Sterling all that well after all.

Or perhaps she would prove herself to be accurate with tarot cards and fortune-telling. His guests would enjoy that.

Slowly, Graham's brows rose as he realized what he had thought. *His guests.*

He made a face in reluctance. "I'll consider it, Miranda. And if it comes to pass, you will, of course, be invited."

"So I should hope," she told him without any gratitude. She did wink, however, and give him a smile. "Now, Francis, I think you may continue to escort me. I'm feeling rather satisfied. Rufus, come, my darling." On cue, the dog rose from his prone position and went to the side of his mistress obediently.

Francis offered his arm with a long-suffering sigh as he looked at Graham. "Now you've done it."

Graham shrugged. "Did I have a choice?"

"Not really," Francis admitted as he and his aunt continued to walk, "and that, I fear, is the worst of it." He tapped the brim of his hat with a smile, leaving Graham alone once more.

Graham exhaled to himself and continued on his way as well, though for the life of him, he couldn't remember his course or his reason.

If any of that mattered in London.

"Mistress…"

Edith turned away from her enjoyable tea with Amelia, finally getting close to discovering the identity of her friend's secret love, all warmth evaporating through the tips of her fingers. She knew that tone.

"No…"

Owen nodded tightly. "Afraid so, mistress."

"No what?" Amelia demanded looking between the two. "What is it?"

"Sir Reginald," Edith murmured, looking back at her friend with a mixture of regret, resignation, and, she would admit, fear.

Owen cleared his throat. "He's in a right state, mistress. Verra upset."

"Of course, he is." Edith sighed, putting a hand to her brow. "Amelia, go upstairs, I won't have you present for this. Owen, have a message sent to Hensh. At once, if you please. I'll want him here quickly. Do we know where Lachlan is?"

"Nae, mistress. He hasna left his London address for us yet." Owen made a face, which echoed Edith's sentiment.

Lachlan had visited semi-regularly, but he hadn't found a lasting residence to his liking. It seemed her brother was changed with regards to his actions towards her, but his nature was not so changed as to render his life vastly different.

No matter.

Edith shook her head. "We'll deal with that later. For now, Hensh will do, and with Amelia hidden away…"

"No."

Owen stepped into the room, his hands going to his hips. "Miss Perry…"

Edith was on her feet and beside him in an instant. "Amelia, you must hide."

But Amelia shook her head very firmly, her jaw set. "No, to both of you. If Lachlan can take a stand despite his injuries against you, then I, your friend, can certainly do so. I may not be an imposing Scot, but I think my own will may surprise us all."

"I canna let ye see him," Edith insisted, her heart leaping into her throat.

"You will," Amelia told her without concern. "He has no reason to harm me or to cause me difficulty. If he knows anyone in Society, he will realize the danger I present. I think you might be too close to the situation and take too much upon yourself." She stepped forward and took Edith's hands. "Hide yourself upstairs and let me take control of the situation."

Edith shook her head frantically, unable to voice her objection, but needing to refuse adamantly somehow.

Amelia gave her quite a stern look. "Edith, from what I can tell, Sir Reginald wants you, not me. He takes care to have you be alone when he comes, despite his claims of going public, because he knows how to unnerve you. You have dealt with him on your own up until now and have done most admirably. Now please, let me try my way. Owen will ensure I am safe."

Owen grunted once and crossed to Amelia, stepping behind her in a show of support.

Edith could only gape at her friend, who suddenly possessed more mettle than she did, then looked to Owen, who only inclined his head towards the stairs.

Unable to fight anyone at all on this, Edith did as they suggested, but not before writing a quick note to Hensh and sending Simms out with it.

Edith bit her lip as she heard Owen go to the door and sat herself on the floor of the corridor above, staying close enough to hear what transpired below. If anything happened, if Sir Reginald did not behave appropriately with Amelia, Edith would rush down and give herself up. She could hardly do otherwise.

"Took you long enough to admit me," Sir Reginald grumbled as he was let in. "Is Lady Edith growing particular as to her guests?" He chuckled at his own words, and Edith could hear the sound of his walking stick hitting the floor in time with his shoes.

Why did that sound so ominous now, rather than the ridiculous charade it always was?

The clicking suddenly stopped, as did the feet.

"Who are you?" he demanded.

"Miss Amelia Perry," Edith heard her reply in a calm tone.

"Where is Lady Edith?"

"Not at home."

Edith could hear his snarl from her position. "I don't believe you. You would not receive callers if she were not at home."

"Lady Edith is a generous benefactress, and said I may receive callers without her, so long as Owen was close."

Edith smiled to herself, imagining how Owen must have looked standing there as a chaperone. She covered her mouth to keep from laughing nervously.

"Your benefactress?" Sir Reginald asked. "How can she be so when she has nothing?"

"She has connections and gentility, sir, which is all I have need of."

"When will she return?" he demanded.

"I don't know, sir. She did not say."

How in the world could Amelia remain so unmoved in the face of this man? So collected, so bold, when she had professed to simply being a silly girl like any other in Society. There was nothing silly in this, and no other woman in Society to compare.

"How long will you be here, then?" Sir Reginald's voice sounded more irritated than irate, but there was an undertone that had Edith curling into a ball where she sat.

Amelia, however, remained unruffled. "Some time, I should think. As long as Lady Edith allows me to."

Steps echoed once more. "You will leave this house tomorrow."

There was no mistaking the venom in his voice now, and Edith pushed to her hands and knees, teeth pressing down painfully into her lip.

She could not believe his audacity. To threaten a young woman with no connection to him? Whose family was influential and popular? Either he did not know of the family, or he did not care.

The first would have been understandable, the second terrifying.

"I will do no such thing," Amelia insisted in an equally harsh tone. "I have been invited to stay, and stay, I shall. We have a great many things to accomplish together, and I don't believe any of them include you."

"Take care, Miss Perry. You don't wish to make an enemy of me."

"I have no wish to make an enemy of any man, sir, but that does not mean I do not have them. And *you* should take care, I think. My uncle is the Earl of Wicklow, Lord Frenway, and unless you have completely mistaken your histories, you will know that means he is one of the most powerful men in Ireland, and a personal friend of the prime minister, whom I am to have tea with tomorrow. Perhaps I should tell him of your visit?"

Edith's mouth popped open. Amelia had said nothing about influential relatives, and for her to give such a threat, veiled as it was, to Sir Reginald was unfathomable. What he wanted most was to have standing and place in Society, and to risk that was to risk ostracization.

He could not have that, surely.

Sir Reginald's shoes clipped in the corridor almost immediately. "Good day, Miss Perry. Do forgive my rudeness. I am only disappointed. I beg you to inform Lady Edith of my call, and that I would be pleased to find her at another time more convenient to her."

Some scuffling was heard, and then the door closed soundly, leaving the house in complete silence for a moment.

Edith raced down the stairs and rounded into the drawing room, looking at Amelia in shock. Her expression was much the same.

"Where did that come from, Amelia?"

"I have no idea," she whispered.

The two suddenly burst out laughing, nerves and relief blending in hilarity, and were quite insensible.

"Mad as hares, the both of ye," Owen grumbled. He shook his head and moved back to the door as frantic knocking echoed there.

Edith wiped tears of mirth from her eyes as familiar voices filled the air. Henshaw and Lord Radcliffe appeared in the drawing room, looking as if they had run a very great distance.

"What in God's name...?" Henshaw asked, looking between the still laughing ladies.

Owen explained what had happened hastily, and the men looked at each other in confusion.

"Edith, are you all right?" Henshaw asked, coming to take her arm once she was calmer.

She nodded and gestured for them all to come more fully into the room. "I am verra well. I've not had to deal with Sir Reginald in so long, I almost forget what it is like."

Henshaw gave her a shrewd look. "Don't make light of it, Edith. This has to stop."

Edith sighed and rubbed at her brow. "I know. I canna stop it on my own, but Amelia's quick thinking today will no doubt change things."

Lord Radcliffe stood nearby, looking at her with some interest. Edith finally looked at him, and his focus seemed to intensify.

Her cheeks heated. "My lord, it is good to see you again."

His mouth quirked only slightly. "You as well, Lady Edith, though I had hoped for better circumstances."

"How did you come to be here?" she asked, looking between him and Henshaw. "I sent a note to Lieutenant Henshaw, but—"

"I saw the weasel, and he looked distressed, so I made the logical conclusion." He shrugged. "Henshaw and I arrived at the same time."

Edith smiled at his attempt to lessen his response. "Trying for another mark, my lord?"

"Perhaps," he replied, his eyes becoming amused.

Henshaw looked over at Amelia, who had said very little. "Well, thanks to Miss Perry, there was nothing for us to do. That was very smart, Miss Perry."

Amelia flushed a little. "No doubt, it was the first time I have told a lie of such magnitude, but I trust it shall not count."

Edith reached out a hand and covered hers. "If you hadna told him I was out, he would have been far worse."

Amelia smiled a bit shyly. "Oh, no, that was not the lie I meant."

The room looked at her in confusion, waiting.

She snorted a bit and covered her mouth. "My uncle is a gentleman, with a fine heritage, richly tied to Ireland." She looked at Edith quickly, her smile growing mischievous. "As blacksmiths. Then in trade. My mother's entire fortune was from shipping. I have never met anyone close to the prime minister, and I have not, nor likely will ever, have tea with him."

Edith stared at her for a long moment, then burst out laughing again. Henshaw and Lord Radcliffe grinned, while Owen applauded and cheered as loud as any Scotsman ever has.

"This could prove interesting," Henshaw said, looking back at Lord Radcliffe. "Sir Reginald will have a difficult time slandering Lady Edith while she is in Miss Perry's company, particularly if he thinks she has ties to the prime minister."

Lord Radcliffe nodded slowly. "How much time will that buy us?"

Henshaw hissed. "Hard to say. Enough time to figure out a better course, I would think. He's shown he is willing to torment Edith at events, so that avenue is not open to us.

They continued to converse among themselves, and Amelia leaned over to Edith. "What are they talking about?"

Edith shrugged and reached for the tea she had put down before. "I have no idea. I have completely lost control of my life. I only do what others tell me. But handsome would-be heroes are tolerable compensation."

Amelia giggled and took some tea herself while both waited to be addressed again.

Chapter Twelve

A little interference may go a long way.

-The Spinster Chronicles, 12 July 1815

"Tell me more about your brother, Edith. He's a baron, yes? I find him enormously intriguing."

Edith looked at Charlotte with some alarm. "No. Absolutely not, Charlotte."

"What?" Charlotte replied, dark eyes wide, looking around at the room of Spinsters. "I merely wish to learn more about the family member of one of my closest friends. Where is the harm in that?"

"A young, handsome, by all accounts, vigorous Highlander who has recently come to London to make amends and reconnect with his sister," Grace mused aloud as she poured her tea, smiling to herself. "Yes, your interest would be quite innocent, would it not?"

Prue snickered to herself, raising her teacup and sipping slowly.

Edith did not find the idea so humorous, her mind spinning on the idea of Charlotte taking an interest in her brother. They would kill each other, she had no doubt, though the journey they took to that point would likely be an interesting one.

"Charlotte, he has no fortune, minimal manners, and no holdings to speak of," Edith assured her friend with all possible bluntness.

Charlotte raised a brow. "Is he your father's heir?"

Edith cringed, her hands folding tightly in her lap. "He is."

"Then I say let me meet his lordship, Baron Halsey." Charlotte folded her arms and lifted a daring brow. "Lachlan MacDougal would be a wonderful addition to my coterie."

"Oh, stop," Georgie protested, putting a hand on her cheek. "Must we admit so frankly that you collect suitors?"

Izzy snorted softly. "What else would you call it, Georgie? That's exactly what she does."

"If you want a Highlander for a suitor," Edith said with a weak smile for Charlotte, "I can give you the names of several others who are far better candidates."

Charlotte grinned in her usual mischievous way. "But they are not your wicked brother, Edith. That is the most appealing aspect."

Edith leaned forward in her seat and leveled a hard look at her. "Lachlan is the reason I was forced into marrying Archie. His debts and my father's debts ruined us, and Lachlan absolved a decent amount of his particular debt by using *me* as a bargaining chip. He may ask for forgiveness now, Charlotte, but you should be fully aware of who he has been."

The room was silent, and Charlotte's suddenly pale complexion made Edith regret saying anything about it. How could Lachlan truly make amends if she continually brought in the reminder of past sins and misdeeds?

"Then bring him into my fold," Charlotte managed, trying for another smile, "so that I may give him a proper dressing down."

Edith smiled. "I will consider it. You might do a better job at that than me."

"Of course, I would." Charlotte winked. "I have no shame."

"Well, soon, neither will I," Edith admitted, "and no pride to speak of, either."

Georgie looked at Grace then, rather significantly, and so obviously that Edith stared at them both in return. She looked only slightly abashed, and Grace snickered.

"What is this all about?" Edith finally asked, reaching for a biscuit on the tea tray.

Again, they shared a look. Then Georgie spoke up. "We have something to tell you, Edith, that concerns you and Amelia."

That piqued her interest, and she wished she had brought Amelia to the meeting today. "Oh?"

Grace looked rather smug for a moment, smiling about some secret or other. "You are not to argue, and not to worry, either."

Edith felt the first prickle of dread begin to start, wondering what was going to be said. There was no question it would be about Sir Reginald or her situation, and anything in those veins would undoubtedly make her uncomfortable.

"We are all leaving London," Georgie said with a smile, "including the both of you."

"What?" Edith cried. "No! No, we canna possibly…"

"We will be going to Berkshire," Grace said loudly, "to a house party."

Edith looked at the others in bewilderment. "Whose house party, and how did I manage an invitation? I've never gone to a house party before, and I wasna aware of any invitations of late."

Grace grinned a bit mischievously. "That is because the invitations to this house party are very exclusive and very private. Only a select few members of Society even know about it, and discretion is the key."

"Why so discreet?" Izzy asked, looking a bit suspicious.

That surprised Edith. So, not everyone was aware of what was being proposed? Interesting… Then who was behind it all?

"Because if more people knew, they would all wish to go," Georgie told her. "People have been known to randomly show up at Merrifield Terrace without invitation when a house party is in progress."

"Merrifield?" Edith repeated, her brows rising. "I don't know that house at all. I've never heard of it. Who is hosting?"

Now, Grace looked positively gleeful. "Lord Radcliffe, of course."

There were no words for such an answer, at least as far as Edith was concerned. Charlotte, on the other hand, clapped her hands and dissolved into laughter.

"Oh, this is perfection!" Charlotte cried. "Absolute perfection!"

"He does not seem like the sort to put on such an event," Prue said, looking a bit embarrassed by her words.

Grace shrugged. "He's not. But his late brother and his wife were."

The silence in the room was deafening. Mortification rose within Edith, for her thoughts had been very similar. Prue turned so red, one could be worried for her health.

"Oh…" was all Prue managed to say before her eyes welled up with tears. Izzy moved to sit beside her, putting an arm around her shoulders and rubbing soothingly.

Grace reached out a hand and smiled softly. "No one talks about it. It was a great loss to Society."

Georgie cleared her throat. "The late Lord and Lady Radcliffe died three years ago. She was elegant and refined and hosted the most glorious house parties. He was devoted to her, social and charming, the perfect match for her. Everyone wanted to attend, would vie for months and months to be invited. Every year was better and better, and if you weren't invited to the Radcliffes' house party, something was amiss with you."

"So," Grace said with a sigh, "after all this time, the new Lord Radcliffe has decided that this is the year to bring back the house parties that made his brother and sister-in-law so famous, and made his country estate the envy of all humanity."

"It is a glorious place," Georgie said with a heaving sigh of her own. "Woods and trails and such lush nature all about you, and the house itself is massive. So elegant and majestic, the most absolutely perfect place in England."

"Perfect, is it?" Edith murmured, not knowing what else to do but make light of all this. "Well, well. Why shouldn't we all venture thus, indeed? I've yet to see perfection in England. What a notion."

"You jest if you will," Grace said with a warning finger, "but Georgie is not exaggerating. The ballroom alone in that place would make angels weep for its beauty. There is a lake nearby, excellent stables, a library to end all libraries…"

"Well, that's enough to convince me," Izzy muttered as she took a bite of a cake.

"Gardens that one can get quite lost in," Georgie said with a touch of longing and a sly little smile towards Edith.

Edith blinked at it. "What? What need have I to get lost in a garden?"

"Who doesn't have a need to get lost in a garden?" Charlotte insisted, fanning herself for good measure.

Georgie rolled her eyes. "I'm getting your invitation revoked, Charlotte. You're just going to create a scandal."

"One can only hope," came Charlotte's quip.

They all giggled for a few minutes, and then Grace gave Edith a smile. "Mr. Copeland and Mr. Tomkins will be invited, as will Mr. Gaither, and several other men whom you may wish to meet."

Edith blushed a bit. "So, you are saying I should use Lord Radcliffe's party to find the protection I seek, yes?"

Grace shrugged. "In a word, yes. Henshaw is coming, and several other ladies have been invited, too. Radcliffe didn't want to make it seem as though all of this was for you, though I do believe you were the motivating factor."

How could she take that? How would anyone? He'd said that he had an idea for how to help her, but he hadn't said what it was. Just the other day, he and Henshaw had been discussing time and options, though nothing specific had been shared with Edith. Now, he would invite her, and others, to his home, despite not being particularly social, in an effort to help her.

How was she to feel about that?

"Are your husbands invited?" Edith asked softly, needing to say something, anything.

Grace nodded with a smile. "Of course. Ingram and Lord Sterling will be delayed for a time, as they are fighting the law for you. It is quite tricky."

"They are?" Edith cried, feeling her blush fade into paleness.

Grace winced. "Yes, and I was not supposed to say that. They are in Kent at present, dealing with the lawyers and folk who set up Sir Reginald's ridiculous scheme. Apparently, there is an associate of theirs and Henshaw's who is doing some other things." She waved her hand, dismissively. "I don't know all of the particulars, but there it is. They shall all meet us at Merrifield."

It was too much, all too much, and Edith could barely comprehend all the moving pieces involved in her situation now. So many people working for her and on her behalf, stepping away from their own concerns and lives, purely with aims to improve hers.

"Stop frowning, Edith!" Georgie scolded. "We would all do

more than this if we could."

Edith barely managed to nod, feeling grateful and humbled to have such friends. "Is there anything else I should know about Merrifield before we go?" she asked, forcing a smile.

Grace gave a rather devious grin. "Just one thing. Sir Reginald is not invited, and he is not to come within fifty miles of the house. You can be worry-free, Edith. No need for heroes at Merrifield."

The thought of three weeks without Sir Reginald nearby sounded like the very image of heaven.

Edith grinned at her friends and said, "When do we leave?"

"Yes, I received your note, Graham, but I was sure you could not be serious."

"Unfortunately, I was and am serious." Graham winced, shaking his head, and looked over at the pale, fair-haired woman sitting in the parlor. "Is all prepared?"

Eloise laughed once and leaned her elbow on the armrest of her chair. "Of course, it is, darling. It took some work, as we haven't hosted anything here in an age, but it is done. When do you anticipate your friends?"

Graham grunted and turned to the fireplace, resting his arm against the mantle. "They aren't my friends, Aunt."

"Whose fault is that?" she demanded without any venom.

He glanced over his shoulder at his aunt, really more of an age to be a much older sister than the sister of his father. "What exactly are you implying, Eloise?"

She met his look with frank eyes. "I know you, Gray. You could walk into a room with twenty people holding out their hands to you, and you will only see a roomful of people."

"That's hardly fair," he protested, slightly stung by the accusation. "I have Tyrone, and I am not... unfriendly with others." Even to him, the words sounded weak.

Eloise shook her head slowly. "My dear boy, it is time to come out of the shadows in which you have hidden yourself."

Graham returned his attention to the fire. "I have not been

hiding. I am simply more reserved than perhaps I should be."

"Gray, the wallpaper says more than you do."

"Then we need less complicated wallpaper."

Eloise laughed her warm, engaging laugh, reminding him of Penelope, his mother, and oddly, Edith.

He had to laugh at himself, feeling his tension easing away every moment he spent here at Merrifield. This was home, and it was the only place that would feel like home. He was never more himself than when he was here. It was easier to breathe, easier to laugh, easier to be.

Easier to admit he had only one friend he could name.

"Fine," he grumbled with a wry smile, pushing away from the fire and moving closer to her. "Those that are coming are... potential friends. Well, there are some among them that I could count as friends. Is that better?"

Eloise lifted a brow in amusement. "Marginally."

She suddenly began to cough, and the rasping, deep, resounding sound of it chilled Graham and sent him to the seat beside her.

"Eloise..." he said, eyes wide, taking in her body as though it would tell him what he wished to know.

She held up a hand, turning her face away into a handkerchief and coughing further. "Wait," she managed to choke out before coughing again.

Graham scooted his chair closer, resting a hand on her back, familiar feelings of helplessness pouring in.

At last, she began to breathe more freely, though she was pale and glistening with a sheen of perspiration.

"Apologies, Graham. How mortifying!"

"How long has it been like this?" Graham asked, keeping his voice low. "Why didn't you say anything?"

Eloise favored him with a dark scowl.

"It has been damp, Graham, and I've never quite felt myself after the winter. Don't fuss yourself over a little cough."

"Little cough?" he repeated. He shook his head at her. "Eloise, I think you just coughed with the entire capacity of both lungs, and it sounded painful in the extreme. Are you feverish?" He laid a hand on her brow only to have it swatted away.

"Stop that," she insisted. "No, I am not feverish. If I were feverish, I would be in bed requesting a dish of soup. As it is, I am perfectly capable of walking here and there, sitting where I like, and behaving as I bloody well please."

Graham sat back, his brows rising. "Well, then. Pardon me."

Eloise rolled her eyes with a heavy sigh. "Don't take that tone, Gray. I've grown tired of being pitied and treated like an invalid. Just because I haven't been well the last few weeks..."

"You haven't?" he interrupted sharply. "Why didn't you write to me? I was wasting my time out in London when I could have been here to take care of you and Molly. You have been wearing yourself out taking care of her, which I should never have allowed. It's too much effort for you, and you are in no state to do so. She is too much work, has too much energy, and you should never have been put in this position. I'll cancel the house party, tell everyone it is no longer happening, and I'll give all this up so you might recover, and..."

Eloise pushed up to her feet, a tower of indignation, despite her slight frame and paleness, a muscle at her jaw ticking as she glared at Graham, silencing him without a word.

"What?" he asked with some hesitation.

"I am not sickly!" Eloise insisted, a fist clenching her side while the other clutched at her shawl. "I'm simply not well."

Graham sat back roughly, giving his sweet aunt a sympathetic smile. "I know."

Her look turned scolding. "Then stop treating me like I'm a fragile thing that will break if I fall! I love being here with Molly, and you need a life away from us, or nothing will get anywhere."

"But..."

"No!" She softened her interjection by returning his smile. "I've never been the picture of health, Gray. You know this."

He nodded, not seeing a need to elaborate on it. She had always been what they called 'delicate', even in her youth, which was likely what had made her his favorite aunt. She had always been able and willing to read to him as a child, and she'd watch him engage in whatever activities he wished to display. She had talked with Graham as an equal and for such a length of time when every other adult in his life had dismissed him, albeit kindly.

"But," Eloise went on, tucking her shawl around her and brushing back a long, wispy tendril of hair, "I have learned how to live my life fully despite that. I do not stop my life, or pause it, to indulge in my moments of feeling indisposed, as so many other fine women likely do."

"Oh, they do," Graham assured her with a quick grin. "Quite dramatically."

Eloise nodded in acknowledgement. "I am not going to stop minding Molly in favor of being unwell. And I forbid you to give up your life thinking you must be here to mind us both." Her eyes narrowed as she looked at him. "Or use us as an excuse to avoid the world."

Graham winced and wrenched his gaze away. He knew that was a particularly accurate barb but hearing it out loud made him feel more ashamed of it.

"It's the comparison," he admitted to her, sliding his hands along the armrests of the chairs.

"Between you and Matthew?"

He nodded and waited for Eloise to situate herself back in her seat.

She sighed once settled and offered a kind smile. "Comparisons are natural. You mustn't blame people."

"I don't." He shrugged. "It's only that every single one of those comparisons would find me lacking. I am not as engaging as Matthew; I have not his easy temperament or his favorable looks. I'll never be Matthew, and it's clear to everyone, including myself, that he should be here instead of me."

"You might feel that way, and there might be a handful of idiots in Society who would agree." Eloise made a face that indicated clearly just what she thought about that. "But I believe you will find that the majority of people are quite used to the changing of a title from one holder to the next and anticipate an adjustment in the manners and personality of the title bearers."

Graham had to smile. "I suppose you are right."

She dipped her chin in acknowledgment. "Don't live your life wondering what Matthew would have done, or thinking you are unsuited to your tasks. Own your place and make it what *you* wish.

That is what is required of you, not fulfilling your brother's plans."

There was no sound then but the crackling of the fire, and there was something impossibly comforting in it. Something that burned the truth of the matter into his heart.

"If you feel you must invite guests to Merrifield to live up to something," Eloise added softly, "then you are mistaken. If you regret doing so, revoke the invitations, by all means. There is no expectation in the minds of others that should matter to you."

Graham smiled to himself and shook his head before Eloise had finished. "No... No, that had nothing to do with the invitations."

"It didn't?" Eloise sat forward, her brow furrowing as she stared at Graham. "Then what in the world were you thinking? This is not like you. I felt sure you were being pressured into doing this because of Matthew and Penelope, I didn't..." She laughed to herself and clapped once. "Oh, this is divine. I've never been more surprised by anything in my life."

"Are you going to let me explain myself?" Graham asked, his tone mild, but amused. "Or should I wait for your declarations to reach their full potential?"

Eloise glowered playfully. "Take care, nephew. I am still your aunt and ought to command some degree of respect."

Graham chuckled and nodded with all due deference. "Very well, then. Respectfully, aunt, I invited these people because of two women."

His aunt coughed again, this time without the same severity and purely out of shock. "Two?"

"One," he went on without pausing, "because I have found myself at her service time and again when she required assistance during some particular difficulty. Her situation grows more and more dire, so much so that a few of us have decided that London ought not to be her location at present. In order to get her away without raising suspicions, a house party was the only legitimate option. I had the nearest estate, so this is where they are coming."

"Oh, Gray," Eloise murmured, reaching out a hand to him, which he instantly took. "That is so lovely. You are giving her a refuge from the trials of her life. Of course, she should come here. What better place? Who is she? Do I know her?"

He shook his head, smiling fondly. "I doubt it. Lady Edith Leveson. You'll like her. She's Scottish, and she speaks her mind in such a way…"

"She's pretty, isn't she?"

"She is, yes."

Eloise laughed at once, her clasped hands going to her lips. "Not a moment's hesitation. This is too marvelous. And who is the second woman?"

Graham's smile turned rueful. "Miranda Sterling."

"No!" Eloise gasped, breaking out into a wide smile. "Miranda is coming?"

"She is, indeed," Graham confirmed. "She invited herself before I had settled on anyone coming at all. I had, of course, been considering the idea for Edith's sake, but Miranda's opinion certainly gave me some confirmation of the thing."

Eloise leaned her head back against the chair, shaking it back and forth slowly. "It must be a significant thing indeed, Gray, for you to call Lady Leveson by her Christian name. But I can easily see how Miranda would be useful in deciding on a particular course."

Graham chose to ignore his aunt's assertion of significance on his forgetting Edith's title, or dwelling on the fact that he had not used it in some time in his mind. Had he made such a mistake publicly? He couldn't recall, but as he hadn't been corrected or called out yet, he could not bring himself to worry.

Besides, he rather liked removing formality where Edith was concerned.

He groaned and covered his eyes with one hand.

"Miranda," he growled to himself.

"Yes, Miranda, indeed," Eloise quipped on a giggle. "You've done it now, Graham. When do they arrive?"

"Three days," he murmured as he dropped his hand, giving her a tired smile. "I'm going to need your help in this, Aunt."

Eloise dipped her chin. "You have it. But I think you will surprise yourself, Gray. In the meantime, I will do what I can to entertain the likes of Miranda Sterling during this house party. Heaven knows, that will take some effort."

Graham could only groan again in response.

Chapter Thirteen

The country is far and away better than Town, and I defy any who would argue otherwise. London may have more events and people, but the country has more freedom, beauty, and life than any city or town could ever boast. One must occasionally, if not frequently, take time in the country. It will do a person good.

-*The Spinster Chronicles, 8 November 1816*

Edith could not say that she had seen much of England, her exposure limited to the travels from Scotland to York and from York to London, and only the trip to Withrow, the Ingrams' country estate, beyond that.

Taking all of that into account, she would have to admit that Berkshire might have been the most beautiful county in England. So green and lush, with rolling hills and grand expanses of nature at almost every turn. It reminded her of the lowlands of Scotland, and despite being a Highland lass, she had felt those faint pangs of longing for her home, though she had not been back for several years.

Her awe and appreciation only increased when she caught sight of Merrifield Terrace. The house itself surpassed what Georgie and Grace had described it to be. A massive expanse of Tudor architecture and style, the stone an idyllic golden color that made the contrast against the green of its countryside all the more lovely. Decorative battlements lined the façade, drawing one's eyes up without any hesitation, and the enormous windows cradled between stone glistened in the morning light. Ivy crept up the lower levels of the place, but instead of looking wild and unkempt, it added an air of romance to the building.

Never had she seen a place situated so perfectly, with elegant design and arrangement of every detail of the exterior, with its gardens and lake and unassuming elegance.

Edith could have stared at the house for hours and never gotten tired of what she saw. She could scarcely draw breath for looking at it, and Amelia had been much the same. Grace and Georgie laughed at their expressions, but they could not contain their excitement, either.

All were greeted by Lord Radcliffe, who was as reserved as ever, though he was polite and accommodating, as a host ought to be. He looked Edith over carefully as if checking for new injuries or distress, but he seemed perfectly satisfied by her appearance. The housekeeper, Mrs. Bates, was pleasant and cheerful, showing them all to their rooms and making sure everyone was comfortable. She even provided Amelia and Edith with their own ladies' maids, since Edith had left Simms in London and Amelia did not have one.

Amelia was given the bedchamber next to Edith with an adjoining sitting room, which they would be sure to enjoy.

The formality of their greeting and the arrangements were strange to Edith, though understandable. There were several other guests due to arrive, including the rest of the Spinsters and Miranda, and there likely wasn't time or need for a more personal greeting or treatment.

But why should Lord Radcliffe treat her differently than any other guest here? Who was she to be deserving of anything out of the ordinary?

Sitting in her bedchamber, which was certainly lovely and perfectly elegant and comfortable, Edith could only feel restless. In this beautiful house, this lovely escape from her struggles in London, she wished to be free. Pushing up from her bed, Edith moved into the sitting room.

"Amelia? I am going to walk about the house. Would you like to join me?"

"No, thank you," came the cheery, if tired reply. "I will rest a while, I think."

For a moment, Edith tensed at her words. Could she go alone? Would she be safe without someone else? Would Amelia be safe by herself here?

Then she recollected her location and the seclusion that being here provided. Merrifield Terrace was far from the reaches of Sir Reginald, or anyone else who might cooperate with him. The only person in London who knew she was here already, apart from her own household and Prue, who couldn't travel in her condition, was her brother, and even that admission had made her uneasy.

If Lachlan wished for her trust, this would be the time to prove his loyalty.

Eventually, word would get out of the house party and its attendees, but for now, all would be well.

She had no idea what measures the men had put in place to keep Sir Reginald from coming to Merrifield, but she would trust that they were enough.

Inhaling slowly, then exhaling the same, Edith left the sitting room and ventured into the corridor, her steps timid. She could hear the others unpacking, laughing, and talking, but didn't stop to converse. Georgie and Grace would no doubt be anticipating the arrival of their husbands, who hadn't travelled with them, and Edith, for one, didn't care to see the reunions.

Joyous though they were, the evidence of such love and bliss made Edith painfully jealous. And she was no romantic.

The corridors and rooms of the guest wing at Merrifield were no less lovely than the rest of the estate, which should not have surprised her in the least. Here were ages of family history portrayed in every stone and wall, in every portrait and carpet, every tapestry and tile. How many of the Radcliffe ancestors had put their own particular tastes on grand display in this place? What guests had stayed in these rooms, and of what station and influence did they belong?

Moving down the grand staircase, her fingers tracing the surface of the dark wood railing, Edith took in the Great Hall with more intensity than she could have managed when she entered. The grandeur of the space was understated, which she could appreciate, and the immaculate windows stretched nearly to the height of the ceiling. Dark wood spanned the ceiling and the lower portion of the walls, with ornate carvings in the corners and along the beams above. One might have considered Merrifield a hunting lodge, if its size were condensed and antlers dotted the walls.

As it was, the whole place felt particularly comfortable to her, as opposed to many fine houses that seemed more a display of finery.

Tapestries hung along the southern wall, and Edith found herself admiring each. It seemed that the Radcliffe family had a taste for legends, as she could see Robin of the Hood, King Arthur, and St. George with his dragon among the stories portrayed. The work was impeccable, though there were signs of aging in each, if one looked close enough.

This was no home on display for the fine Society of London. This was a family home in every respect.

Which begged the question: why had it been so very popular among them?

Edith frowned in thought as she continued to explore, moving further into the house. She passed two parlors and a breakfast room, then paused at the sight of a woman standing out on the terrace. The grand windows at the rear of the house, which belonged to no room to speak of, offered an unhindered view of the terrace, and the woods and gardens beyond.

There hadn't been others arriving when Edith had, apart from the rest of her party, and she wasn't aware that anyone else had come since their arrival. There was something about this woman that made Edith curious.

She stood at the railing, a deep blue shawl wrapped around her slender frame. Fair hair barely contained in a low chignon, stray locks dancing on the breeze, and a pale complexion provided such a contrast to Lord Radcliffe that it seemed impossible for her to be a sister of his.

Searing pain lanced at Edith's throat, and her hand flew there as if to soothe it. Could it be that Lord Radcliffe had a wife?

She had never asked; he had never said. Their limited conversation hadn't provided an opportunity to express such things, and all that her friends had told her had been related to the title, not the man. The tragedy of his brother, but not himself.

The woman turned then, her dark eyes falling on Edith almost at once, leaving her no opportunity to flee undetected. She smiled at Edith, a warm and gentle smile, though Edith felt no comfort from it.

"*Jings crivvens, help ma boab*," Edith muttered as she forced a smile and strode forward.

There was no help for it now.

The fair woman was remarkably pretty, though clearly older than Edith or any of the Spinsters. She moved to a door close by, entering the house.

"Good morning, my dear. Have you made yourself comfortable?"

Edith smiled, the low tone of the woman's voice settling on her rather like a sip of brandy might have done. "Aye, that I have. I canna take a rest after riding in the carriage so long, so I fancied a walk. I hope ye dinnae mind," she said.

"You're Lady Edith," came the bemused reply, the smile turning almost mischievous.

"I am," Edith admitted, her cheeks heating. "It isna hard to tell, in some respects."

That brought a light giggle from the other woman. "No, it is not." She stepped forward and smiled further still. "I'm Lady Eloise Hastings. For better or worse, I suppose I am the mistress of Merrifield." She shook her head on another laugh. "My nephew is Lord Radcliffe."

"Nephew?" Edith exclaimed before she could stop herself. "How is that...? I mean, my lady, you canna be old enough for that."

"Thank you very much," Lady Eloise said with a playful curtsey. "I am his father's much, much, *much*..." her eyes widened for emphasis, making Edith grin, "younger sister. Not even a dozen years in difference between my age and Graham's. I might as well be a sister." She turned her head to cough weakly, though it seemed to take a deal out of her to do so.

Edith stepped forward, a hand instinctively going to Lady Eloise's arm. "Lady Eloise, are you unwell?"

She waved a hand. "Just Eloise, please," she managed between a pair of weak coughs. "I have never been one for unnecessary syllables in addressing me."

"Eloise, then," Edith amended. "And ye may call me Edith, ma'am, if it please ye."

"It would." Eloise grinned at her, then dabbed a handkerchief at her throat. "And no, I'm not unwell… Simply not especially well." Her smile softened, and her color heightened just a touch. "I'm afraid good health has not been my companion throughout my life. Delicate, I believe they call it, though I hardly find that flattering."

Edith rubbed her arm gently, attempting to soothe what she knew she could not. "Would ye like to sit for a spell? Or perhaps return to the terrace? The day is verra fine, and the fresh air may do ye good."

"That was my thought before," Eloise admitted as she extended an arm to Edith. "Will you walk with me, Edith?"

"Gladly." Edith looped her arm through hers, and let Eloise lead her out to the terrace. "This is a beautiful estate, Eloise."

Eloise dipped her chin in a nod, her gaze spanning out over the gardens. "I'm afraid I cannot take credit for any of it, but I do consider it home. My nephews have been kind enough to invite me to remain as they have inherited my brother's title, and so I have never had to look elsewhere." She inhaled deeply, her eyes closing, then exhaled very slowly, the sound full of satisfaction. "I could not imagine anywhere so perfect. But then, I am not particularly objective on the topic."

Edith snickered and tried to take in the view as a whole; rolling hills, forests, and all. "I'm afraid I have examined some of the house myself, exploring this and that from my room until I met you. I was restless, and the spirit of this house is so inviting…"

"You don't need to explain yourself," Eloise interrupted, turning to Edith and putting a hand over hers. "Or excuse yourself. You are an invited guest at Merrifield, and we have no secrets here. No locked rooms or forbidden halls. Walk and wander as you will; it will not upset or offend any of us. Merrifield is the most comfortable fine estate to be found, and I have several witnesses to swear to the claim."

"Thank you." Edith sighed and returned her attention to the grounds. "*Och*, this view reminds me of Scotland. I didna think I would find anything like home in England, except perhaps in the north, and here I find loveliness to compare. I would like to walk every square inch of it, let it seep into my soul until I forget that I am far from home."

Eloise hummed softly and tucked one of her flying fair strands of hair behind an ear. "Well, my dear, I am not a great walker, so I cannot accompany you for every inch. But I could, perhaps, tolerate a stroll in the walled garden, if you are of a mind to see it."

A burst of warmth lit Edith's chest, and she could have cried with joy. "I would enjoy that verra much, Eloise. Verra much, indeed."

"I can't believe I'm doing this."

"Indeed, my lord."

Graham glared at Morgan as the latter brushed out his coat. "That wasn't a conversation starter."

Morgan did not look troubled in the least by this. "Sorry, my lord. Just adding in my opinion."

"Your opinion is not necessary." Graham huffed and fidgeted with his collar in the looking glass. "We have time before I need to look presentable again, yes?"

There was no response from his valet.

Graham glared at his back through the looking glass. "Morgan."

"My lord?" he replied, looking up innocently and meeting his gaze.

"That was addressed to you."

Morgan's brows rose in mock surprise. "Was it? Sorry, my lord, I thought I wasn't necessary."

Graham grumbled incoherently under his breath before repeating the question clearly.

"Yes, my lord," Morgan replied. "I believe the rest of the guests will not arrive until just before dinner. Shall I have the young mistress informed that you will attend her?"

"No," Graham said slowly, shaking his head. "No, she will have her lessons now, and I don't want to disrupt that. I'll seek out my aunt, make sure she is well enough for supper and cards this evening."

"Was that in question?" Morgan asked as he hung Graham's coat over his arm. "I thought Lady Eloise was always ready for supper and cards."

Graham glanced back at his valet, amused when he ought to have been scolding. "That'll do, Morgan."

Once Graham was out of the room, he undid the top button of his shirt, sighing with relief when the choking sensation was gone. Finery might have enhanced the look of ladies, but Graham was convinced it was designed to include weapons of torture and confinement for men.

Only here at Merrifield could he ignore the strict standards of dress, even if it were only for a few minutes. His guests, though few in number at the moment, would be taking a respite in their rooms, leaving the corridors and billiards rooms free from any who would find him improper.

He was abysmal at billiards, but he did find them an adequate activity to quiet his mind when he had too much on it. He'd never seek to play in earnest with other men, but alone, he could easily pass the time there.

He might do so, once he found Eloise and saw to her. She'd seemed more fatigued than he would have liked of late, and more than once, he had considered cancelling the house party. But between his determination to help Edith and his aunt's insistence on having the event, he'd let it all continue.

Time would only tell if it was a worthy endeavor.

He strode down to the main level only to find that Eloise was nowhere to be found. None of the servants had seen her recently, and she was not in her rooms. Considering she was no horsewoman, and never walked to the village, there could be only one place left.

Shaking his head, Graham left the house, wanting to laugh and growl at the same time. His aunt refused to accept that she had limitations and that she would do well to obey them. She would walk the gardens and then be nearly bedridden the day after in recovery. For all her declarations of not being sickly, her constitution was not one of strength on even the best days. More than once, he had considered bringing her to London to see better physicians than what they had in nearby Linfield.

Eloise would not hear of it and swore by Dr. Benson and his treatments. Graham had no complaints about the man himself, but his aunt had not had improvement to her health and stamina in some time. It was entirely possible that nothing could be done by any physician, but he would have given a great deal to try.

"Good day, milord!" one of the gardeners' assistants called from the hedgerow with a wave.

Graham nodded with a smile, enjoying the fact that he did not have to force it or remind himself of politeness. Here at Merrifield, Lord Radcliffe smiled at his tenants and servants, and could even be prevailed upon to speak with them.

The same could not necessarily be said for his neighbors, but there was no sense in giving up his reserve on all fronts.

He ducked as he entered the garden through the smaller entrance, not wishing to circle all the way around to the main gate. Scanning the paths and low bushes, he frowned, seeing nothing and no one. His aunt would not have gone through the maze, unless she had completely lost her ever-sharp faculties, so she must have been on the other side of the garden behind the roses.

With all the meandering paths his mother had laid down during her renovation of the garden some twenty years ago, it would take him as long to reach the roses as it would have done to go around.

Nothing for it, though.

Graham walked quickly on the stones, hopping over the low bushes where he could, glancing up at the windows purely out of habit. Any of his guests would have thought him unhinged, and Molly would have found him laughable. He wasn't sure which of the impressions he would prefer to have left, but it would be best for all concerned if he were not seen at all.

Eloise would pay dearly if he were.

Rounding the last of the bushes and lifting the low-hanging wisteria out of his way, Graham moved into the last part of the garden, only to stop in his tracks.

Eloise sat on a bench at the end of the lane he presently stood on.

And she was not alone.

Striking green eyes raised from the private conversation and widened as they clashed with his gaze.

Holy heavens.

Graham swallowed, his fingers sliding against each other by his sides. Edith looked even lovelier than she had upon her arrival, a simple cream calico gown enhancing every aspect of her. She had forgone the deep green traveling cloak from before. The brilliance it had lent to her already magnificent eyes had left Graham unable to present the warm and welcoming greeting he had intended. All he had managed was his habitual reserve, bare politeness, and looking her over as though something might have happened to her since he'd seen her last.

He'd meant to ask her about her state rather than look it over. He'd meant to show her how pleased he was that she had come, that she was here, and that he could spend some time getting to know her in this place. He'd managed none of those things.

And now she was sitting in his garden with his aunt.

And he was barely dressed. Fully clothed, but hardly respectable. Morgan would kill him. Provided Graham recovered enough to face anyone ever again.

Seeing Edith's reaction, Eloise turned and smiled brilliantly. "Graham! Come join us, won't you? You see that I have met Edith, and we have been walking the gardens. She has been so generous to keep to my pace and insists we rest far too often. I've a mind to keep her as my nursemaid; do help me to persuade her."

Graham informed his feet that they ought to move, and they did so, albeit with a touch of awkwardness, and he forced his hands into his pockets, more to keep them occupied than anything else.

"I don't believe a woman of such a status as Edith would be acceptable as a nursemaid, Aunt, no matter how qualified she may be."

Edith swallowed, and her hands twitched as they lay in her lap. "Status is as status does," she murmured, averting her gaze.

"True enough, dear," Eloise chimed, smiling at her new friend. "Who said that?"

Edith's lips pulled into a smile that tugged at something behind Graham's navel. "Edith Leveson. Widow, Spinster, and Scot."

"Spinster?" Eloise replied with a laugh. "Darling Edith, you are scarcely twenty-five, if you are a day, and you are a widow. Nothing spinsterly about you."

Graham quite agreed, but he also knew full well to what Edith was referring. Yet it was not his secret to tell, so he merely remained silent, watching.

"No' that kind of spinster, Eloise," she told his aunt. "I write for the Spinster Chronicles. A Society paper in London."

"Oh, I know all about the Chronicles!" Eloise retorted with a wave of her hand.

"You do?" Edith and Graham said together, sharing a stunned look.

Eloise looked between the two of them. "Of course! Miranda sends every edition on to me. I adore every word. Brava, my dear."

Edith blinked and looked back at Graham in bewilderment.

He could only shrug. "They are quite clever. I cannot claim to have read every word, but what I have read, I enjoy."

"I'll be sure to pass that along," Edith said with a small smile, her eyes nearly dancing. She looked at Eloise again. "And I am twenty-seven."

"Pah!" Eloise shook her head, making a face. "Still a child, I'd say."

"Because you are so aged," Graham pointed out, giving his aunt a severe look. "I have no idea what makes you a capable judge of age."

Edith snickered behind a hand, and his eyes flicked to hers as he smiled. The sound of her laughter could have danced on the breeze, and he felt like a fool for thinking so.

A charmed fool, but a fool all the same.

"I am older than my age," Eloise insisted, narrowing her eyes at him, though her lips still quirked in a smile. "And I am still your aunt. I am entitled to the wisdom of my generation."

"Your generation." Graham pretended to consider that, looking up at the sky. "Your generation. Wouldn't that practically be the same generation to which Edith and I belong, hmm? You are closer in age to us than to your closest sibling, after all."

Eloise exhaled a short breath through her nose, though he could see her fighting laughter. "You see what I must put up with, Edith?

The impudence! What shall I do with him?"

"I canna say," Edith told her, once more looking at Graham, almost shyly this time. "A bit of impudence has always endeared a body to me, personally. Shows a canny mind, does it not?"

Graham smiled at her, a slow curling of his lips that seemed to cause the same sensation in the soles of his feet. A compliment from Edith was worth any teasing that would be forthcoming from his aunt, and any awkwardness on his part.

The playful streak in the woman was damned attractive.

"I suppose it does," Eloise admitted reluctantly. She slowly rose, her breathing shifting as she did so in a way Graham did not care for. "Stay right there," she ordered, pointing a finger at him. "I am only stiff. Edith, will you see me back into the house, love? I believe I have walked enough for the day."

"Of course," Edith said at once. "I do not know the way to your rooms, but..."

Eloise waved a hand at her. "I am not going to lay down, my dear, only take some tea. We will go to the parlor and share a pot together. I want to hear all about you without this brat of a nephew ruining things."

"I beg your pardon?" Graham protested mildly.

"Continue to beg," Eloise shot back. "When you deserve my pardon, I daresay I shall give it." She winked at him, then gestured for Edith to lead her away, passing Graham.

"I like her," Eloise whispered, patting his arm as she went by him.

Edith smiled at Graham but said nothing as she and his aunt proceeded through the garden to return to the house.

How long Graham stood there after they left, he couldn't say, but he suddenly felt like playing a very long game of billiards.

There was entirely too much on his mind.

Chapter Fourteen

———⟨⌘⌘⌘⟩———

Intrepid voyagers may meet the most valuable allies. They may also find a heap of trouble. The chances are roughly the same.

-*The Spinster Chronicles, 19 December 1817*

Edith forced a smile for what felt like the fourteenth time that morning, and her face was beginning to ache for it.

How was she so out of practice?

Her friends had arrived, saving Prue and Charlotte, as well as the other guests, and it was the other ladies among the party who were to blame for the painful smiles. They were, for the most part, ridiculous.

The Miss Bradfords, Felicity and Diana, were particularly intriguing. Both stood to inherit a great deal of money, had charming enough looks and manners, but had no real designs for matrimony. They were well-educated, well-spoken, and shockingly well-versed in gossip.

Adaline Chesney wanted nothing more than to be on Lord Radcliffe's arm at all times, but she would settle for any eligible man in the room. She lacked tact and attempted to cover the flaw with giggles and fluttering lashes. Every other lady, married or not, was competition, and she left no doubt about it.

Catherine Tillman barely spoke, but Edith could hardly call her shy. She had a gaze that would leave any person unsettled, and her fortune and breeding were impeccable. The only person she spoke with was Mr. Gaither, and she seemed to do so in only low tones.

Edith appeared to trouble her somehow, though they had only barely been introduced.

At the sound of another of Miss Chesney's grating laughs, Edith quietly rose and turned to Georgie with a slight smile. "I think I will take some air for a moment or two. Will you make my excuses if I am noticed?"

Georgie returned her smile, knowing full well what Edith was up to. "Of course."

Edith nodded her thanks and walked as sedately as she could, although she was desperate to run out to the terrace and down the steps.

It was a rather pleasant day, a mixture of sun and clouds in the sky, and with a breeze just chilled enough to keep one from feeling too heated. It was a rarity for England, or Scotland, for that matter, and it seemed a shame to remain indoors rather than take part in it. Besides, being alone was such a delight after being forced into social activity all afternoon, evening, and now this morning.

On occasion, one simply must be alone.

Edith chose to go around and beyond the walled garden, lovely though it was, and though she had much to explore still within. The landscape and grounds of Merrifield were quite the glorious spectacle from her bedchamber windows, and she wanted to traipse them all before she returned to London.

Wildflowers dotted the grass and hedges, some places forming natural canopies of wisteria, and even some honeysuckle. Their fragrances filled the air, a heavenly scent only nature could provide, and with a richness that could not be described adequately. Edith slowed her pace, pleased she hadn't bothered with a bonnet to shade her from the warmth of the sun or the experience itself.

She closed her eyes, inhaling and exhaling slowly and deeply, a marvelous cleansing sensation filling and refreshing her.

There was nothing like Merrifield in all the world, and she was convinced of it.

A sound disturbed the beauty of the moment then, and Edith frowned at hearing it. A rustling came from off to her right, and it was far too vigorous to be a rabbit or bird. Muffled cries of distress soon accompanied it, not to the extent of tears, but certainly involving effort.

There were no children in the party at Merrifield, so it had to be a local from the village or a servant, though her first inclination was to declare the person younger than any servants she had seen. She moved around the hedge and saw a small, dark-haired girl trying desperately to untangle herself and her yellow frock from a bunch of brambles on the other side. She was so determined that she was ripping a hole in the garment.

Edith hurried forward. "Here, lass, let me help you."

The girl jumped as if she had not known anyone was there, her striking blue eyes widening sharply.

Edith smiled at her kindly. "It's all right. I just want to help you out of there. My name is Edith. What is your name?"

"Molly," she replied after a moment, still looking at her warily. Then, she rolled her eyes and dipped into a light curtsey among the brambles and thorns. "Lady Molly Hastings, if you please, ma'am."

There was nothing to do but grin at her attempt at manners, and Edith responded in kind. "Lady Edith Leveson, at your service, Lady Molly. Now, might I help you?"

"Yes, please," she said heavily, forgoing any sort of nerves or shyness. "I'm making a mess of my dress."

"Yes, well, that can happen," Edith conceded as she worked to disentangle the girl. "Particularly with brambles. What were you doing?"

Molly wrinkled her nose up and pushed some of her dark hair out of her face. "I was so bored and so hungry, I thought I could sneak out and get some berries before anybody discovered I was gone." She frowned and shook her head. "I got stuck picking some of the berries up high."

Edith gave the girl a bemused look, though it likely should have been more disapproving, as she helped her step out of the bushes. "You snuck out of your house? I can understand the desire to on such a day as this, but I'm afraid, my dear Lady Molly, sneaking just isna done."

"I know," she admitted with a sigh too heavy for a child, "and you can call me Molly. I don't like being called 'lady'. I much prefer to be a child." She sighed again and shuffled her feet. "Gray is always telling me to behave like a lady, and I try. But I was so bored…"

It was said with such longing, Edith had to smile. The memory of childhood was faint, but the same enthusiasm and liveliness was still clear as the day itself.

"That can happen, I fear. How old are you, Molly? If ye dinna mind me asking."

"Almost seven," she said proudly, "but I am very smart for my age."

"Aye, I can see that," Edith murmured, pulling some small leaves and twigs from her curly locks. They had no doubt looked pretty enough before, but with her running around, they now looked an untidy mess.

It suited her well, though no doubt her parents wouldn't agree.

Then, her name echoed in Edith's mind again, and her eyes widened. "Did ye say your name was Lady Molly Hastings?"

Molly gave her a disparaging look. "Yes, Edith, I did." Then she looked down at her dress, and her expression paled considerably. "Oh, no. My dress! There is a hole in my dress. Oh, I am going to be in so much trouble." She put her hands over her face and whimpered with what seemed to be real distress, more so than even when she had been stuck.

"It isna so bad, Molly," Edith told her as she looked at it. The hole was hardly gaping, though it was rather front and center. Noticeable, yes, but hardly disastrous.

Again, Molly favored Edith with a look, one that would have terrified anyone of her age. "You don't know Gray."

"That bad?" Edith asked, thinking she had a fair idea of who Gray might be, but fearing to inquire.

"Worse," the girl moaned dramatically.

"Well," Edith said, biting back a smile, "then I suppose there is just one thing to be done." Keeping her eyes on Molly, she took hold of her own skirts and began to tear the fabric in exactly the same place.

Molly stared at it, and Edith, with wide eyes.

"Edith, what did you do?" she breathed.

Edith shrugged, fighting the desire to laugh wildly.

"It's only a dress, Molly. We can mend them."

"Do you want to pick some more berries with me?" Molly asked, beaming. "Then, I promise I'll go straight back home."

Edith laughed and agreed, stepping forward to pick a few berries, and eating quite a few of them as she went.

Wild blackberries had never been part of Edith's childhood experience, but they added perfectly to her present circumstances. Molly talked her through the process of finding perfect ones, and her knowledge of it all was really quite impressive, considering her age.

When they had finished, Edith took Molly's hand. "Come on, lass. Let's get ourselves back to Merrifield. I'll walk with ye at least part of the way."

"I like your accent, Edith," Molly told her with a smile as she took her hand and began to skip. "It's fun. It sounds like dancing."

"I have never heard it described that way," Edith replied, "but it may be my favorite description yet."

Molly giggled, then looked at the path ahead of them, her expression falling at once.

Edith looked as well and swallowed.

Lord Radcliffe was storming towards them, his expression tight, his gaze fixed on the small girl next to her.

"Oh, dear," Molly sighed, tucking some hair behind her ear. "Gray."

Crivvens. Edith looked down at her. "He looks upset."

She nodded and scooted a little closer to her. "He's my uncle."

Edith looked heavenward, afraid this was not going to go well at all. Eloise might have given her the freedom to go where she wished, but that likely had not extended to interacting with Molly. There had to be a reason why her existence was so little known. If Lord Radcliffe were the overbearing, overprotective guardian she imagined, he would not take kindly to this particular introduction.

Was Edith going to unearth all the secrets of Merrifield? Or simply the ones Lord Radcliffe felt particular about?

But there was nothing for it.

"Where have you been?" Lord Radcliffe asked when he was close enough. "I have been looking everywhere for you!"

Molly looked appropriately apologetic. "I'm sorry, Gray."

He sighed and folded his arms, his eyes still fixed on her with the same intensity he used with everyone. "Answer the question, please."

"I was picking berries," Molly replied obediently, "and eating them."

Edith clamped down on her lips to keep from giggling at the girl's openness and honesty.

Lord Radcliffe's gaze flicked to Edith's without emotion, then back to his niece. "And?" he prodded.

Molly sighed heavily. "And I didn't tell Nanny Florence where I was going, and as punishment, I got stuck in the bush." She scowled and shuffled her feet again. "If I were taller, or able to wear breeches, this wouldn't be a problem."

Edith had to close her eyes for a moment, ready to lose all composure.

"And you, Lady Edith?" Lord Radcliffe asked, sounding nearly as severe, though a good deal more amused.

Edith's eyes popped open, and she looked at him as innocently as possible. "Yes, my lord?"

His lips quirked. "What part do you play here?"

"None, my lord," she replied. "I was walking the grounds, found her in distress, and freed her from it." She let herself smile ruefully and tilted her head rather as Molly did. "And then I ate some berries, as well."

He stared at Edith for a long moment, his mouth tightening as if he were not sure if he were angry or amused. Then, he looked back down at Molly.

"I don't know what to do with you," he sighed, unfolding his arms and setting his hands at his waist. "I am supposed to be hosting this nonsense, but instead, I'm out here hunting for you."

Molly started to pout a little, looking down at her stained slippers, shifting uncomfortably where she stood.

Edith felt for the girl and put a hand on her back.

"If I may, my lord," she murmured as gently as she could.

Lord Radcliffe looked at Edith again, one brow raised in silent query.

"I suggest that you return to your guests and host as you must," Edith proposed, "and I will return the child home. I'll sneak her back in before anyone can see anything."

He snorted softly and gave her a bemused look. "You don't know how to sneak through my house."

"No," she said simply. Then she indicated his niece beside her. "But she does."

He looked down at Molly, his face softening, then back at the house with a bit of reluctance. "Point taken." He hesitated, then exhaled roughly. "All right," he finally agreed, turning back to look at Molly, "but we will discuss this later, young lady."

Molly took Edith's hand. "That means I'm in trouble," she whispered loudly.

Edith bit back a grin and looked at her uncle. "Does it?"

He looked at her quickly, then back at Molly, his brow furrowing.

"Edith will protect me, Gray," Molly said staunchly.

"Will she now?" he asked, again looking at Edith.

There was something in his gaze now that caused the strangest tingling in Edith's toes, and a slow burning began in her cheeks.

"Yes," Molly insisted with a nod. "She's my friend."

Lord Radcliffe smiled at the girl before raising a brow. "And does your friend think sneaking out of the house is a good idea?"

Molly looked up at Edith, and Edith gave her a knowing look in return. Then she pouted. "No, and she said as much when she found me."

Edith squeezed her hand and winked at her, then looked up to find Lord Radcliffe watching her with interest. "She did, did she? Seems to me you were lucky to have Edith be the one to find you, Molly."

"I think so, too, Gray," Molly told her uncle with sageness beyond her years.

Lord Radcliffe chuckled, the deep sound giving Edith a falling sensation. He ruffled his niece's hair, stroked her cheek, and said, "All right, back to the house. I'll come see you later."

"Yes, Gray," she said, smiling despite her previous attempts to pout.

He looked at Edith once more, and she could see gratitude expressed in his eyes.

She smiled in return and nodded once.

His smile lingered, something he saw clearly amusing him, then he turned back for the house.

"Whew," Molly exhaled heavily, and with some relief. "That could have been so much worse. Come on!"

With a tug on Edith's hand, Molly resumed her skipping towards the house, and Edith, not to be outdone, joined in, though skipping had never been one of her more accomplished talents.

Molly surprised her by taking a small door just off the kitchens to reenter the house, pulling Edith past the pantry without disturbing the kitchen staff in the slightest. They moved down a long, narrow corridor, surprisingly well lit, and then up a particularly narrow set of stairs.

Edith stumbled once on the hem of her skirt, snorting a laugh to herself at the thought of tearing another hole in her gown, this time unintentionally.

It would be only too perfect a picture for Lady Edith Leveson, who sought connection and protection at this very house party she was at present avoiding.

Her intrepid guide opened a door that Edith would have completely passed, letting them both into the gallery. The walls were filled nearly from floor to ceiling with grand portraits and sweeping landscapes depicting soldiers in battle and fine horses running wild on the land.

"Heavenly days," Edith breathed, looking around at them all.

Molly, however, was far less impressed. "Come *on*, Edith! We're nearly there!"

Edith found herself tugged along again, moving down one corridor, then another, then somehow still another before ultimately reaching a quaint, comfortable nursery.

Molly finally released her hand as they entered the room, twirling a little in the center of the space. "Gray says I can change the furnishings for my next birthday! I want everything to be blue. No, green." She frowned, her lips twisting. "Blue and green, perhaps. And gold. Things that sparkle, too."

"Sounds marvelous, lass." Edith smiled at the child, still so full of energy. "Now, let us change your frock before your nanny or a maid sees you. That way, it will be our secret."

Quickly, they switched her gown to a checkered green with a

simple pinafore over the top.

"There, Lady Molly," Edith praised with a teasing wink. "Much more presentable, and none the wiser."

Molly curtseyed. "Thank you, Lady Edith."

"I must change my own frock, lassie," Edith sighed, "and return to your uncle's party."

"Oh, must you?" Molly pouted without shame. "I never get to go to parties. Gray has never had one, either."

Edith smiled sadly. "I am sure ye have lessons to attend to, and I have tasks myself. I dinna much care for parties, but it is the polite thing to do, and so I must." She made a face to indicate how she truly felt about it.

The girl giggled at the expression. "Could you come and see me later? After I've finished my lessons?"

"Ye'll have to ask your uncle, Molly, lass," Edith told her. "But if he agrees, I would be delighted to."

Molly grinned at her and nodded. "I'll ask him! I'll ask him as soon as he comes! Thank you, Edith!" She dashed over and hugged Edith tightly around the waist.

Suddenly awash in emotion, Edith patted the girl's back, swallowing with difficulty. "There's a good lass. Now fetch a book and sit yourself by the window for Nanny. I daresay she'll come 'round soon enough and be surprised to find ye here."

"Not that surprised," Molly told her with a dry laugh. "She's grown accustomed to my doing all sorts of things." She waved and darted over to the window seat, picking up a book from the floor.

Edith shook her head as she left the nursery, shutting the door softly behind her.

What a delightful surprise Lady Molly Hastings was turning out to be! Lord Radcliffe would certainly have a time of it as her guardian; there was no doubt about that.

Chuckling to herself, Edith turned to go back to her rooms to change, if she could remember the way. She had not taken more than two turns before another set of footsteps met her ears.

Lord Radcliffe turned down the same corridor, coming towards her, his head lowered as though in thought. He stopped when he saw her, then looked her over, his mouth working as if he did not know what to say. Then his focus remained on her skirts, and his mouth quirked.

"Why is your dress torn?" he asked without premise.

Edith looked down at the hole she had made and laughed, cheeks flaming yet again. "Molly was so upset about the hole in hers, I tore one in mine to match."

He shook his head a little. "Why would you do that? I was told you did not have much by way of worldly possessions."

Edith shrugged a shoulder. "I don't. But I can mend this well enough, and relieving Molly's distress was well worth putting a hole in my frock."

That seemed to surprise him, and he looked quite as if words were beyond him.

"She asked if I could see her later," Edith said, suddenly feeling self-conscious. "I told her to ask you. I willna do anything without your consent, particularly if ye do not wish her presence to be known."

"I'm only protecting her," he murmured softly. "I don't hide her. I don't speak of her, and I probably should. But I just… I can't seem to find my way around guardianship without…"

"Her parents," Edith replied, her voice very low, her heart suddenly pounding too hard.

He nodded once, looking away.

"I am so sorry," she murmured, not knowing what else to say. "I canna begin to imagine."

His throat worked on a swallow. "It has been difficult, it is true." His attention came back to her, and compassion radiated from him. "I understand you have been separated from your family for some time. That cannot be easy, either."

"It is hardly the same thing," Edith protested weakly. "My family… Well, they would still be there if ever I were permitted home."

"Permitted?" Lord Radcliffe repeated softly. "Do they forbid you?"

Edith winced, wishing she had chosen her words with more care.

"Aye," she whispered, looking down at the rug beneath their feet. "From the day of my wedding, I've been cast off, ye might say.

It was hoped that my marriage would last a bit more'n a day, but there was naught to do about that. Unless one takes the view of my father, in which case it is my fault."

"How in the world…?" he started to argue, his voice rising.

"I didna do my duty proper if I couldna keep my husband to our marriage bed," Edith overrode bluntly, her hands balling into fists at her side, the confession a release, so long it had remained buried within her. "If I had, he would ne'er have suffered his accident, and we might still be wed."

Lord Radcliffe's eyes were wide, his lips parting ever so slightly. "Surely, you jest?"

Edith nodded once. "I wouldna have the creativity to invent such a ludicrous statement."

"Well," he muttered under his breath as he ran a hand through his hair, "as long as you realize it is a ludicrous statement…"

"I ken verra well," she assured him, smiling ruefully. "It is one of the reasons I dinna miss my family over much. Ye've a much stronger right to missing yours than I do."

A crooked smile crossed his lips. "I don't believe it is a competition, but thank you. Besides," he tilted his head in the direction of the nursery, "Molly keeps her parents very alive in many ways."

"Well, she is a delightful child," Edith told him, stepping away a little, "and if you'll permit it, I should like to see her again. But I will abide by your wishes. I do owe you that much, for being my hero."

His smile faded just enough to be bewitching, his eyes still fixed on hers.

"I am no hero, Lady Edith, not even for you. And I would like you to see Molly again. Whenever you like, as you wish, now you know where she is."

"Thank you." A giddiness began to well within her, something she didn't understand but found a ticklish delight in. "Provided I can find my way back to the main of the house at all. I think Molly must have taken precautionary measures not to be followed by anyone, for I canna remember a single thing about how I ended up here."

Lord Radcliffe chuckled warmly. "She does enjoy her adventures, even if they involve servants' stairs, ancient tunnels, and several rounds of backtracking." He gestured back the way he had come. "Come with me, and I'll see you back in a much, *much* more direct route. Far easier to recollect later."

Edith smiled and dipped her chin, falling into step beside him. "Are you trying to tell me your niece enjoys making things unnecessarily complicated?"

"Molly thrives on making things unnecessarily complicated," he insisted with an earnestness that had Edith laughing. "My life being chief among them. Only three months after I had assumed guardianship, she decided that she was only going to speak in rhyme. It was the most miserable three weeks of my life, and I tried everything…"

Chapter Fifteen

I am not particularly certain that I believe in love at the first sighting. I rather think that one is far more likely to love a person after the second sighting, in the proper setting. Or the third, when one is laughing. Or the fourth, in absolute perfection. But then, this author is a Spinster, so all this conjecture could simply be false.

-*The Spinster Chronicles, 25 October 1819*

"Would it be possible to do a house party without a ball?"

"I don't believe so. There is a certain level of expectation."

"Why can we not defy expectation?"

"Because we are a boring family, and we thrive upon tradition."

Graham looked at his aunt in mild surprise. "Do we indeed? Why does that not sound like a compliment, I wonder?"

Eloise gave him a playful sneer. "Behave yourself, Gray. You've led a different woman into dinner every night so far, and you've been very good about keeping up conversation. Do try to dance this evening."

"What else would one do at a ball?" he asked, raising a brow.

"You didn't set up gaming tables, did you? The gentlemen must remain for the dancing. There aren't enough to ensure every lady has a partner every time." Eloise looked towards the ballroom in apprehension, biting her lip.

Graham chuckled at her dismay and rubbed her arms gently. "No, Aunt, I did not. And we are rather evenly paired, considering the number of married couples in the house at present. Not all the ladies will wish to dance every dance, and everything is furnished beautifully. Will you do something for me?"

Eloise nodded at once, her attention coming back to him rapidly. "Of course, what is it?"

He offered her a smile. "Enjoy the evening? You look lovely; the lavender does suit you well."

His aunt gave him a dubious look. "Who told you this was lavender? You aren't that conscious of shades, so you must have had help."

"Morgan," he admitted without shame. "He asked Capshaw what she was dressing you in this evening."

"Traitor," Eloise grumbled, though she smiled. "I cannot promise to dance, but I do think I shall very much enjoy a chair by the terrace door. Watching dancing can be nearly as enjoyable as participating in it."

Graham made a face. "I don't know, I've never found much pleasure in either."

Eloise rapped him on the arm before looping her hand around it. "You cannot have that attitude this evening. I forbid it."

"Yes, ma'am." He winked as he led her into the ballroom, his chest swelling with pride as he took in the pristine appearance. The walls had always been a brilliant white, and it took a good deal of upkeep as the house aged, but moments like this were worth it. The vast array of elegant chandeliers and sconces dotted about filled the space with luminous candlelight, each reflecting off the bright walls in their turn. A hint of gold leaf detailing along engraved surfaces traced upwards into the ceilings and the murals painted thereon.

It was the finest ballroom he had ever seen, and it happened to belong to him.

Not that he'd had anything to do with it, but now he could fully appreciate what a fine space it was.

"Stop gaping at your own rooms," Eloise hissed with a nudge in his side. "The musicians await your cue, and if you would look about you, you would see your guests are eager to dance."

Graham glanced around and saw, shockingly, that his aunt was correct.

The married couples stood close together, smiling at him as though they had known him for ages. They were, of course, all members of the Spinsters and their husbands, so they had only known him a short while, but somehow, he had been adopted. There was something equally satisfying about that.

Strange.

Graham gave a nod to the musicians, who immediately struck up a jaunty tune. The Bradford sisters and Miss Chesney were quick to form lines with their partners, and they were joined there by Lord and Lady Sterling, Tony and Georgie, and the Mortons.

"Why are you not opening the dance?" Eloise asked with just as much exasperation as her last question had held.

Graham sighed. "So many rules for being the host, I seem to have forgotten that one."

She narrowed her eyes at him. "I highly doubt that." She sniffed and looked around the room. "Now, where is Miranda? I simply must... Oh, there she is!" Tapping his arm with her fan, she disengaged herself from his hold and moved away.

"What happened to finding a chair?" he asked after her, knowing a response was unlikely.

No matter.

Graham smiled at Lady Ingram as he neared her, his eyes casting around for her husband. "I was going to congratulate you on the return of your husband, my lady; only I do not see him near."

Lady Ingram laughed, her head tilting back in a charming fashion, highlighting her beauty in an entirely natural way. "Aubrey has gone to fetch me a drink. He will return momentarily." She smiled at him, her hands folding elegantly before her. "I do wish you would call me Grace, Radcliffe. With all that you are doing for Edith, I'd feel much better calling you a friend."

Graham inclined his head in a nod. "If you wish it, I would be honored to do so, if the familiarity will not earn me an eye blacking from your husband."

She grinned quickly. "No, he would never. Besides, Tony, Cam, and Sebastian call me by my name. I daresay Hugh Sterling will as well, once he adjusts to being part of the group. We are all on quite familiar terms, Radcliffe. Rather like a family."

"I see that," he murmured, watching Mrs. Morton laugh merrily while briefly partnered with Tony. "Rather remarkable, I must say."

"It has become so, and I am ever so grateful." Her smile turned wistful, though there was a fond edge to it. "My own family gives me little enough reason to smile or laugh, apart from my husband. But with the Spinsters, I have never felt bereft of anything."

"Who's feeling bereft?" Ingram asked with mild alarm as he approached, his eyes tracing over his wife as though looking for injury.

Grace rolled her eyes. "No one, Aubrey. I was just saying that I do *not* feel bereft. Radcliffe was commenting on the Spinsters."

"Ah." Ingram nodded once, flashing a quick smile. "Bereft is most certainly not a word to describe the Spinsters."

"So I see," Graham murmured, watching the various members of the group around the room, all of whom were full of good cheer.

Yet he did not see Edith anywhere.

Suddenly, bereft was the only word to come to mind.

"Looking for someone?"

The suspicious note of curiosity in Ingram's question brought Graham around to look at him, sardonic expression in place.

"Looking for everyone," he corrected easily. "As host, I could hardly have guests avoiding the ball, could I?"

Ingram made a face, accepting the lie as accurate reasoning, no doubt. "I suppose not. What a dreadful idea."

"Avoiding a ball?" Grace asked on a laugh.

Ingram looked at his wife with open honesty. "No, hosting."

Graham choked a laugh into a fist and took a glass of champagne from his footman with a nod of thanks before turning back.

"How did your business in London go?"

Ingram sobered at once and stepped closer. "Not as well as I had hoped, but not as bad as I expected. The solicitors we've hired are now poring over every possible document and working on a solution that might not leave Edith so destitute. Mr. Chadwick, who is Camden Vale's brother-in-law, has been working especially tirelessly, when he is available."

"Available?" Graham repeated. "I thought he was a scholar."

"So did I," Ingram said with a shrug, "and yet he seemed to have many conflicts in his schedule. Still, he has a brilliant mind, so I have complete faith that if anything can be found, Chadwick will find it."

"Good," Graham grunted in satisfaction. "Tony was with you in that?"

Ingram nodded. "And Francis. Cam made the introductions, but the law is not his particular friend."

"Now that, I can understand," Grace commented dryly. "The man is a paradox in every legal respect."

"Cam is perfectly respectable, love," Ingram insisted. "A gentleman of the highest degree."

Grace blinked at her husband once. "We are talking about Camden Vale, aren't we?"

Ingram's expression soured. "Funny, wife."

"Just because he is your best friend of late does not change his stripes," she laughed, linking her arm with his. "I adore him, but even you must allow that he rather enjoys being defiant."

"I know I do," chimed in another voice.

Graham smirked as Tyrone joined them, bowing politely to the Ingrams. "Making a tardy appearance, Tyrone?"

His friend appeared unruffled by the accusation. "I didn't realize we were emphasizing punctuality at your soirée, Radcliffe. How interesting." He turned his attention to Grace while Graham and Ingram snickered. "My Lady Ingram, might I claim the next dance?"

"Naturally, Mr. Demaris," Grace said, smiling warmly. "And will we be competing against your cousin for best dancers in our set?"

Tyrone grinned freely. "I knew you were my favorite of the Spinsters for a reason, my lady."

"Watch yourself," Ingram growled good-naturedly. "Just for that, I think I'll partner with Janet."

"Then we are assured of winning," Grace shot back. "Remind me to fetch a compress for Janet's toes later."

The Ingrams glared at each other, both on the verge of laughing, and Graham only shook his head, chuckling to himself. It was rare to find a couple in Society that adored each other, let alone one that could banter with each other so skillfully. Yet, in his admittedly limited experience, that was the standard for the Spinster couples.

Had none of them made comfortable matches for the sake of it?

No, that was part of their foundation, was it not? To marry for love, if at all? To avoid forming a marriage out of desperation?

What, then, of Edith and her venture?

Protection and security were what she sought. If the rumors were true, if she had a lover, she could have found it. Or, if she wished, she could find it in such a way with more powerful men. It was far less respectable, but many respectable widows did such.

Even some respectable wives did such, with more discretion, of course.

The thought left a bitter taste in his mouth, but he had to admit the possibility was there.

"Oh, she looks wonderful, does she not?"

Graham turned at the sound of Miranda Sterling's voice near him, bowing in greeting. "Miranda, good evening."

She smiled, her eyes bluer for the nearly matching shade of gown she flawlessly wore. "Good evening, dear. Lovely decor and arrangement. What a marvelous room!"

"Thank you." He returned her smile, then returned his attention to the dance. "What were you saying? Who looks well?"

"Edith, dear. Edith." She indicated the dancing with her fan. "There, in the green silk. And she doesn't look well; she looks luminous."

His eyes caught sight of Edith then, and all sound in the room ceased.

How had he missed her entering? Her gown was the color of nature in the spring draped in a delicate lace overlay, both forming to her frame and person with a perfection that would make any dressmaker weep. Matching cream and green ribbons weaved in and out of her dark curls in an almost teasing manner, bringing the itch of temptation to his fingers. Tracing those ribbons within those locks, dislodging some and disheveling the appearance, yet losing nothing at all in the experience.

But more captivating than all of that, as incomparable as it was, had to be the brilliant smile upon her perfectly full lips. She seemed to be constantly on the edge of a laugh, every step of the dance appearing lighter and fresher than he had ever seen. She was everything that any miss in Society would wish to be.

Graham could not look away.

He was transfixed by her, and it took him far too long to notice the unsteady beat of his pounding heart. As well as the dotty smile currently affixed to his lips.

He couldn't help it; anyone witnessing such a sight would have to smile at it. The fact that he felt as though every inch of him smiled along with his lips was beside the point.

"Such a vision," Miranda praised on a delighted sigh. "It's been an age since I have seen her so full of joy. And that gown! Janet Sterling brought it for her, you know, along with three new gowns, all perfectly tailored, by way of apology."

"What for?" Graham heard himself reply, his voice sounding rather distant.

Miranda tsked beside him. "Oh, she felt so horribly burdened with guilt for not being more present for Edith during her time of need. I did try to tell her that with Francis working towards the betterment of Edith's position, Janet was beyond all blame, given that *someone* had to see to the baby, but alas…" Miranda lifted her fan to murmur to Graham. "She swears it did not cost her much at all, though I do not believe her one bit. Such exquisite gowns as that one would have cost a fortune."

"Well worth the expense, I should think," Graham said to himself without thinking.

There was a soft laugh from beside him that ought to have given him cause for worry. "Very true, my boy, and I do believe she looks even prettier up close. Perhaps you should join the dance."

He flicked his gaze to Miranda, knowing precisely what she was doing, then back at the dance. "Hmm," he rumbled with some thought. "Perhaps I should."

"You're agreeing with me?" came the shocked response. Then, in a much flatter tone, "Why?"

Graham smiled again. "I make a point of agreeing with anyone who makes suggestions that benefit me. Don't take it personally."

"Never do, Radcliffe," Miranda laughed, sauntering away. "Believe me, I never do."

Despite the obvious proposal, Graham did not dance the next. Or the one following. Or even the one after that.

He watched, however, with great interest.

Edith's enthusiasm did not change with a new partner and did not alter with the variation in dance. Her liveliness and contagious spirit seemed to invigorate the other couples and even the other guests in the room. It really was remarkable. She hadn't said much by way of conversation in any of the other activities they'd had at this party, and based on his previous encounters with her where dancing had occurred, she hadn't seemed particularly elated by the thing.

As far as he could tell, she had enjoyed it well enough, but nothing beyond.

This, however, was unfettered joy.

Yet there was nothing silly about it. There were plenty of young ladies in Society that were giddy in the dance, whirling about and flirting shamelessly, taking too much to drink, and behaving without thought. This was far from such a tasteless display.

This surpassed any other joy Graham had seen before in his life, and he was suddenly envious of it. Envious of the joy. Envious of the lightness. Envious of the laughter.

Envious of every damned partner.

He exhaled very slowly, the admission sinking its way down his throat with the warmth and weight of brandy. *He* wanted to be the one making Edith smile, laugh, dance with such lack of inhibition. He wanted to be the reason she looked thus.

He wouldn't have a chance of that standing here against the bloody wall, however.

Idiot.

"I do believe the wall will stay there now. You may step away."

Graham looked at his aunt almost coldly. "I'll have you know I was just thinking the same thing."

"Were you?" Eloise made a soft, noncommittal sound as she watched the last movement of the dance at hand. "And did you also think it time to stop being so unnervingly observant of one person in particular? I nearly had the magistrate summoned for her protection."

"I have yet to find amusement in your statements," Graham grunted, downing the last of his drink.

"It's staring you in the face, Gray," she assured him. "Right before your nose."

He shook his head slowly. "Are you going to your rooms, Aunt?"

"Of course not, why would you say so?"

Now Graham looked at her in surprise. "You haven't been to a ball in years."

Eloise raised a brow, her lips quirking. "You haven't had one."

"Matthew did."

She waved her hand, scowling. "Matthew had too much fuss at his. This is much more sensible."

"Sensible?" He gestured to the pilasters, the plants, the sheer volume of candles. "Sensible?"

Eloise lifted a shoulder, smiling fully now. "Very sensible, Gray. As always." She leaned closer, her eyes narrowing. "Perhaps you ought to be a little less sensible. Just a thought."

"Thank you for that wisdom," Graham told her as the current dance finished. "If you'll excuse me, I'm going to do the most sensible thing I've done all evening."

He strode away, unsteady heart pummeling his ribs as he neared Edith, smiling and laughing with Amelia, who was a picture herself, smiling more than Graham had seen her in their entire acquaintance.

Was that Edith's influence? Or simply the dance?

"Lady Edith, Miss Perry," Graham intoned, wincing at the formal, almost stiff manner he had adopted.

Both ladies turned to him, smiles still in place. They curtseyed in time with each other, and he belatedly bowed in response.

"Lovely evening, Lord Radcliffe," Amelia told him with an earnestness that made him smile. "Truly, this is beyond anything."

"Well, it is not Almack's, Miss Perry, but I'm pleased that you are enjoying yourself."

Amelia made a face, giggling. "Almack's gets so very hot and crowded. This is far more to my taste." She glanced between Edith and Graham, and her smile deepened. "If you'll excuse me, I believe I have promised this dance to Mr. Demaris." She curtseyed quickly and left with almost silent steps.

He was rather fond of Amelia Perry and made a mental note to thank her later.

Edith stared at him with wide eyes, a slight smile on her lips that distracted him from concise thought.

She bit down on her lip softly, and Graham felt his left knee give a little.

"Dance with me?" he asked with the bluntness of an eleven-year-old schoolboy.

Her smile deepened, sending his right knee quivering. "I would love to."

The musicians began to play again, and the bright, almost brisk melody made Graham frown, shaking him out of his haze. "This… wasn't exactly what I was hoping for."

Edith covered her mouth on a laugh, her barely exposed shoulders shaking. "Nor I."

Still, he had to smile, the corners of his mouth steadily spreading the more he stared at Edith. "This is unnecessarily complicated…"

Her hand dropped, her full lips straining to avoid laughter as she tried for somberness. "We'll just have to muddle through."

"Well, I do have *some* practice…" He held his hand out to her, his breath pausing in his lungs.

The moment her hand laid in his, heat surged into his center, and the desire to dance rose with an intensity he had never felt before. Jaunty country dance or not, dancing with Edith would never be anything less than a delight.

They took their places and began the first movement, matching each other's patterns perfectly. Edith moved forward to go around Graham, smiling almost shyly up at him as she did so.

"You're smiling," he murmured, his eyes tracing her as she circled him.

"Aye, I am," she quipped with a faint brush of her shoulder against his as she moved back to her place.

He tilted his head at her while the man to his left circled his partner. "Why?"

Edith giggled to herself. "Should I not?"

"I'm not accustomed to anyone smiling like that in my presence."

The admission caught him by surprise, and he gnawed the inside of his lip to keep himself from wishing it back.

Edith's brows quirked just before they moved towards each other, hands extended. "I dinna mean to upset what ye are used to, my lord," she purred as her fingers hooked into his.

"It's not upsetting," he managed as they turned in a circle, life itself at the tips of his fingers.

"But," she continued without a break, "I think ye mus' grow accustomed to smiles in your presence."

Graham swallowed as they parted, backing into his place. "Must I, Lady Edith?"

She nodded as the woman to her right circled around her partner. "Aye. From me, at least." Color began to tinge her cheeks a lovely shade of pink. "And it's just Edith. Ye've gone wi'out the title before, and I'd prefer if ye did again."

It was all Graham could do to keep his forward motion to the pattern of the dance rather than going directly to Edith herself. His eyes, however, would go nowhere else. "Then smile as you please, Edith. I look forward to the prospect."

Chapter Sixteen

Once in a very great while, speaking one's mind can have quite convenient advantages.

-The Spinster Chronicles, 30 August 1816

"Amelia, are you ready?" Edith asked as she adjusted her lace fichu in the looking glass.

There was no response.

Peering around the doorway into the sitting room, she saw Amelia standing at the window, somehow looking fragile in her white and blue sprigged muslin. Her face was hidden from view, but one hand raised to brush against her cheek.

Edith sighed sadly and moved into the room. "Amelia?"

It said a great deal about their friendship that Amelia turned to face Edith without hesitation, another tear slowly coursing down the same cheek.

"Oh, lass," Edith murmured, going to her friend and taking her in her arms. "What is it?"

"I can't go down there today," Amelia whispered in a choked voice. "I can't..."

Edith rubbed her back. "What happened?"

Amelia shuddered in her arms. "Adaline Chesney criticized me for only dancing with married men and Hensh. She told me I was wasting my opportunities, and if I had any understanding with a gentleman, I should forget it if he were not present."

Edith ground her teeth together, irritation rising. "Did she?"

"I don't want to forget Edmund," Amelia hiccupped in a whimper. "I don't know why I haven't heard from him, but I want to believe the best! I must. I can't let him go, Edith, and I just…" Her words dissolved in a mass of tears, her face suddenly burying against Edith's shoulder.

"Oh, Amelia…" Edith sighed, holding her closer. "I didna mean for this retreat into the country to be painful for ye. Would ye like to return to London?"

Amelia shook her head. "No." She sniffled and pulled back, eyes red and watering. "No, we need to stay. This is good for you." She dabbed at her cheeks with her sleeve and sighed. "But I cannot face the ladies this afternoon. I'm likely to burst into tears. Will you make my excuses?"

Edith rubbed her arms once more. "Of course, lass. Take your rest. I'll come to fetch ye before supper."

Nodding, Amelia managed a weak smile and moved to sit in one of the chairs near the fire. "And if you could find a way to trip Adaline somehow, I would not complain."

The image made Edith chuckle and nod. "I'll do my best, lass." With a wave, she left their sitting room, her smile and amusement disappearing the moment the door was closed.

How dare Miss Chesney say such things to Amelia! How dare she suggest Amelia go against any understanding she might have had for the sake of convenience and availability! There was no excuse for such behavior. Edith was very much afraid that Miss Chesney was aware of Amelia's attachment and was using it to cause pain.

Moments like these were when Edith wished she were far less proper and less well-behaved.

"That's a terrible expression before tea," Miranda stated without hesitation as she exited her rooms and joined Edith in the corridor.

"The feelings beneath it are far worse," Edith assured her.

"Do tell, my dear." Quickly, Edith related the basics of the situation, and Miranda's face hardened at hearing it. "I see," Miranda said simply once the telling was done. "Well, I am not entirely sure how I feel about Adaline Chesney having any sense of Amelia's *tendre* over Andrews, but this is…"

"Andrews?" Edith interrupted in shock, her pace faltering. "Edmund is Mr. Andrews?"

Miranda had the maddening ability to look completely unruffled by Edith's outburst. "Of course. Did you not know? Those two have been circling each other for ages."

The image of the tall, dark, almost aloof man appeared in Edith's mind, and she could not, for the life of her, see what Miranda was describing. But she had no reason to doubt the statement, especially since Miranda Sterling always seemed to know the truth of any given situation at any given time.

One could always trust what Miranda was saying.

"Amelia and Mr. Andrews," Edith mused aloud as the pair of them continued down to tea. "What a thought!"

"They will have beautiful children," Miranda said on a pleased sigh. "Provided Andrews reappears in the world."

Edith smiled ever so slightly. "I suppose I must hate him less for abandoning Amelia, now that I know who he is."

Miranda smiled back, nodding. "Indeed. One could never hate Andrews."

They neared the drawing room, and Miranda took Edith's arm, pulling her to a stop just outside of it.

She gave Edith a very thorough look. "The same need not be said for Adaline Chesney."

"It's no' me she's injured," Edith reminded her.

The older woman's expression did not change. "The girl is a spiteful cat who would trod on a child if it would improve her station. She will try to injure you, as you are beautiful, amiable, and marriageable. You do not have to take it with good graces."

Edith's brows rose in surprise as a smile crossed her lips. "Are you telling me to behave badly, Miranda?"

"I am telling you to stand for yourself, my love," Miranda corrected, now moving them both forward into the room. "The good Lord knows you deserve to."

Edith swallowed and patted her friend's hand as they moved to the others, the tea service just arriving.

"The gentlemen are to take tea with the ladies, are they?" Miranda chirped with some delight, though the note of surprise was evident. She smiled at the gentlemen seated around tables or standing nearby. "How marvelously forward-thinking of us."

"They will be playing at cards, Mrs. Sterling," Catherine Tillman said in the clipped tone Edith had grown accustomed to. "We are not so far removed from Society as to forget our places."

Miranda gave the young woman a surprised look as she sat gracefully on the divan beside Janet Sterling. "My place is at tea? How peculiar."

Edith barely avoided snorting a laugh as she took a seat beside Grace, glancing over at Tony, Francis, and Henshaw, who all looked heavenward in a silent plea for deliverance.

"Miranda's on her mettle," Grace murmured as she took a cup of tea from Felicity Bradford. "How marvelous!"

Edith could only nod her agreement.

Catherine Tillman, however, was not amused.

"The lady's place is separate from that of the gentleman," Catherine insisted. "It is widely accepted, and Society does expect it."

"I have learned not to pay too much attention to Society's expectations," Miranda told her, and, by extension, the rest of them. "If I did, I would have to consider myself a failure for not having given my husband a child. And I can assure you, Miss Tillman, that I am not a failure."

There was no way for Catherine to refute that statement, not if she wished to maintain her reputation and position.

Edith took a cup of tea herself from Miss Bradford and sipped slowly, the desire to laugh rising steadily.

Miss Bradford looked at Edith with a sympathetic look. "It must be such a relief for you to be away from London, Lady Edith. I can only imagine what painful memories must exist there for you."

Edith jerked slightly, barely avoiding upending her tea. There was no knowing for certain what pain she was speaking about. She swallowed her tea and chanced a glance at Lord Radcliffe, who had heard, and his eyes were steady on her.

"Oh, yes," her sister chimed in beside her. "How you must miss your husband, Lady Edith."

Edith breathed a faint sigh of relief and was certain she was not the only one in the room to do so. "I suppose I must," she replied, smiling with all politeness. "It is a very peculiar trial. But I think Sir Archibald would wish me to move on with my life in the best way possible."

Sympathetic nods were all around, and Grace and Georgie hid snickers behind their fans.

"You poor thing," Adaline Chesney simpered. "But I heard that you have quite got on with your life, and in a most intriguing way."

Edith looked at her in surprise, not caring at all for the tone in her voice. Out of the corner of her eye, she noticed Lord Radcliffe stiffen slightly.

"Hush, Adaline," Felicity hissed in a rather surprisingly dark tone. "Idle gossip is not suitable."

"It is not idle," Adaline sneered. "Ask anyone."

"What have ye heard?" Edith managed to ask, trying to look only merely interested though her toes were suddenly ice. "I hope it is at least entertaining. Imagine being accused of tedious rumors and no' exciting ones."

The women laughed easily, and again, Lord Radcliffe relaxed a bit, though his tension was still evident. Clearly, he was minding the conversation carefully when he ought to have been focused on his cards with Mr. Wyndham.

Adaline gave Edith a smug smile, her eyes glinting. "We all have heard that you have taken on a Scottish lover in your time of distress. That he is a rather large and imposing fellow, and quite barbaric. Tell me, truly, does he wear the kilt in your bedchamber?"

Diana Bradford gasped. "You have said too much, Adaline," she chided.

"You heard that, too?" Felicity asked, looking over at her.

She nodded. "I did not think it appropriate to repeat!" she said with a pointed look at Adaline, who ignored her.

Lord Radcliffe rose, drawing Edith's gaze. His expression was rather murderous, and he began to come to the gathered ladies.

Thinking quickly, Edith only smiled at Adaline. "My, my, a Scottish lover? That is a bit predictable, is it no'? One of my own countrymen for a taste of home, was that it? Does the rumor say if he had money? I canna countenance taking a lover simply because one has need of primal comfort when there are no other advantages to the situation."

Grace coughed a surprised laugh into her tea, and Felicity Bradford looked at her with wide eyes.

"You... you are saying the rumor is false?" Adaline asked, looking disgruntled.

Lord Radcliffe had stopped and was now only perhaps three feet behind the group, though no one marked him.

Edith flicked her eyes up to his and saw that he was watching her with interest. Perhaps he had also heard the rumors. She smiled at him, then at the rest. "I'm only saying that I shouldna be so crass as to parade any illicit relationship for comment."

Cheeks flaming with outrage, Edith now directed her attention entirely upon Adaline. "And while I have no notion why Society finds my personal relationships so verra intriguing..." A few ladies flushed and averted their gazes while Edith continued. "...I can honestly say, no' tha' it matters on the whole, that I havnae taken a lover of any sort, nor should I, unless I was fortunate enough to marry again, and then it should only be with him. Does tha' make me so very prudish to you, Miss Chesney?"

She looked positively appalled, her small mouth working soundlessly. Grace and Georgie grinned, Janet hid a smile behind her cup, and Miranda silently applauded.

Diana Bradford sat back and murmured, "Well, well, a true lady after all. I am delighted to hear it."

Edith seethed silently, barely maintaining her tight smile, and rose to her feet. "If you will excuse me, I mus' see if any other imaginary Scottish lovers are waiting for me in my bedchamber. They do so hate to be kept waiting."

Grace snorted and pulled out a handkerchief in an attempt to feign blowing her nose, while Adaline merely looked ill and scowled.

Edith curtseyed to the group and moved to leave but stopped only three steps from her seat. Exhaling, she looked over her shoulder and said, "And the thing about kilts, Miss Chesney, is that it makes all sorts of things verra convenient. And vastly more entertaining."

Her friends seemed to crumple against each other in mirth, while the Bradford sisters gleefully grinned. Catherine and Adaline, however, were both quite red in the face.

Lifting her chin, Edith continued to move away, glancing up as she passed Lord Radcliffe. He met her gaze with a great deal of pride and a hint of a smile.

"Brilliantly executed, my lady," he murmured.

She inclined her head. "Thank you, my lord. I think I should visit my special friend now, do you agree?"

He did smile now and nodded. "Absolutely. She is waiting for you."

"Thank you, my lord." Edith smiled with genuine warmth, then left the room without a backwards glance.

She made her way back through the corridors and up the stairs, the pathway clearer now than the day before, and soon she was at the nursery, knocking on the slightly ajar door.

"Come in!" chimed a sweet voice.

Edith pushed the door open further and smiled at Molly, seated as she was on the floor with her dolls. "Is there room for one more?"

"Edith!" Molly darted over and hugged her tightly around the waist. "Do you want to play with my dolls? I have enough for us both."

"I would love to," Edith told her, situating herself on the floor.

The two of them soon lost themselves to their imaginations, playing all sorts of things with their dolls, including story time, school lessons, and dance instruction. Edith told a few stories she could remember from her childhood, letting her brogue ring out proudly, as befitted the tales. Molly was a strict dancing instructor but said Edith showed great promise.

What a relief.

Molly's nanny appeared then, a tall woman with a kind face and soft voice, and she offered to procure some crumpets from the kitchen if the ladies would like a tea party.

The places were quickly set, and Edith was named Princess Zara to Molly's Queen of Spain, with many dolls as their additional companions. Warm water with lemon served as tea, and the conversation among the table was highly amusing from all assembled.

They had been at it for quite a while, and were giggling madly, when suddenly Molly looked past Edith at the door and frowned.

Edith turned to look and found Lord Radcliffe leaning rather casually against the open door, watching them with a bemused expression. Granted, they were sitting on the floor, and it was not the most elegant of situations, but surely, he had seen worse.

Not from Edith, but all was decent and proper, even so.

She lifted her chin proudly. "My lord."

His mouth quirked as he took in the sight before him. He winked at his niece, who went back to speaking with her dolls. Then, he looked down at Edith with a raised brow.

"You've been up here quite a long time, Edith. Shouldn't you be down with the others?"

She shook her head at once. "I would much rather be up here having tea with her majesty, the Queen of Spain," she said, gesturing grandly to Molly, who dramatically bowed at least three times, "than anything else at the moment. The crumpets are delicious, and the conversation is far better than downstairs."

"Hear, hear," Molly cried, only half listening, but smiling at Edith anyway.

Lord Radcliffe grinned at Edith, a full, true, glorious grin. Her heart raced at the sight of it.

"You can't hide up here forever," he murmured.

Edith shrugged nonchalantly, or at least attempted it with her heart and breath being what it was. "Who is looking for me? Besides you, I mean. Despite all your best efforts, my lord, I am exactly the inconsequential lass I was in London, with far less worry, and with one new friend who means more than anyone else I have met since being here."

She smiled at Molly, who popped another bite of crumpet into her mouth and grinned with her cheeks full.

"At any rate," she continued, tracing patterns on the lace tablecloth before her, "I canna bear to hear more of the rumors about me. I've heard quite enough, and the only one who knew about my brother being in my home was… you know who. If everyone believes what he said about him, they will believe anything else he says, so my chances of finding a protector have likely run their course. I might as well enjoy myself while I can. Besides, no one suits so well as…" She trailed off as she realized that the name she had thought of belonged to the man before her.

Crivvens…

Clearing her suddenly clogged throat, she said, "Spending time with Molly is far more important than that."

He did not respond, did not so much as move.

Edith glanced over at him and found his smile had faded; his eyes so arresting she could not find a single word in her vocabulary.

His throat worked, and he looked at Molly. "Sweetheart, I need to take Edith away now. She will come and see you tomorrow, all right?"

The little girl pouted but nodded. Lord Radcliffe came to help Edith to her feet, and Edith leaned down to Molly to give her a hug and a kiss on the head.

"Until tomorrow, lassie," Edith murmured with a wink.

Molly attempted to wink back. "Good night, Edith."

Smiling, Edith turned and allowed Lord Radcliffe to escort her out into the corridor. He turned to shut the door, facing it for a long moment, his back to her.

"He was your brother?" he murmured softly.

Edith stared at his back, the strength in its breadth powerfully evident, making her flush from head to toe. "Who? Oh, Lachlan? Aye, my idiot brother who frightened the weasel one day, and apparently, now the whole world thinks he's my lover."

He released a low sigh, then turned, his eyes dark, saying nothing further.

Edith began to shift uncomfortably under his gaze. "Are ye troubled that I spend my time with Molly?" she asked in a timid voice. "I'll no' do so publicly; her reputation will be untarnished."

He slowly shook his head, then pushed away from the wall and strode towards her. One hand went to the side of her face as he pressed his lips to hers. It was gentle, so soft, and yet perhaps the most intense kiss Edith could have imagined. It called to the depths of her soul, sent ripples down her spine, and she trembled at their connection. He set his hand at her waist, holding her firmly rooted, his fingers sliding against the suddenly shockingly thin fabric of her gown.

The kiss was over quickly, and Edith found herself gasping softly as he broke off. His mouth hovered a hairsbreadth above hers, waiting for her response, his unsteady breath tingling against her tender lips.

Edith could barely think, barely breathe, but in that moment, she felt as though she had been waiting for him to kiss her for an age. And she was not done yet.

She slid her hands along his jaw and into his thick, dark hair, forcing his lips back to hers. This time they were not as gentle, and her back was pressed against the wall rather abruptly, his hold on her increasing. She arched into him, his lips sending a spell through her that left her dizzy and elated, yearning for more of this flurry, more of this tide. It was heaven, and she prayed it would never end.

There was so much in his kiss, beyond any words she knew. This was heat and longing and truth, purity and passion and poetry. Her heart seemed to burst into flames within her, and all she wanted in the world was him. Was this. Was them.

He broke the kiss again, though she would happily have continued, and his erratic panting echoed her own. His hand moved from her face to wrap around her fevered frame, cradling her in his embrace.

Edith rested her forehead on his chin, her hands sliding from his hair down to his shoulders, gripping him for balance as they breathed in the silence together.

"I have wanted to do that for so long," he finally said, his voice unsteady.

She chuckled in a low tone. "Really? You didna say anything about it."

He snorted softly, and his hold tightened. "In case you haven't noticed, I am not the most sociable person."

Edith pulled back a little and smiled at him. "No, I suppose not. How long?"

He returned her smile, his eyes warm. "Since that blasted waltz. It was infuriatingly short for what I suddenly wanted, and I was so used to not feeling anything for a woman that it took me by surprise."

She moved her hands back to his neck and gave him a look. "You did a fair job of hiding it."

His smile turned quizzical. "Have you never wondered why I was always around when you were in need? I don't have perfect timing; I was quite simply unable to stay away."

Her ignited heart began to dance at his words, and she had to fight to swallow. "And now?"

His eyes somehow grew darker and elicited a shiver that brought her closer to him still. "And now, I refuse to stay away. I don't care what you or anyone else says, I will defy all expectations and societal dictates. I will dance only with you, call you Edith in public, and probably stare at you for an inappropriately long time, as nothing else is worth looking at when you're there. And I will kiss you again and again, as often as I can." As if he needed to emphasize the point, he did so again, and it was gentle, long, lingering, and tempting beyond reason.

Incineration would be her constant state for the foreseeable future.

When she was able, she swallowed again and pretended to be unaffected. "And what am I to do?"

He sighed and touched his forehead to hers. "Let me? Encourage me if you like. Tease me, so I don't lose myself. And call me Graham. All the time."

"Your Christian name?" she asked, eyes wide.

He nodded against her, brushing his nose against hers. "Try it."

Face somehow flushing further still, toes curling, her fingers began to toy with the hair at the nape of his neck. "Graham," she repeated softly.

He groaned a deep sigh and kissed her. "Nothing should sound that good," he whispered.

There was nothing to do but tremble at such a statement, and Graham held her closer, his lips grazing and dusting where they would.

Eventually, they made their way back down to the others, though Edith was unable to focus on anything except his proximity to her. With every clash of their eyes, her stomach curled most disconcertingly, her lips tingled with exhilarated memory, and her body shook, remembering the warmth of him, the hardness of his chest, and the strength of his arms.

As if he knew, Graham smiled a slow, heated, devilishly attractive smile at her each and every time.

Chapter Seventeen

———— ⟞⟐⟐⟐⟞ ————

There is something to be said for comfort. There is some debate as to what it is that should be said specifically, but surely something should be said.

-The Spinster Chronicles, 27 June 1815

Graham was whistling as he ambled through the family wing of Merrifield. Whistling. He didn't think he knew any song well enough to whistle it, but here he was. Whistling.

Edith had done this to him. There was no other possible excuse.

He smiled to himself as he thought of her, images running through his mind from the evening before. They had been partnered for cards and had spent the entire evening giving each other meaningful looks while touching their feet together beneath the table. And the night before, they had been incapable of staring at anyone else during the musicale.

Of course, that had been the evening after they'd kissed.

His chest tightened to a mixture of pleasure and longing at the memory, and his pace quickened. The morning was almost completely without structure today, one of the first in the entire house party, and he knew exactly how he wanted to spend it. And with whom.

"Going somewhere, Gray?"

He barely paused as he glanced over his shoulder at Eloise. "Yes. The library."

Eloise frowned as she came out of her rooms, folding her arms over her shawl. "The library? Gray, you have guests. You should be spending your time with them, not on your own, alone with the books."

Graham grinned, raising a brow. "Who said anything about being alone?"

His aunt's mouth dropped open, and Graham chuckled as he rounded a corner to head down the stairs.

She would be running all sorts of scenarios through her mind on that statement, and he would certainly be paying for it later this evening.

It had taken him a good deal of time to determine where Edith would be on a morning such as this. She was not one to spend the morning lying about her rooms and requesting her meals on trays, but he wasn't sure what, exactly, she would be doing. Molly had been the one to give him the idea during their breakfast together.

"Well, that's easy, Gray," she'd said around a bite of toast with jam. "Edith loves stories. I told her all about the library yesterday, and she said she was going to go." She'd shrugged and gone back to the meal as though that were the end of the matter.

For Graham, it had been just the beginning.

The library was soon before him, and he grinned in anticipation. How had a matter of hours apart from her felt like days?

Finding the door to the room open, Graham slipped in, eyes scanning around with an eagerness and curiosity he hadn't felt in so long he'd forgotten the sensation. The library didn't have many places to hide, yet there was no sight of her initially. A movement near the tall window drew his attention, and he turned silently towards it.

Edith stood against the curtains there, blending in with the fabric almost to the shade with her simple cream gown, leaning towards the window for as much light as possible. In her hands was a book, and if her expression was anything to go by, she was completely, totally engrossed in its pages. Graham watched for a moment as page after page turned, as Edith's breathing increased in pace, and he would swear her eyes got wider.

For only seeing part of her face with her present position being what it was, he could read her perfectly. There was nothing here, nothing around her, but the words on those pages, and the story they told.

Which meant she had no idea he was here.

Slowly, carefully, he moved towards her, his shoes making no sound as he did so. When he was immediately behind her, barely breathing, Graham reached out and placed both hands on her upper arms.

Edith shrieked a deafening sound, the book flying out of her left hand, her right gripping the curtains for her very life.

Graham couldn't help but laugh, and he gently pulled Edith to him until her back was to his chest, then wrapped his arms around her.

"I'm sorry, Edith," he managed, still laughing softly. "I couldn't help myself."

"Saints and aunties keep us," Edith whispered in a shaky, unsteady breath, releasing the curtain and placing her hand on his arms. "Graham."

A jolt of pleasure shot into his chest, and he kissed her hair. "Did you have many aunties to protect you?" he asked against the soft, sable tresses tickling his lips.

She exhaled slowly and hugged his arms to her. "I have an extended family tha' would fill Merrifield wi'out even inviting the lot." She leaned into him, sighing. "I havnae spoken to any of them in an age."

There was a sad note in her voice that made him ache, and he leaned forward to press his lips to her cheek. "If it makes you feel any better, my family is small. Only Eloise is left, and there were no others that took any interest. But I always had Matthew."

Edith hummed in his arms, then turned to give him a warm but mischievous look. "Did you have a reason for scaring the devil from me, or were you simply feeling impertinent?"

"A bit of both," he replied. Smiling, he touched his brow to hers. "Would you ride across the estate with me?"

"I havnae been on a horse in years." She kissed Graham gently on the lips, smiling. "But if ye've the mounts to spare, I would love to go."

Graham kissed her in return, much less gently, a low groan rising

184

within him.

"Perfect," he murmured. "Come on." He slid his hand into hers and entwined their fingers before heading for the door.

"I dinna have a riding habit, Graham," she pointed out, sounding hesitant even if her steps were not.

Laughing, he glanced at her. "I won't tell if you don't."

As he'd hoped, Edith laughed in return and squeezed his hand. "Then I willna say a word."

They hurried out to the stables, and horses were quickly prepared for them.

As it happened, Edith was more than accomplished as a rider, and the exhilaration on her face from almost the moment they began was worth more than the entire house party. They galloped almost recklessly at first, raced for a bit, then let the horses walk while they engaged in free and relaxed conversation with each other. It was so easy to talk with Edith and even easier to listen to her. The sound of her voice was soothing, but it was more than that.

It was so much more.

She spoke of her home in Scotland, her older brother and younger sister, and the sort of life they'd had as children of an earl without much to recommend him. He spoke of his brother, of their rambunctious youth, and of the sort of marriage Matthew had found. She told him about her grandmother, by all accounts the only member of her family to always treat her well. He told her of the life he had imagined for himself before he'd inherited.

"But I suppose there is no use in remembering that life," he admitted, nudging his horse closer to her. "I have the title, I have Merrifield, and I have Molly. Responsibilities all, though Molly is easily the best and brightest of them."

Edith beamed at him, her dark hair having tumbled from its style on the ride and now hanging in waves around her shoulders and down her back. "I can easily see that. She is the loveliest lass. I'm quite fond of her, Graham."

He smiled softly. "And she is of you. She asks me every morning when you are coming."

"You see her every morning even with the house party?" she asked with a smile.

He nodded. "We have breakfast together. I cannot attend her all the time, and she knows this, but I was in London so long, I want to make up for it." His smile turned sheepish, and he shrugged. "And she seems to enjoy eating with me."

"Yes, I can imagine she would." Edith considered him with a tilt of her head, her lips curving into a fond smile. "You are a fine father figure, hero."

He snorted and gave her a look. "Passable, at best. And don't call me that, Lady Edith Leveson."

"Don't call me a Leveson," she retorted, shuddering a bit. " 'Tis the only thing I share with the weasel, and I detest it now."

Now that was something he could understand.

He shook his head, staring at this miraculous, impetuous woman he had come to know, wondering how in the world she had come to this.

"How did the weasel obtain such power over you?"

Edith looked at him with wide eyes as she rode, clearly stunned. "You don't know? I'd have thought the others would have said something afore this."

"I know a little," he admitted, patting the horse's neck as the animal nickered beneath him. "I know he is the cousin of your late husband, and I know what he wants of you, but beyond that…"

Edith looked away, staring off at the grove of trees in the distance.

Graham winced and reached out to take her hand. "Forgive me. I didn't mean to sadden you. It must be very hard at times, and if you still miss your husband…"

"On the contrary," Edith informed him with a smirk, returning her attention to him, "I have not missed my husband from the moment he was taken from me. Does that shock you?"

He shook his head. "Not as much as it should. I had heard, of course, of Sir Archibald and his ways, but I wasn't at all sure what…" His cheeks flamed in sudden embarrassment. "That is… if your relationship was…"

Edith took pity on him and exhaled shortly. "I was bartered to Sir Archibald, and I do not say that lightly. He received a titled bride in exchange for a moderate fortune, less than he'd have liked, that was very shortly spent upon nothing of particular value." She managed a weak smile, though Graham could see real pain behind the façade. "The rumor goes that I was married for about five minutes, but in truth, it was really about the space of an hour. Perhaps two, at most."

Graham pulled his horse to a stop, barely able to blink at what she had said. "You're joking."

She shook her head, her smile fading as she stopped as well. "Not at all. We were married long enough for him to do his marital duty, no breakfast or luncheon after the vows, and then he died in a horse-riding accident directly after he left our marriage bed."

He hissed a wince. "That's terrible."

"Oh, no, it was quite a relief," she assured him without much emotion. "It was the most horrifying, painful, terrifying hour of my entire life, and then, suddenly, I was freed from it all. His will had not been amended to include provisions for me, which my father should have overseen, but…"

"I meant the manner of his death," Graham interrupted with a short laugh, "and that he died so quickly following the wedding."

Edith flushed and laughed, tucking a dark curl behind her ear. "Oh. Oh, that." Her brow furrowed briefly with thought, then cleared. "Yes, I suppose it was. It probably didn't help that he was so drunk he couldn't remember my name."

"He was *what?*"

"Drunk," she said again, her eyes somewhere on his horse's mane. "Completely and fully soused. Could barely make his vows intelligible. He drank his way back to his house after the wedding, drank his way through his duty, and called me four different names throughout, none of which were mine. Then he called me a fifth name as he stumbled out of the bedchamber, yet another bottle in hand."

Graham couldn't believe what he was hearing. Was disgusted by what he was hearing. Would have probably killed Sir Archibald himself, if the blackguard were alive today.

But he never would have met Edith if he were alive today.

There was no telling where she would be or what her life would look like. Graham's life would have proceeded along as it had done with all the same tragedies, responsibilities, and tasks. Everything would have been the same up until one night at the Martins' ball during a particular waltz.

He wouldn't have danced it.

He wouldn't be out riding with her now.

Wouldn't have…

"I didna even like Archie," Edith murmured aloud, seeming somehow unaware she was doing so. "I loathed him and feared him, and I didna understand why Da would drag me down the aisle to wed him. Why Ma didn't come. Why Lachlan had done this. But the thing that fully cracked my heart in two was that my husband couldna remember my name on the day he made his vows."

Graham would have sworn his own heart cracked, hearing her admission. How could any man alive, having simply seen Edith, treat her that way? How could a man having *met* Edith not remember her name?

What sort of hell would Sir Archibald Leveson be damned to endure for eternity? Surely, there was no pit of fire and brimstone deep enough or hot enough to adequately house such a man. That such a creature still left such a wound upon the heart of this woman.

Graham could scarcely breathe.

"Edith…" he eventually managed.

She raised her emerald eyes to him, uncertainty and vulnerability written in them.

"I could be *five* sheets to the wind, absolutely insensible with drink, and I can assure you, I would never forget your name."

Her eyes widened, and she swallowed before wetting her lips. "Even if we had only been wed for five minutes?"

Graham reached out and brushed his fingers along the curve of her cheek, shaking his head in disbelief. "Even if you had been my wife for all of five seconds, I could never have forgotten your name. I would be acutely, exquisitely, painfully aware of it."

He heard her breath catch and leaned in, kissing her full lips slowly, savoring the taste and feel of them. She cupped his jaw and molded her mouth more perfectly to his, wringing out any sense he possessed with an ardency that undid him.

One of their horses nickered again, and they were forced to part to steady them.

Graham glanced at Edith and found her watching him, rosy-cheeked and smiling, almost on the verge of laughter.

"What?" he demanded, near to laughing himself.

"Have you ever been five sheets to the wind, Graham?" she asked, her smile widening with the glory of a thousand suns.

He sniffed with mock effrontery and nudged the sides of his horse, sending him into a trot. "I'm not going to dignify that accusation with an answer," he called back to her.

The pounding of horse's hooves brought his head around. Edith thundered up, her smile now challenging, but no less attractive. "If I beat ye back to Merrifield, ye're honor bound to answer the question, my lord!"

"You know better than to call me that, Edith," he scolded, pushing his horse further to catch her.

"If ye beat me, *my lord*," she said with stronger emphasis, "then, and only then, can ye make demands. *Twig?*" She quirked her brows and urged her horse on, the animal gracefully and skillfully obeying as though they had ridden together for years.

Graham threw his head back and laughed, then did his utmost to match her, the thrill of her challenge coursing through his veins. Win or lose, this was one competitor he was well motivated to take on, though he was not entirely certain if he wished to win or wished to lose.

Both could have rather pleasant advantages.

Edith, however, proved victorious, leaving Graham with no alternative but to relate to her the one and only time he had gotten intoxicated beyond reason. She had assured him, after her laughter had subsided, that his story would pass for an average evening for a Highlander.

Whether that was designed to make him feel better or worse, he could not say.

Once they returned to Merrifield, they were forced to part, he to change and resume his hosting duties, and she to being one of his guests. When the party left to go for a shoot, most of the ladies with the gentlemen, Edith was not among them.

This time, Graham had no difficulty finding her.

He went up to the nursery, where Edith and Molly were lounging together on a chaise while Edith read fairytales. Molly had snuggled up against her and fallen asleep, completely at ease.

"And the princess wondered..." Edith read, softening her voice before stopping, glancing down at the sleeping girl with a tender smile.

Molly's breathing shifted with the silence, and she stirred.

"The princess wondered," Edith continued, "how to do as the fairy had said."

Graham entered the nursery, his eyes sliding from Molly to Edith and back again as he moved to stand in front of their chaise.

Edith continued to read, leaning her head against Molly's, and looked up at Graham, smiling.

He swallowed with some difficulty, moved beyond description to see her like this with his ward, and the warmth in Edith's eyes brought on a fire within him.

Edith must have felt it too, for she dropped her eyes back to the page, her cheeks coloring.

Slowly, Graham stepped closer, then began to move around the chaise, his fingers trailing along the arm of it and barely brushing against Edith's arm as he came to her side.

She lifted her head from Molly's but did not look at him, continuing to read, though her voice was not quite as steady.

Helpless to resist, Graham bent to cup Edith's chin, turning her face to his. She kept her eyes lowered for a moment, then dragged them up to his, the rich darkness in the green depths robbing him of breath. There was so much tenderness in her look, so much emotion, so much that he felt unable and unworthy to express.

Edith's lips quirked in a bare smile, and he bent to kiss her. She kissed him slowly, maddening in the softness and stirring in the certainty.

He let his fingers stroke the underside of her jaw absently, the texture of her skin almost addicting to the touch. She sighed against him as he did so, encouraging him to repeat the motion with more pointed attention.

It was not a long or particularly passionate kiss, but there was something deep and intimate to it. Something that terrified Graham, yet cried within him as perfection.

A terrifying, beautiful perfection.

When he broke the kiss, he cupped Edith's cheek, and he smiled at her softly.

She gave him a dreamy smile in return, and he knew for certain that he would do a great many impossible things to receive that smile again.

Chapter Eighteen

———⟨∞ ∞⟩———

Confessions may give the heart wings and free the soul.

-*The Spinster Chronicles, 6 July 1818*

"Of all days for it to rain, it had to be a day when I wished to walk. It is always the way."

Edith glanced up from her drawing to smile at Eloise, sitting as she was in the parlor and looking forlornly out of the window. "We walked yesterday, Eloise."

That earned her a scowl. "Yes, and it was so lovely, I wished to do it again. That is all."

"I can walk with you, Aunt Ellie!" Molly exclaimed, beaming up from her own attempt at a sketch, having seen Edith drawing a time or two over the last few days. "We can walk inside and pretend it's outside!"

Eloise smiled at the girl. "A perfectly capital idea, sweetheart. When you have finished your picture, we may do so. How is it coming?"

Molly frowned down at it. "It doesn't look like anything. I'll never be able to draw like Edith."

"It takes many years of practice, *nighean milis*," Edith assured her. "With patience, if ye work at it, ye'll be far, far better than me."

Molly looked at Edith's drawing, her eyes wide, then looked back up at her. "Really?"

Edith leaned forward and playfully touched her forehead to

Molly's. "Aye. Really."

That made Molly snicker, which made Edith giggle, and even Eloise, watching on, laughed at the pair of them.

A gong sounded from somewhere in the house, and Edith sighed at hearing it, glancing at Eloise.

"Already?"

The older woman wrinkled her nose up with a reluctant but understanding smile. "We are all formality tonight. Gray has been overseeing details all day, which is likely why you haven't seen him."

Edith blushed and shifted her eyes to the window, heart leaping to her throat. How could Eloise know that they had been seeing each other during this house party? That Edith had been wondering why Graham had not sought her out, or sent her a note, or any of the other sweet and surprising signs of affection he had made use of over the last several days? She hadn't felt hurt, only curious. After all, tonight was a ball, and she was assured of at least one dance with him.

But more than anything, she anticipated the look on his face when he saw the gown she would wear tonight. Janet had brought it to her yesterday, and it fit Edith to perfection.

She'd already discussed ideas for her hair with the maid Eloise had set her with, and, apart from generally disliking grand affairs like balls, she found herself eager for the night's activities.

But not yet.

"You have to go now?" Molly whined, somehow pouting without actually doing so.

Eloise rose, her complexion pale, but her smile warm. "Come along, pet. We'll take that fine walk of ours, and tomorrow, Edith will come and tell you all about the ball, eh?"

Molly nodded and curtseyed to Edith. "Good night, *mo charaid*," she said softly, fumbling over the pronunciation of the word Edith had taught her only yesterday.

Tears sprung to Edith's eyes, and she gave Molly a quick hug before hurrying out of the parlor.

If nothing else good came from this stay at Merrifield, the friendship she had found in that precocious girl would be worth it all.

"Edith, there you are!"

Whirling in surprise, Edith's jaw dropped at the owner of the voice. "Charlotte? When did you get here?"

Charlotte beamed and hurried to her, kissing both cheeks and taking her hand. "Just arrived. I may have missed the rest of the party, but why should I miss a ball at Merrifield?"

"But in the middle of the Season?" Edith demanded, smiling in return as Georgie, Grace, Izzy, and Amelia soon joined them. "How could you get away from your admirers?"

"Oh, they bore me, simply bore me!" Charlotte waved a hand and scoffed, then took Edith's hands in her own. "Besides, when I had the letters from the girls regarding your remarkable absence from certain moments of this party, and a certain increase in warmth from the host, I had no course but to come here and root the secrets out of you."

Edith's eyes widened, and she swallowed hard. "The what?"

"Letters," Georgie repeated, smiling with a quirk of her brows, "that we wrote."

"Kindly," Izzy added for emphasis.

"Because you've disappeared more often than you've appeared," Grace insisted brightly. "We can almost never find you."

Had she really been so absent? She'd not known anyone was looking for her at any given time, apart from Graham, and had presumed she hadn't been particularly missed.

They'd noticed she was gone?

Did they suspect…?

Edith swallowed again and looked at Amelia with wide eyes. "Oh, Amelia… I am so sorry; I have completely abandoned you, haven't I? This was meant to be an escape for us both, and I've only been thinking of myself."

Amelia snorted and waved it off. "I don't care about that, I have been well enough off with this lot and trying to find information about Edmund. Although now, I demand to know where you have been, what you have been up to, and what the devil Lord Radcliffe has to do with it."

She folded her arms and raised a brow in query.

Edith nearly laughed, as all the rest looked at Amelia in shock.

"I knew I liked you, Amelia Perry," Charlotte stated with a broad smile. "Edith has to answer the question now, as you are far more likable than myself. She will not disappoint you."

Izzy cleared her throat, looking around. "Perhaps we should adjourn to a more private room? This is not exactly a conversation for a corridor."

As one, the group moved to the nearest available private space, the library.

Within its walls, Edith could only think of Graham. Of his kisses, of his scent, of his embrace…

And now she had to speak of him to her friends. By way of explanation, if nothing else.

But what to share? Graham had given her no indication of his intentions or of his feelings. He had said nothing of the sort, but she could easily sense an admiration and a degree of desire, but should it be called love on his part?

She did not dare to hope.

But she had to tell them something, so she told them all, apart from her feelings, and was very cautious regarding Molly. Despite her attachment, the girl was not her child, and it was not her story to tell.

The general outcry was as she had expected.

"You have tamed the earl," Charlotte crowed, clapping her hands.

Georgie rolled her eyes. "Charlotte, for heaven's sake, do try to show some decorum."

"I knew it," Amelia breathed, collapsing against the nearest chair. "I knew there was something between you. I knew he could not look at you so for nothing."

"I dare not assume…" Edith protested as she shook her head. "That is, he hasna said…"

Grace reached out and put a hand on hers. "Of course, he's said. You're only thinking of words, Edith."

She stared at Grace in shock, words failing her. Had he shown her? Had she missed it?

"Aubrey told me something last night," Grace went on, still smiling. "He said he is coming to know Radcliffe rather well throughout this party, as well as in caring for you in London. I think, based on what he said, that you can be assured of feelings on Radcliffe's part, that those feelings are stronger than what he can express, and that you need only be patient." Her smile spread, crinkling the corners of her eyes. "He will make it perfectly plain."

Edith felt her heart pound with a fervency that stole her breath, spreading warmth throughout her body with every beat. Emotions swirled and built within her, near to choking her as the truth made itself known.

"I love him," Edith confessed breathlessly, tears clogging her throat and filling her eyes.

Grace grinned and leaned back. "I know, Edith. I can see it. We all can, and we see the way he looks at you, as well."

"Indeed," Georgie agreed. "And I, for one, think you are in very great danger."

"Danger?" Edith cried with a laugh. "How can I be in danger from Graham?"

Georgie quirked a brow at the use of his given name and smirked. "The best kind of danger, my dear. The very best."

Again came the sound of the gong, and Charlotte clapped her hands. "Excellent. Time to dress for the ball, and to see just what sort of display Radcliffe will have for our dear Edith."

"Charlotte!" Izzy scolded, eyes wide.

Edith could only laugh. She wondered the same thing.

Only an hour later, wreathed in shades of lavender, in fabric too fine for her finances, Edith made her way down the stairs, her fingers grazing the railing in her borrowed and pristine gloves. She had spent too long at the looking glass, fussing over attempted perfection, wanting to be more than she had ever managed to be in her life.

Hoping he saw beauty where she saw flaws.

Had her hair curled as well as she'd wished? Were the ribbons and pearl combs going to improve her looks or take away from them? Did the shade of her gown complement her eyes?

Did any of this matter?

It was all a distraction, this fussing and preening. Graham had seen her with her hair tossed and down, windblown while on horseback, and he'd kissed her then. He had seen her in a plain day dress, hair in a simple chignon, and he had kissed her with passion.

He had held her in his arms without seeing what she was wearing and kissed her hair all the while.

Nèamh pray he might love her half as much as she loved him.

Heart thudding in her throat, Edith made her way to the ballroom, smiling as she caught sight of others milling about, the music not having begun. What in the world could anybody be waiting for?

There was as much glory in the ballroom as there had been the first ball of the party, but somehow, more magic. Every lady was dressed in somehow finer gowns than before, and every gentleman looked pristine in stark eveningwear. Candles were everywhere, and the gold detailing of the ceiling and walls positively sparkled.

It was enough to make one breathless in mere appreciation.

Edith looked around for something else she wished to appreciate, more specifically someone, but he was nowhere to be seen. He was the host, so he would be in attendance soon, and in the meantime, she could settle her nerves with her friends.

She smiled at other guests as she moved to Charlotte and Grace, both of whom praised her appearance enough to settle her.

Amelia looked forlorn as she stood apart from them, her attention on her gloves, though the rose-colored gown did lend her cheeks more color than they had in them naturally. Edith sighed as she watched her friend, noticing that she brightened the moment someone spoke to her, in an attempt to disguise her hurt. Somehow, it seemed wrong to be so full of hope, love, and joy when Amelia was feeling the loss of them.

Grace and Charlotte suddenly grew silent, their eyes widening.

Edith frowned at them. "What is it?"

Charlotte clamped down on her lips, giggling softly, and indicated Edith turn around.

Edith did so, her breath catching, heart pounding. As she had hoped, Graham stood there, more elegant, refined, and handsome than any other man in heaven or on earth. His eyes raked slowly down the length of her, then back up, and anyone looking at him would know his regard for Edith.

There was no mistaking it now.

He bowed, holding out his hand, and murmured, "Will you take the waltz with me, Lady Edith?"

A few people nearby gasped, no doubt from his suggesting the waltz, and others that he would open the ball with her, of all ladies.

Edith could have professed her love for him then and there, but for the sudden impulse to tease him.

She tilted her head in an almost coy fashion. "A waltz, my lord? Do ye no' find the waltz rather distasteful?"

Grace snickered next to her, and Amelia grinned beside her.

Graham, however, continued to look only at Edith, his hand still outstretched. "I do, Lady Edith, under usual circumstances. But it is my personal opinion that the right sort of partner could make the waltz a glorious thing. If I am proven right in this, I shall have no qualms about dancing every waltz at every event with that precise partner."

More gasps echoed, and Edith's cheeks flamed in embarrassed pleasure. It was nearly a proposal, and there was no mistaking it.

Her knees quivered, but she *had* promised to tease him, and she aimed to do so. "And you are under the impression that I could be such a partner for you, my lord?" she inquired, unable to keep the smile from her face.

His mouth curved into a dangerous half-smile. "I am quite assured of your suitability, Lady Edith. I will have no other. Now, will you waltz with me?"

Heart fluttering, Edith put her hand in his and let him lead her out into the middle of the room.

"Now, Edith," he murmured as he took her waist in hand, raising their arms over their heads, "we will waltz." He paused, tilting his head from side to side. "Again," he added.

"Without me pushing you," she reminded him as she placed her hand on his back, her fingers rubbing the fabric.

Graham smiled at her and dipped just a bit closer. "Yet you did render me without words once more. A pattern, I think, is being established." He exhaled softly, shaking his head as the music began. "A full waltz with you, Edith. I can think of nothing so close to perfection."

Edith sighed and was swept into the movements of the waltz, Graham's steps sure and his hold strong. She couldn't look anywhere but his eyes, couldn't believe she had lived any moment before this.

He smiled then, as if he knew something amusing that she did not.

"Tell us your secrets, then," Edith encouraged, delighted by such a smile.

"I was thinking," he mused in a low voice, "that I just might find myself becoming a dancer after this."

Edith laughed at the image that presented. "Graham, why have you only ever danced with two other women before me? You do it so well."

He seemed to shrug as they turned in a great swell with the music. "I never found any other reason to. If I was to make a fool of myself, it had better have been worth my while."

"And this is?" she asked with an impertinent tilt to her head.

The look he gave her was a kiss in and of itself. "I don't know that anything has ever been more worth my while than this."

Edith bit down on her lip to hold back a whimper of the most pleasant distress, longing to fly away from this room and these people, to just be with him and no one else.

Graham's eyes drifted down to the exact place where her lip puckered beneath her teeth. When they returned to her eyes, the intensity pulled her closer to him, the hand at her waist sliding further around, anchoring her there as much as any dance could allow.

She'd have gone closer if she could have.

And then, far too quickly, the waltz was finished, and the respectability of their proximity could not last.

"Graham..." Edith whispered as their hands lowered, fingers lacing.

He brought her hand to his lips, lingering in a manner that made Edith shiver. "Save me the supper set, sweetheart. I want to spend as much time with you as I can."

"You can have them all, *mo chridhe*," Edith breathed, knowing he wouldn't understand the endearment, but needing to say it.

As if he knew, he kissed her hand again, before returning her to Grace and Charlotte, neither of whom had words for her, though both took her hands.

The ball proceeded another hour or so without much fuss, Edith dancing with Henshaw, Aubrey, Tony, Francis, and Sebastian. Graham danced with her friends as well, but nothing made Edith happier than watching him dance with Amelia. She smiled more brightly than Edith had seen her do in months, and Graham was doing it for her.

If Edith hadn't loved him before, she certainly did now.

Suddenly, there was a ruckus at the front of the ballroom, disrupting the music and the dance. Edith grabbed Georgie's arm, fearing the worst for herself, and for Graham.

Then, through the crowd, came a man dressed too casually for a ball, breathing as if he were desperately winded, and his eyes scanned the entire company eagerly.

As soon as Edith could see his face, she gasped and released Georgie's arm, turning to her other side, where Amelia had gone very still, her eyes wide.

"Amelia?" she asked gently, very concerned that she would swoon.

Graham came to them as well, though he bore a small smile on his face.

The man's eyes suddenly caught Amelia, and he froze as completely as if he had been a statue.

Amelia ignored them both. "Edmund."

Mr. Andrews looked her up and down without shame, his generally reserved countenance gone in the face of agony and ecstasy. He swallowed once, and then marched towards her just as her feet carried her forward. They clasped each other tightly, Amelia sobbing against his shoulder, and he clutching her to him as if nothing in heaven or on earth would ever take her from him.

There was no helping the tears streaming down Edith's cheeks as she witnessed their reunion, the love between them palpable as well as visible.

Graham wrapped his arms around her and kissed the side of her neck softly, holding her close.

"You did this?" she whispered, running a hand over the arms that held her.

He rested his head against hers. "I received a fascinating letter only yesterday, inquiring as to whether Amelia Perry might be in attendance, and if one Edmund Andrews might be admitted to see her. I replied in the affirmative, and Ingram related the whole situation to me."

"Tell me," Edith murmured.

Graham chuckled softly. "As it happens, Andrews has been working for the government. His latest assignment was in Portugal, and he fell into a spot of trouble, which is why he stopped writing to Amelia. Vale and Ingram discovered this while working with Chadwick on your particular matters, and the three of them were able to get him back. As I understand it, he came straight here after giving his report and seeing his duty fulfilled. His biggest concern was that Amelia had thought him indifferent and uncaring, when quite the opposite is true, as you can see."

Edith nodded and leaned back against him while they had this moment.

Graham kissed her again, this time at her ear, very softly. "I'd hold you the same way in this company if they were not already doing so. You are too beautiful, too lovely to resist. It is only the promise of sitting next to you at supper that is keeping me from stealing away with you right this minute."

Her eyes fluttered, and she pulled his arms more tightly about her. "I'd go," she admitted without shame. "I'd fly away wi' ye, Graham, and ne'er look back."

He groaned, his lips still at her ear, scorching the tender flesh. "Don't tell me that. How can I be respectable now?"

Edith laughed breathlessly. *"Dinna fash.* I ken ye'll think of something." She cocked her head as she watched Andrews and Amelia whisper together, all eyes still on them. "Graham, surely there is somewhere they can be alone…"

"Unchaperoned?" he teased, nuzzling her a little. "Perhaps you are right. Pardon me, darling, while I tend to my hosting duties." He kissed her again before clearing his throat and striding over to the still embracing couple.

He spoke to them softly, and then turned to the gathering with a smile. "Ladies and gentlemen, our newest and most honored guest, Mr. Andrews, has something he would like to say." He gestured for Andrews to do so.

Mr. Andrews turned to Amelia with a breathless, wild grin and said, for all to hear, "Amelia Perry, I've loved you from the moment

I saw you, and only more ever since. I have waited too long to ask, but will you forgive me and be my wife?"

Tears still streaming down her cheeks, she took the hand she still held and kissed it fervently. "Yes, Edmund. Yes, yes, yes."

Andrews swept her up again, kissing her soundly, and the ballroom as a whole cheered and applauded, several ladies wiping tears from their eyes.

Graham gave them a moment, then winked at Edith as he turned and escorted them from the room.

The music struck up again, and the dancing resumed. Edith, for one, thought her heart might burst from her chest, so filled to the brim was it.

A hand settled on her arm, and she turned to see Miranda smiling at her, eyes moist. "You'll be next, my lamb. I feel sure of it."

Edith exhaled a satisfied sigh. "Ye think so?"

Miranda nodded once. "And so do you, Edith. Mark my words, the next few days will be quite interesting." She gave Edith a knowing look and moved to speak with Georgie and Izzy.

Edith looked at the door to the ballroom where Graham had disappeared, smiling in anticipation.

They had the rest of the evening together, and, if she got her wish, the rest of their lives, as well.

Chapter Nineteen

———————⌒⌘⌒———————

Alterations to any plans one has made can be a disruption that, in one stroke, may throw all into upheaval. It should be avoided at any cost, if possible. If not possible, one should attempt to make the best of it. Again, if at all possible. Which it may not be.

-*The Spinster Chronicles, 4 January 1819*

"Gray said the ball was really nice. He said you looked beautiful, and that you danced a lot, and that supper was the best one Cook has done yet."

Edith smiled and watched the girl fiddle with wildflowers in front of her, sun in her hair. "It was lovely. I could barely dance at all after supper, the food was so delicious. I was fair to bursting, but I just couldna keep myself from completely stuffing my gob."

Molly giggled and glanced up at her. "Scottish is funny, Edith."

"Aye, a wee bit," Edith admitted with a wink. "But it's a bonny language, lass."

"And you're a bonny lady, *mo charaid*," Molly told her, beaming proudly.

Edith ruffled the girl's dark curls before kissing her head. "*Tapadh leat*, lass. It warms my heart to hear you call me friend in my own tongue."

"Teach me more words!" Molly exclaimed, clapping her hands.

Laughing, Edith nodded. "Verra well. When you want to say 'cheers', you say, '*slàinte*'."

Molly repeated the word firmly, then tipped back an imaginary glass of something or other.

"*Slàinte*," Edith repeated, doing the same.

"What else?" Molly demanded as she turned towards Edith, flapping the skirts of her pale blue calico before settling her hands in her lap. "Tell me something I can tell Gray."

Edith thought about it for a moment, then said, "*Teaghlach*. It means family."

Molly tried the word, but fumbled around it, making herself giggle. "My family is strange," the girl admitted. "Aunt Ellie is my great-aunt, but she's not that old. Gray is not my papa, but he sometimes acts like he is. I don't have my mama or papa anymore…" She looked down at her fingers, the short, uneven nails tinged green from her toying with flower stems. "I barely remember them now."

"That canna be easy for ye," Edith murmured softly. "I havnae seen my mother or father in years, and sometimes I miss them very much. Is there a portrait of them in the gallery?"

"Yes. I go there sometimes to remember what Mama looked like." Molly shrugged her slight shoulders, still looking down. "But it's not the same. I miss having a mama here with me."

Edith sighed and reached out to touch the girl's cheek, bringing her attention up. "I'm quite certain that wherever she is, she misses you terribly."

Molly gave her a very small smile. "Can we play a game, Edith? We're almost at the village, and there are all sorts of hiding places. I can hide, and you find me."

"It sounds lovely." Edith got to her feet and helped her up, giving her a serious look. "Stay close, though. I'm not going to explain to your uncle how I lost you in a game."

Molly agreed and took her hand, skipping alongside Edith as they moved further away from Merrifield down the worn grass path.

Edith smiled when Molly disengaged and began to twirl in the open space. There was something so vibrant about her, so full of life, and it was contagious. She was the sweetest girl, and clever beyond her years.

"I'll hide first!" Molly cried, suddenly dashing towards the abandoned blacksmith's shed.

Edith obediently turned her back, smirking to herself. "I'll count to thirty, lass, and then I'll be coming to get ye!"

"If you can find me!" came the laughing reply.

Commencing with her counting, Edith looked up into the cloud-dotted sky, smiling at the beautiful day. After the exquisite experience of the ball, dancing with Graham enough times to draw comment, sitting next to each other at dinner, brushing fingers and legs against each other, sleep was near impossible to come by. Dreams could not be better than the reality she had experienced.

Graham had spirited her away before the final dance of the evening, kissing her sweetly in the corridor, and holding her close. "We're on the brink of something, Edith, if only we can catch it."

Another long, slow kiss had finished the conversation, and they had danced together one final time.

She hadn't seen him yet this morning, but Molly had told her they had breakfasted together, which made Edith smile.

He was so good to his niece. So good to all of them.

"Thirty!" Edith called out, turning around to face the shed.

She came closer, keeping her tread light, looking around the back of the building for possible alternative hiding places and finding none.

Molly was near the shed somewhere, if only Edith could find her.

There were only so many places she could be, considering the state of the place, and after only a few moments of looking, Edith surmised that the girl had come to the far side of the building, likely crouching in a cupboard on that side, or some such. Edith pressed her back to the building, grinning to herself. She would silently count to ten, then leap out with a cry that would startle Molly, whether she was inside a cupboard or not.

Feeling more like a child than she had in years, Edith grinned in breathless anticipation, then sprang around the corner with a roar and a grin.

It faded in a heartbeat.

Molly stood not far off, beside Sir Reginald, two large men standing by, restraining her. The men had their hands on the butts of guns, and one had a hand over Molly's mouth. Her eyes were wide with terror, sending jolts of fear into Edith's stomach, the urge to be sick clenching at her.

"Lady Edith," Sir Reginald said with a smirk, his voice so sneering it made her skin crawl.

He looked her over very thoroughly, his eyes lingering in obvious places, and anyone alive would have felt filthy by the time he was done.

"What are you doing?" Edith hissed, clenching her fists. "Let her go."

He clucked his tongue and shook his head, reaching out to touch the girl's hair. "Not a chance."

Molly struggled fiercely, and the men holding her clamped on harder. There was something menacing about the look in their eyes, in their manner, and there was obvious impatience with her. She was entirely expendable to all three of them.

"Dinnae struggle," Edith told her firmly, trying her utmost to remain calm for her sake. "Dinnae fight them. Be still."

She looked at Edith, her eyes filling with tears, but she nodded and went still.

"Playing with village children, Lady Edith?" Sir Reginald clicked his tongue in disapproval, shaking his head. "And during a house party? That is not very polite of you. How disrespectful to Lord Radcliffe, after all he has done for you." He touched Molly's hair again, smiling at her.

"Don't touch her!" Edith spat, coming closer.

He gave her a hard look. "Do you think I have any interest in this child?" he replied, losing his false congeniality. "I could not care less. I only took her to convince you of the gravity of your situation."

"My situation?" she asked, feeling her body grow cold at the look in his eyes.

He nodded once. "It is very simple. It has always been very simple, but you have chosen to complicate matters. You come with me back to London now, and this child is free to return to her village and parents."

Realization dawned on Edith, rippling across her frozen skin with some measure of comfort.

Sir Reginald had no idea whose child he had taken, or of her identity at all. If he had, he would not have been so willing to part with her. Had he known who her family was, he would have devised a far more cunning plan.

And that, Edith could not have borne.

"What will you do with me?" she asked, unable to look at Molly, her mind reeling in an attempt to form some sort of plan.

The look in his eyes was so lewd it brought bile rising to Edith's mouth. "That list is not suitable for a child's ears, my dear."

She shuddered and put a hand to her mouth, closing her eyes, forcing herself to breathe.

Every threat, every touch, every image he had painted in her mind suddenly revisited her *en masse*, causing her to sway almost unsteadily. How could she submit to him? How?

How could she not, with what was at stake?

"Come, come, Lady Edith, we haven't all day."

She opened her eyes and looked back at him in disgust. "You swear to me that she will be free? No repercussions?"

He nodded. "None, unless you raise an alarm about this. She is free to go as free as she came. But if you scream, if you alert anyone to what you are about, we will come back for her."

Molly whimpered, and the sound reverberated in Edith's soul. She looked at her for a long moment, knowing what she was going to do, but utterly loathe to submit to his will. "May I have time to pack my things and say my farewells?" she asked him, her attention still on Molly.

Sir Reginald snorted in derision. "And have you leave word for Lord Radcliffe to hunt you down? I think not. I'd rather let him stew in wondering where you went, assuming he cares, and your dear, devoted friends thinking the worst. No, your things can be sent for. We leave right this moment or not at all."

Edith closed her eyes again and took a moment to breathe again.

To have one final moment of peace. To resign herself to her fate.

Then she met his cold, sneering eyes again. "Very well," she said clearly, without any hint of her natural brogue. "I consent."

Molly cried out behind her captors' hands.

"Hush!" Sir Reginald snapped as he turned to her. "I've had quite enough of you."

"Sir Reginald!" Edith said immediately, throwing as much firmness and coldness into her tone as she could, taking two steps forward.

He and his men looked at her in surprise.

"Leave that child alone," she ground out, her jaw tight. "I have agreed to your terms, now let her go. I willna condone you treating her thus."

He sneered at her, mocking laughter oozing from him. "You are in no condition to dictate anything."

Edith folded her arms and firmed her stance. "Perhaps not, but I can and will make your life a living hell from this moment on if you dinnae do as I say."

His expression darkened, "I own you, you little baggage!"

"Then I have nothing to lose, ye ken?" she replied, his words frightening her more than she could show.

He owned her.

At long last, she had become nothing more than a possession.

He muttered something under his breath and nodded at his men, who released Molly. She ran at Edith and flung her arms around her, quivering against her legs. Edith sank to her level and pulled her close.

"It's all right, wee one," she whispered, intentionally keeping her name from being said. The more she could save her, the better.

"Don't go with them," she pleaded tearfully. "I'm scared."

Edith rubbed her back soothingly. "I have to, sweetheart."

She pulled back and looked at Edith, rubbing the tears from her face. "What do I tell... my papa?" Her eyes widened at the lie, her tone uncertain. "You were... You were supposed to bring me home."

Edith glanced over at Sir Reginald, who gave her a look of ultimate warning.

"Tell your papa that I was called away urgently, and my cousin and I must return home at once." Edith smiled as gently as she could. "*Teaghlach*, lass. Remember?"

Molly blinked once, then nodded. "I remember, Lady Edith. Family."

Edith could have kissed her for translating so clearly. Hopefully, it would keep Sir Reginald from suspecting any sort of secret word.

Which, of course, she had intended it to be at the moment, but not one that would anger him.

She glanced over at him with some trepidation, most of it for effect.

Sir Reginald nodded and gave a signal to his men, who departed.

"Can you be brave, darling?" she whispered to Molly, taking her hands. "Can you do that?"

She nodded, though her lips trembled.

Edith smiled and kissed her hands. "Go on, then. Run home."

Molly gave her one last, fierce hug, and then darted off without looking back.

Edith watched her go, tears welling and falling in one smooth motion. Her heart was breaking into a million pieces within her, the shards falling down around her with icy pangs. She couldn't look after her, and she could not look at Sir Reginald. She could only stay in her place, near the ground, and wish to God that the earth might swallow her whole.

Molly was safe and would be safe. That was the most important thing.

The less important things, however…

Edith gagged and choked on the still rising tears, her fingers clawing at the ground.

"Sentimental, my dear." Sir Reginald spat in disgust before chuckling with some secret, dark humor. "How very Scottish of you to treat village children as if they were your equals. It's no wonder you haven't attained anything in your life. Not even marriage to my cousin could have brought you up. No matter. Your station will change soon enough."

He seized her arm and hauled her to her feet.

"What do ye mean?" she asked as she started moving with him, still not looking at him.

His hands started wandering over her backside as he chuckled. "You are to be my mistress, Lady Edith. Did you doubt that was my ultimate plan?"

"My, my," she murmured morosely, "ye must want me dreadfully to fight so hard to get me."

That earned her a vicious blow across her face, sending her stumbling back to the ground. "Want you?" he all but screamed. "I've damn near lost my taste for the sight of you. You're not worth the trouble."

He hauled her to her feet again, taking her chin in hand hard, shaking her, his eyes narrowing. "Or perhaps you are. Time will tell just what that spirit of yours, that willfulness, will bring to me. But make no mistake, Lady Edith, you are mine. You belong to me. And no one gets to take what belongs to me." He kissed her then, harsh and rough, biting down on her lip without mercy. His hand moved to her back, then shoved her towards the carriage, nearly causing her to stumble again.

"So, what are we to do, then?" Edith asked with a murderous glance back at him, wiping at the blood at her mouth, fighting the urge to spit as her tears of despair turned to tears of fury.

His smile curved as he followed her. "The whole world will know that you have become my mistress." He quirked his brow with insinuation. "Suggestion is a powerful tool. You will be at my beck and call, whenever I decide I want a piece of rough Scottish blood." He laughed to himself, either at the prospect, or finding amusement in something Edith did not understand. "I am half tempted to move you into my London house, but I hardly think my wife would approve."

"You have a wife?" she asked, almost stumbling as she tried to enter the carriage.

He forced her inside, his hands yet again where they ought not to be. "My business, not yours."

"Am I to be a prisoner in my own home?" She sat in the furthest corner of the carriage she could manage, wondering with horror what he meant for her. What she was to do? How she was to act?

What would happen?

"Yes," he said simply as he followed her into the coach, happily not moving closer to her. "My men will watch you, accompany you, and are full well free to touch you as they please. But the best part of you is for me alone." He smiled as if that would be of some comfort to her.

Edith shuddered and looked out of the window as the carriage moved.

"Your so-called friends will not be permitted to see you," he went on. "And I will know if you defy me. Things will be far worse for you if that is the case. I will call on you at any hour I wish, stay as long as I like, and do as I will. Your funds will be cut off entirely, and only what I give you when I am generous will be yours."

"That will be a great change," Edith muttered. "Imagine not having funds."

Sir Reginald kicked her sharply across the shins. "When I come to call, you will wear what I direct and only that. You will have no guests and no change in your servants. Your own servants may stay, but they also belong to me. Nothing will go on in that house without my saying so. And if your filthy Scottish lover comes around? I will have him beaten to within an inch of his life for daring to touch what is mine."

Edith smiled faintly to herself, tears still slowly falling. "I would dearly love to see ye try," she whispered.

Sir Reginald somehow didn't catch the words, staring as he was out of his own window now.

Edith wiped at her still-bleeding lip, closing her eyes on fresh tears.

Oh, Graham...

She clasped onto the memory of every dance the night before, every moment in his arms, knowing she would never have another like them in her life.

It would be enough. She longed for more, ached deeply for it, but here at the end, she knew it was enough. More than that, it was hers forever.

Not even Sir Reginald could take it from her.

Chapter Twenty

———— ✦~✦✦~✦ ————

There is nothing so bad as waiting when one would rather do anything else.

-The Spinster Chronicles, 29 May 1817

Agony was a word upon which Graham had been pleased to dwell for the past several days. Even the sound of it was one that seemed to be pulled from the darkest depths of one's soul. It should have been a more reverent word. Always spoken in a hushed tone. Bearing the weight of its burden at all times. Never used in vain.

Agony was all-encompassing.

He thought he'd known agony, but he was wrong. He had known grief; he had known pain; he had known sorrow, anger, hopelessness, and numbness.

He had not known agony.

Not until now.

For as long as he lived, he would never forget the moment Molly had torn into his study and told him that Edith had gone off with her cousin. A man with cruel eyes and a slender frame, travelling with two larger men who had held Molly while they waited for Edith. That Edith had sent Molly home with one word.

Family.

The weasel was part of her former family by marriage, but even without that word, Graham would have known who had taken her just by Molly's description and the manner by which the event had taken place. That was not a family.

They were a family — Graham, Molly, and now Edith. There were no legal ties that bound Edith to them, but there were cords of love winding around them all and bringing them together.

She had sacrificed herself for family.

And Graham could only sit here.

Edith was gone. In danger, undoubtedly, and there was no telling what she could be enduring now.

And he was here.

He didn't have a choice. There was nothing he could do in London that would solve the issue. Or so Henshaw, Ingram, Sterling, and the others had told him when he had gathered them all to discuss it.

He'd hotly reminded them that he could storm her house and be married to her in less than a day, thus giving her legal protection from the weasel.

Ingram, having spent too long looking at the finer details of the law lately, was able to point out that such an act might stop the abuse, but would not get Sir Reginald out of her life.

Nor would it help Graham's ward when her time to come out eventually came. If her guardian was married to a woman whose reputation was so particularly smeared by ruin, Molly would never be accepted in Society.

Graham had been about to retort that he didn't care when the next words stopped him.

"...which is why we have to ruin him first."

An intriguing notion, which was why the group of them had spent the rest of the night and many of the early morning hours discussing their options and resources. Tony had suggested they bring Andrews into the discussion, but no one thought he needed to be brought in at that time.

He had only just come back from assignment, and he and Amelia were never seen apart.

But eventually, they had brought him in, and Graham was ever so grateful they had. The man's mind was beyond impressive, and his strategic agility was unmatched by anyone of Graham's acquaintance. He'd left almost immediately, Amelia accompanying him, to return to

London to start working on the matter, as well as letting Amelia, and by extension, her mother, begin their work on the plans for the wedding.

Graham had wanted to shut down the house party and send the lot of his guests home, given that there was no reason for any of them to be there now. But every one of his friends had advised against it, suggested that such an action would do more harm to Edith than good, as it was. They could spread her own story, that her cousin had come to fetch her on urgent family business, and that her belongings would be sent for.

The truth would come out eventually, but they would have time to put various pieces in motion before that.

Henshaw had argued, alongside Graham, that Edith could suffer considerably at the hands of the weasel while the lot of them moved their chess pieces into position. What, he had countered, would be left to save of her if they waited so long?

For a man not in love with Edith, Henshaw did a fine job of behaving like one. His scowl could have matched Graham's. His surly nature from the moment she had gone *was* Graham's. His desire for revenge actually rivalled Graham's. And no one was on Graham's side with the same passion, drive, and fierceness as Henshaw.

What a pair they would have made had they nothing to risk and time enough to give Sir Reginald what he deserved.

Both of them were reminded of Owen, Edith's brooding and hulking servant, as well as Edith's brother, who had remained in London.

Word was sent to both immediately as to the situation at hand.

Then, one by one, his guests had left, assignments all around, and there was nothing more to be done but finish out his hosting duties. The remainder of the guests had left at the scheduled time, and Merrifield seemed darker and more hollow when no one else was left.

He wasn't naïve enough to think that it was due to his guests that this was the case. They had only been a distraction; sights, sounds, and smells to occupy him while he avoided curling up in his study to give in to the howling creature of despair within him.

Agony called to him, and he could not let himself answer.

214

Edith had been the one to make the place glow and come alive, and it was her absence that darkened it. He'd never thought Merrifield lacking in any respect until she had gone from it.

She made everything and anything better simply by her presence. He was the chief example of that.

"Graham?"

He looked up from where he sat behind his desk to see Eloise entering the room. "Aunt."

She smiled gently, though her complexion was nearly gaunt in its pallor.

Edith's departure had affected her as much as anybody else, and she hadn't left her room more than a handful of times in the days following. She'd insisted that she wasn't taking ill, forbade him from sending for a doctor, and kept to her bed to rest, though she never appeared particularly well rested.

"Eloise…" he murmured, seeing how weak she looked as she struggled to sit in the nearest chair.

She glared, which was the liveliest she had seemed in some time. "I will not crumble, nephew. I may not be strong, but I will not be pitied."

He held his hands up in a show of surrender, then rested his elbows on the desk surface, exhaling slowly.

"Have you heard anything?" Eloise asked in a much softer voice.

Graham shook his head. "Not in days." He rubbed his hands over his face, groaning low. "Every other man in this operation has a task to perform. Why should I be the one designated to wait?"

"Because you feel the most."

He moved his hands just enough to look at her with a frown. "Shouldn't that give me leave to do the most?"

Eloise lifted a dainty shoulder, folding her shawl tightly about her. "I don't know. But I would worry that you would lose your head in an attempt to save her. That you would not keep yourself calm and might behave recklessly. Cooler heads must prevail."

He glared at his aunt. "Cooler heads don't love Edith as I do."

"And I am pleased to hear you admit that you love her," Eloise shot back without hesitation. "But you mean to tell me that Aubrey, Lord Ingram, does not have some love for Edith? Or Captain

Sterling? Henshaw has no love for her?"

Graham stiffened in his seat. "I did not say I was the only one to love her," he insisted quietly. "Only that they do not love her the same."

Eloise tilted her head. "Do they need to?"

The answer to the question was clearly in the negative, but Graham could not bring himself to admit it.

"Lieutenant Henshaw would go to the ends of the earth for Edith," Eloise reminded him. "Mr. Andrews would bring down the wrath of hell. Mr. Vale, as I understand it, would do worse. These are not men standing idly by and waiting for the right time to summon you, Gray. I know you are at your wits' end, wanting something to do to help sweet Edith. But trust that others are doing things and that solutions will come."

Graham eyed his aunt with some admiration, remembering, belatedly, that she had more energy than her appearance suggested.

"Thank you, Eloise," he murmured with a smile.

She inclined her head in an almost regal fashion that reminded him of Miranda Sterling. "You are not the only one being driven to distraction, you know."

"Am I not?" he queried with a quirk of a brow.

"You don't think Molly and I would run off to save Edith if we only knew how?"

The image was a harrowing one, and a humbling one. Why should his aunt and his niece feel anything less than the rest of them did when it came to Edith? Anyone knowing her would want to help her. He'd wager the Spinsters were beside themselves trying to find a way to help, despite what their husbands would or would not allow. Who knew how many other people would have loved to find a way to save Edith?

Despite being almost alone here at Merrifield, Graham suddenly felt rather less alone in the grander sense.

This had to work. Whatever they settled on, whatever was in the works, had to succeed.

It had to.

Footsteps in the corridor attracted the attention of them both, and the arrival of a footman with a tray brought Graham to his feet.

He took the letter from the tray and broke the seal at once, his eyes scanning the words frantically.

All is set. Come to London to begin.

It was signed by Ingram, but it could have come from any of them and had the same effect.

Graham grinned and crumpled the letter in one hand, giving his aunt a triumphant look.

"Well?" she queried with a catch in her voice.

"I'm going to London." He chuckled in his relief. "I don't know what we're doing when I get there, but it sounds as if there is a plan."

Eloise smiled up at him and took his hand. "Go, Graham. And send us word when we may come to London."

Graham looked at her in surprise. "You haven't been to London in years. Will you be well enough for the journey?"

"For Edith," Eloise insisted with a nod, "I will make myself well enough."

The whole city of London knew Edith was tainted now; there was no mistaking it.

She could not leave the house without stares, whispers, and comments following her, not even for a walk, as she had tried the other day. Not a soul would look at her. She had gone out walking with Simms that morning, and it was as though she bore the plague.

True to his word, Sir Reginald had his men always following her, and they had even entered the house and her rooms on occasion. Owen had vowed to protect her at all times, no matter the cost, and he rarely left her side when they were at home. He had begun to sleep in her personal sitting room now, with a gun and blade by his side. According to him, he did not care what anybody said; no one would touch her while he drew breath.

Sir Reginald called upon her at will, but he had not yet made any advances worse than what she had already experienced. He had chosen to stay the night a time or two, staying in a guest room, and leaving in broad daylight so everyone would see. His visits would usually consist of him berating her, touching her, taking a rough kiss or two, and then busying himself with drinking and eating and sleeping.

Edith did not fight it. Did not fight him. She was without feeling anymore, resigned to her fate. She could only hope that he would tire of her soon.

Still, she did not regret her choice. She loved Molly as if she were her own child and would have sacrificed herself to a fate far worse than this to save her. But in doing what she had, Edith effectively had distanced herself from her friends forever.

And from Graham.

There was no thought of him that was not an equal blend of the bitter with the sweet. Her dreams were filled with him, and she woke to tears every morning. What a life she might have had, if only things had been different!

But there was no use in wishing such things. She could cling to memories, but not live in them.

She was on her own now.

A pounding on the door brought her from her thoughts, her heart leaping anxiously into her throat. She rose quickly and flattened herself against the wall while Owen, armed as he usually was now, moved to the door.

"Ye muckle *gomeral*, dinnae point tha' thing so near my face."

Edith gasped, her eyes widening at the blessed sound of the one person she knew was not permitted to cross the threshold.

"Dinnae tempt me, an' ye willna have aught to worry aboot," Owen growled, though the tone was without any threat at all. "An' what in the Devil's purple arse is tha'?"

"If it was fer ye, I'd explain. As it is..." Strong footsteps clomped in the corridor, and then Lachlan was before her in the parlor, expression serious, his frame thinner than when she had seen him last.

"Lachlan," Edith gasped, still flat against the wall in shock.

Lachlan eyed her for a second, his shoulders dropping on an exhale. "Edie." He whistled sharply then, and another sound in the corridor met her ears.

A great, brown bloodhound sauntered into the room, his ears drooping as much as his face. He glanced at Edith blearily, then came

218

to her and dropped himself at her feet.

"Rufus?" Edith stared at the animal in shock, recognizing him from occasional visits with the Spinsters to Miranda Sterling's home. Then she looked back at her brother. "What the devil?"

Silently, her brother handed over a note, and Edith opened it quickly.

Dearest girl, I cannot be with you during this terrible ordeal, but I can send my sweet boy to you for companionship, comfort, and protection. Know that my heart and prayers come with him. Do not lose hope.

It was signed by Miranda Sterling. Edith stared at the name, sniffing back sudden tears.

They hadn't forgotten her.

Of course, they wouldn't, but absolute seclusion could play the very worst tricks on a mind.

Edith stooped and scratched Rufus behind his ears, murmuring softly in Gaelic until the dog seemed to sigh deeply. She grinned, then stood and faced her brother.

"So. You've met Miranda."

Lachlan raised a bushy brow. "I've met so many people in the last weeks, I can barely remember my own name."

"And how did they take you?" she asked. "Well?"

"Well enough. I'm no saint, but I'm no' the devil." He smiled at last and almost looked himself. "But what about ye, Edith? I have heard all sorts of things about you. A mistress to Sir Reginald? At his beck and call? His devoted slave for all eternity?"

She shuddered and looked away. "Only partially correct. I am no' his mistress in truth, and I am no' a devoted slave. But I am a slave of sorts, and I am at his beck and call."

"I ken. And it is why I am here."

"Why are you here?" she repeated, entirely confused. "What in the world have ye to do with any of it? Ye are hardly in a position to change my reputation for the better."

He shrugged once. "Who says I am going to?"

Edith sighed in irritation, not caring for the mysterious tone in his voice. "Why are ye here?"

"Other than delivering the mongrel?" He gave her a rather serious look. "Did ye really think I was going to let my sister endure such a man and such behaviors without doing something? I may be a drunk and a cad and a wastrel, but nobody abuses my family."

Edith folded her arms. "Except fer yerself."

He waved a dismissive hand. "Ye know what I mean. Ye need help, and I am here to help."

She tilted her head, now very curious. "How did ye know that I need help?"

He smiled knowingly. "I hear things. And Owen sent for me, besides."

Edith glared at Owen, who met her gaze without shame. "Where are ye staying?" she asked, returning her gaze to Lachlan.

He looked rather smug. "Right here with ye. Back together under the same roof, Edie."

She gaped, then her mind frantically scrambled. "No. No, you canna. He has forbidden ye from being anywhere near me. He thinks ye are my Scottish lover, and all of London is talking about it."

Lachlan grinned broadly. "I always wanted to be notorious."

"It isna funny!" she told him. "He says he will have ye thrashed and beaten."

Now he looked nearly offended. "And ye think he can?"

Edith snorted. "Of course no'. I know verra well ye could take him and his lackeys at one time while three sheets to the wind under the influence of Uncle Robert's home brew, and almost kill them in the process."

"Almost?" he screeched, truly offended now.

She gave him a look. "Uncle Robert's brew? Aye, *almost* kill them."

He considered that, then nodded. "Aye, tha's probably true. At any rate, I dinnae care what he says or threatens. I'm staying. No one comes near ye."

"He will be furious," she warned him.

"Good." He clapped his hands together and rubbed them. "And now, my dear Edie, we have somewhere to be."

Edith rolled her eyes. "Have ye been listening? He has forbidden me from going anywhere, apart from a short walk."

Lachlan gave her a despairing look. "Edie, you really must learn to break rules on occasion. There can be such fun in rebellion."

Without another word, he and Owen snuck Edith, who had donned a dark, hooded cloak, out of the house through the back door. They marched her down the street, via almost abandoned paths, to a church not far from the house.

She looked up at the façade, then at her brother in bewilderment. "Have ye turned yerself to God, Lachlan?"

He ignored her and pushed open a door, looking behind them as he ushered her in.

The chapel was perhaps half full, and Edith saw some of Society's best, including her friends, all at the front.

She gasped, covering her mouth as Lachlan ushered her into a pew in the back, blocking the escape she was desperate for.

Some of the guests observed them and left no question about their feelings on the matter.

Lachlan sat next to Edith while Owen stood behind them, almost at attention.

"What are we doing here?" she hissed. "No one wants me here; no one will look at me. Are ye trying to embarrass me more than I already am?"

"No," he said softly. "I am teaching ye to rise above their pettiness. And ye're wrong. Someone does want ye here. Someone who has been trying to write to ye for ages, and the letters were intercepted. But we found a way."

"We?" Edith asked quietly.

The doors behind them opened then, and an organ started to play. Through the doors appeared Amelia on an older man's arm, dressed in a pale yellow gown with a gorgeous veil.

Edith put a hand to her mouth and looked up at the front of the church, where Mr. Andrews now stood, smiling as broadly as anything. She glanced back at Amelia, and their eyes met.

Her smile was glorious as she reached out a hand to her and whispered, "I am so happy to see you, Edith."

Edith couldn't say a word, she was so overcome with emotion and tears. There was no helping them as they streamed down her cheeks.

221

Amelia and her father continued down the aisle, and Lachlan put his arm around Edith, pulling her tight as she cried.

They had not forgotten her. They had not abandoned her.

"*Tapadh leat*," she murmured to Lachlan as he ran a soothing hand along her back.

"Ye dinnae have to submit to him, Edie," he replied. "Ye can resist. It's no' over yet."

Edith frowned in confusion. "What do ye mean?"

Lachlan shook his head, a small smile on his lips.

The ceremony was beautiful, and Edith only took a brief moment to hug and congratulate the bride and groom at its conclusion.

Amelia squeezed her hands tightly.

"Keep hoping, Edith," she urged, Andrews nodding his agreement beside her.

"I will try," she assured them both, managing a small smile.

Lachlan and Owen ushered her out of the church and returned her home without any fuss, but Edith did not doubt that word would reach Sir Reginald soon enough.

Had Graham been at the wedding? Her heart seized at the thought, but she did not know if she could bear to see him. She could not bring herself to ask if Lachlan had seen him or if he had tried to write.

She didn't want to know. Not when she ached this way, not when she was so bound up in Sir Reginald's demands.

But perhaps, with Lachlan's help and encouragement, she could learn to resist. She could have no better instructor in resistance and rebellion, and now she knew she was not alone.

Now, perhaps, she could fight.

Chapter Twenty-One

―――――――――⟨∞ ∞⟩―――――――――

A little creativity can change a great deal if one is bold enough to be creative in the face of convention.

-The Spinster Chronicles, 10 May 1815

"Lachlan! Lachlan, stop running about the house with Rufus!"

There was no response but that of the dog bellowing as he thundered down the corridor above her, a much larger, heavier tread accompanying it. Then, she heard a taunting howl that had clearly not come from the canine, which prodded the actual canine to howl, as well.

"*Jeebs, Crivvens...*" Edith muttered, shaking her head, using various colorful words from home silently as she attempted to complete her embroidery in the parlor.

Embroidery.

She could not remember the last time she had embroidered something, and now, here she was, finishing a project.

She'd actually had the time and the peace of mind to take the task on, and had completed four sketches, five watercolors, and three landscapes.

Time and peace.

She hadn't had much of either in years.

For some reason, she had not seen Sir Reginald in some time, which was delightful, but also gave her cause to worry. Not for Sir Reginald, naturally, but that something far worse would be coming.

He had not come by the house since Lachlan had come to stay, and yet he had to know he was there.

What's worse was that Lachlan had begun to challenge Edith to go out on her own, without Owen. She was terrified of the idea, but he continually promised that she would be safe.

It was never entirely clear what that meant, but he had been talking so much about resisting and rebellion that it had begun to sound like a fair idea.

So, she had begun.

She had made a few small trips on her own, just brief walks and errands, keeping her head high and pretending she was not a pariah in Society.

One day, she had found that Owen was still following her, though at a very great distance. He was not exactly pleased to have been discovered, but Edith was comforted by it all the same.

A sharp jab of a needle shook Edith from her reflections, and she hissed, shaking the injured finger out as she looked over the embroidery. No harm done there, fortunately.

Rufus could be heard baying loudly now, and Edith looked up at the ceiling ruefully, Lachlan's low voice audible, but not intelligible.

Lachlan had been wonderful since he'd come to stay with her. He'd kept her from growing despondent, made her smile when she would have been solemn alone, and provided warm conversation with every meal. He did give her time alone and privacy whenever she wished, but if he caught her looking morose, he would do what he could to improve her spirits.

And he was marvelously protective. Sir Reginald's henchmen had tried to come into the house two days ago, and it had only taken a scant few words from Lachlan and two punches to convince them otherwise.

There had been no attempts by any to enter since then.

Edith knew better than to suspect that her troubles were over, but the temporary reprieve was blessed indeed.

A thundering down the stairs brought a smile to Edith's lips, and she glanced through the open parlor door to them. "I ken that Noah had a fair few animals in his ark, but if they came oot of that boat in a stampede, I still think ye'd make more noise than the lot of them."

Lachlan stopped and made a face at her, rather as he had done for most of their childhood. "Dinnae get yerself in a kerfuffle, *mo piuthar*. The stairs remain unharmed, and yer neighbors will only think yer lover is pleased as punch to be wi' ye."

Edith covered her face and leaned forward, laughing in embarrassed hysterics. "*Aich*, ye *gomeral*, *haud yer whist*, and take yer blatherin' off wi' ye."

Her brother chuckled without restraint and came to her, patting her on the head. "Tha's the mos' Scottish I've heard from ye since…" He trailed off, his hand stroking her hair far more gently. "Well, since I saw ye las' at home."

She looked up at him, smiling and taking his wrist in her hand firmly. "Having ye back with me, Lachlan, has brought a wee bit of Scotland back tae me. I thought I'd lost that part of me long ago."

He smiled in return, exhaling. "Ye'd never lose Scotland, Edie. She's in our blood."

She squeezed his wrist in a show of gratitude, and his smile grew at it.

"Let's have a stroll, Edie," he said brightly, patting the hand on his wrist and stepping away. "The evening is verra fine."

Edith glanced out of the window, then back at him. "This late?"

He pretended to look at the window, as well. "It's no' late. I still see the sun."

She gave him a dubious look. "Barely."

"Perfect." He scoffed with a wave of his hand. "Come, a wee stroll will do us both good."

"Are we taking Rufus?" Edith asked as she rose with a groan.

Lachlan shook his head. "No' this time. The lad can stay here with Owen and learn the art of whiskey."

"I have ears, ye ken," called a voice from the hall.

"Aye, and a mouth tae go wi' them! Hasna helped ye much yet!" Lachlan winked at Edith with a grin.

She rolled her eyes. Sometimes, there no explaining Highlanders.

They both donned light outerwear and ventured out of doors, Lachlan surprising Edith by not taking her arm. Not that she minded, but he had always done so before this.

It was such a cool, fine evening, that there were a great many people about. Their usual walk seemed rather congested, so Lachlan nudged his head along another path, and Edith followed, not minding at all.

"Edie," he murmured softly, leaning close, "do ye still carry a *sgian dubh* on ye?"

"Aye," she replied in surprise. "The blade is no' as sharp as it once was, but it would suffice."

He nodded, smiling in his usual carefree way, not bothering to explain the question as they moved towards their new route.

But, it seemed, that path was just as popular with Londoners at present, for there were just as many others about here as there had been elsewhere. Edith frowned as she was suddenly separated from her brother, though it was not terribly surprising, as there were some very pretty young women about. Lachlan must surely have been bored with only her for company, and it was only natural that he should take the opportunity to be introduced to one or two of them.

Edith merely shook her head and kept going, knowing he would find her eventually. The path was a simple one, the route uncomplicated, and she was not very far from her house.

No one would expect Lady Edith Leveson to have an escort for a walk. Not anymore.

Only a few moments later, Edith felt the ribbons of her bonnet cut, the bonnet itself flung off, and her hair seized in a painful grip.

She reached back with a gasp, but she could not dislodge the ever-tightening grip.

"Sneaky little slut," hissed Sir Reginald, wrapping his free arm around her waist while his fingers gripped her scalp with such pain that tears sprang to her eyes. "Did you think I wouldn't find out?"

"I didna send for him," she spat, struggling against his hold. "I told him you forbade it."

"Not hard enough," he insisted as he shook her head by her hair. "You could have cast him off, you could have barred him entry, and certainly to your bed. But you did not."

He forced Edith to walk awkwardly as she was held fairly immobile by him.

Her *sgian dubh* was at her wrist, fastened into her spencer, if only she could get to it.

"I am free to do what I wish," she told Sir Reginald, driving an elbow into his stomach. He grunted at the contact, but his hold remained.

"You are no such thing," he ground out against her ear. "You are *mine*." He hissed against the skin of her neck before running his nose, mouth, and even his tongue along it.

She jerked her head away, but he followed, and his fingers began to tear at her dress. Sleeves first, and then to her bodice, rendering the garment nearly indecent, though not entirely.

Edith growled in distress. "I am not!"

"Don't fight me," he barked. "I have been far too lenient with you, and that will change tonight." He pressed against her forcefully, leaving no doubt as to his intent.

"I will fight you all the way, and you will never make it past the door," she told him, struggling frantically as she reached for her sleeve.

"You're making a scene," he told her, finally moving his face away from her neck.

"Good," was all she replied.

And then Edith screamed, a blood-curdling, ear-piercing scream, and all in the vicinity looked towards them.

People gasped in horror, and women covered their mouths, this time in sympathy, as there was no mistaking Sir Reginald as the one who had rendered her thus, his hold on her aggressive and obvious.

Several men began to rush over with shouts as they saw Sir Reginald manhandling her, and far more than she thought had been around. More of the men were commonly dressed than seemed gentlemen, and some quite dirty, though Edith didn't care, if they would only come to her aid.

One of the men, a tall and imposing one, had gone directly for Sir Reginald, seizing him by the throat while others fastened themselves at his arms.

Edith was snatched from Sir Reginald's hold, and was passed, rather gently considering their roughness and rough treatment of him, from man to man. Finally, the first man who'd reached Sir Reginald, undoubtedly the leader of her rescuers, took her from the others, and his hold was tight, warm, and far too familiar.

"Now, I think," he murmured close to her ear, "you *might* call me a hero."

Edith gasped and turned in his hold to see, beneath the dirt and common clothes, her beloved Graham, smiling despite his exertional breathing.

"Graham!" she whispered, unable to cry out in truth for her disbelief.

He smiled at her, his hold tightening, and her heart surged with delight. She reached for him, but he pulled away. "Not now, Edith, there is too much to do." He nudged his nose along hers with a brief sigh. "I just couldn't help myself."

She tried to argue that it was the same for her, but he silenced her with a look. Then, he turned her back to look more closely as a few others marched Sir Reginald away from the group.

Edith would have gasped again had her lungs the strength to do so. Beneath the dirt and disguise, she could now see Francis, Henshaw, Andrews, Tony, Aubrey, Cam, and, of all people, her own brother, Lachlan. He had changed his clothes and somehow found dirt or soot to dirty himself with.

"*Feasgar math*, Edie," he said cheekily. "I'm sorry for deserting you, but these lads wanted a bit of Scottish blood to get his hands dirty."

The others chuckled, some shaking their heads, while Edith rolled her eyes.

Graham squeezed her tightly for a moment, then released her. "Go with Owen, Edith. I will come to you tomorrow and explain everything."

Edith glanced over to see Owen joining them, nodding at each man with familiarity. She noticed he was not dressed in a filthy disguise as they were, however.

She nodded at Graham, smiling at him, then at the others. "Thank you," she whispered. "All of you."

Aubrey took her hand and kissed it, looking every inch a rough blacksmith. "You should have known we would do something, Edith. Nothing would have stopped us."

"Not a damn thing," Henshaw confirmed with a nod.

Edith could have cried at the firm answer he gave. "Oh, Hensh, you have done so much for me. You have given up so much of yourself and your time."

He shook his head, silencing her. "Worth every moment, Edith. Not another word."

"Mus' ye be so damned noble, Hensh?" Lachlan groaned, clapping the man on the back. "A man resembles the verra devil standing beside ye."

"Someone has to make me look good," Henshaw joked, nudging Lachlan hard.

"Go home, love," Graham murmured gently, guiding her in Owen's direction. "I'll explain everything tomorrow."

Edith glanced back at him, afraid he might disappear. "Promise me."

Graham's eyes stayed firm and steady on hers. "I promise."

Her heart leapt and fell in a quick swoop. She turned and let Owen help her home, though she knew well enough that she would not sleep at all for anticipation of seeing Graham in the morning.

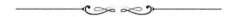

"Lord Radcliffe, mistress."

Graham released the breath he had been holding and moved forward, his heart threatening to break every rib in its vicinity with its pounding. He hadn't slept at all the night before, not with rescuing Edith and the fallout, taking Sir Reginald in to the magistrate, and seeing to all the details they had so carefully prepared.

He wished now that he had taken a moment or two to rest, if for no other reason than to be clearer in this moment.

Graham came in, and his eyes found Edith at once, neglecting Amelia, who had come that morning to wait with her. He said nothing, and Amelia laughed, very low, and excused herself from the room.

He couldn't breathe yet again, staring at her without shame. She was dressed simply, though the shade of her gown and its style did not even register in his mind. She was beautiful, soul-stirring in every respect, and his knees shook with the desire to fly to her.

"Good morning," Edith managed to say, her cheeks coloring.

"Yes, it is," he said simply, leaving no question as to what he was referring to.

Edith only smiled.

He said nothing else; he simply stared at her. He wanted to say everything. He wanted to say nothing. He wanted...

He wanted...

"What happened to Sir Reginald?" Edith eventually asked, her fingers clenching and unclenching in front of her.

He smirked at the question. "At this moment, he is desperately trying to explain to a magistrate why he imprisoned a woman of station and fortune and stole her rightful legacy from her late husband. We discovered that Sir Archibald *had* made provisions for you in his will, none of which were upheld. The weasel is also discovering that many of his friends and supporters are disgusted by his treatment of such a woman, and all of London knows what a villain he is."

Edith covered her mouth, looking torn between laughter and tears.

"Didn't you wonder why he had been absent lately?" he asked, tilting his head. "We have been keeping him quite busy over the last few weeks, working to ruin him in every possible way. I wanted to come to you myself, but Ingram and Henshaw assured me that you would be well enough off with Lachlan, as that rumor was already in full swing. So, we played with the rumors, setting seeds of doubt with the world, and then last night, we set the trap."

"And I was the bait," she answered, not sounding at all upset about being used in such a way.

He nodded, swallowing back the memory of arguing so vigorously against it. Everything had gone according to plan, and Edith was well and whole before him.

"Can you blame him?" He shrugged, smiling at her. "I would have fallen for it."

Edith's smile, in return, warmed him to the base of his spine. "I've missed you."

"I've missed you, too," he admitted roughly. Then, he swallowed again, smiling. "And someone else missed you." He turned to Owen, standing guard as he was, and gave the signal they'd arranged.

A small, curly-headed blur in a green dress burst into the room and latched her arms around Edith's waist.

"Edith!" Molly squealed, clutching tightly.

Edith looked at Graham in shock, tears in her eyes as she held his niece. "Molly?"

He shrugged, still smiling. "She and Eloise wouldn't let me leave them at home, not when I wrote we were ready to save you."

He watched Edith's throat work and felt his heart squeeze as she sank to the floor, pulling Molly fully into her arms.

"Oh, Molly, I am so sorry."

"It's not your fault the bad man got me," Molly said, completely unperturbed. "I didn't hide well enough. You saved me, Edith. I ran straight to Gray and told him exactly what you said. I remembered every word, and it worked!"

"Good girl," Edith praised, her hand rubbing circles on Molly's back as her eyes found Graham's again. "I am so proud."

Graham smiled as well, though the memory of Molly relating the tale was one he would be pleased to forget.

"Will you marry Gray and be my aunt?" Molly asked, pulling back to look at Edith squarely.

Graham could have choked in surprise, or laughed at Edith's tightened expression.

She averted her eyes from him and took Molly's hands. "Oh, you sweet lass. I've missed you so much."

"It's a fair question," Graham said in a low voice, smiling at the woman he loved.

Her eyes shot to his. "What?" she mouthed, the words inaudible.

He shrugged. "You didn't answer her."

Amelia was suddenly in the doorway and cleared her throat. Molly rushed out of the room and took her hand, then stuck her head back in and urged, "Say yes!"

"Shh!" Amelia insisted, giggling herself, leading Molly away from the room.

Graham continued to watch Edith, who hadn't moved from the floor.

"Graham?" she asked softly, emerald eyes wide.

"I find I want to know your answer very much," he mused, taking a few steps further into the room. "I have a distinct personal interest in it, in fact."

"You..." Edith tried, slowly getting to her feet. "You want..."

He took pity on her and smiled. "I was convinced that I would have to give something up if I ever married. There was no possible way I could ever find a woman that would be a good mother figure to Molly and would be someone I needed myself, someone I could love." He shook his head in disbelief. "Then, you came into my life, setting the whole world ablaze with your fire and your fight, your ability to attract trouble and the way you somehow still find things to smile and laugh about. I've been in love with you from the start, Edith. I was never a hero, because my motives were entirely selfish. I wanted you for myself, but I resisted. Until you came to Merrifield. Until I saw you with Molly. She adores you. Then, you sacrificed yourself for her..." His voice broke, and he cleared his throat. "You could have lost your life for her."

"My life was not in danger," she said quietly.

He shook his head fiercely once. "You don't know that. And your life could have been over in so many ways; it chills me to think about it. Yet you did it, the very thing that horrified you, for Molly."

"I would do it again, and far worse," she told him. "I love her, Graham."

His smile was warm and tender. "I know. I know you do. I can see it." Emotion clogged his throat, and he worked to swallow around it. "She told me what you call her. And what she calls you. When she talks about you, Edith, she lights up. Molly lost her parents, and I have fought for years to find ways to fill her life so she wants for nothing. Now I know what she needs, what she wants, and how to make up for her loss. It's you."

"Graham..." she whispered, getting to her feet shakily.

"You love her as much as I do," Graham went on, "and probably better. How could I not love you for loving her like that? I love you, Edith. I would fight anyone or anything in heaven, earth, or hell to have you as my wife."

Edith was crying now, the tears giving him as much pain as they did encouragement. "Oh, Graham... my reputation, the rumors..."

He laughed once. "You think, after all we have been through, that I care about anyone or anything else? The truth, or parts of it, will make its way out eventually, and a long line of people with apologies will be at our door, and perhaps we won't even answer it."

She barked a laugh at that, which made him smile.

"But I don't care, Edith. I've never cared what anybody said or thought about you, because I knew you. I could see you. When you marry me, we'll live at Merrifield anyway." He paused, then tilted his head as he added, "Except for when we live at the Scotland estate, which is sadly in need of a visit."

"Scotland?" she gasped.

He grinned, loving that he could give her this revelation now. "Did I neglect to mention I have a house there? Shameful. It was my responsibility when Matthew held the title. Estate management at the Scotland estate. I was happier there than I had been anywhere else up to that point. I grew to love Scotland." He hesitated before finishing, "I learned a fair share of the native language, as well."

Edith's already wide eyes went rounder still, and one hand flew to her mouth. "You... Did you...?"

"Edith," Graham murmured with all the love in the world, slowly coming closer, "did you think I didn't know? That you called me your heart? That I'd have felt it without knowing the language? Did you think I would not feel the same way? I did, and I do, *mo gràidh.*"

She gasped and reached for the chair nearest her for balance.

"You are my heart as well, Edith," he assured her, nearly to her now. "If you still love me, as I believe you once did, will you marry me?" Fairly certain of her answer, he let himself offer her a teasing smile. "And could you bear returning to Scotland for some months while I see to my duties there?"

Edith burst into tears, covering her face for just a moment before flinging herself into his arms. "Yes, Graham," she sobbed against him. "Oh, please, yes. Yes, I will marry you. Yes, I will go to Scotland with you. And yes, above all else, I love you."

He chuckled, kissing her hair. "I thought you might. Hoped you might. But you are constantly taking me by surprise, so I thought it best to be sure."

She pulled back with a broad smile and took his face in her

hands. "Then let me make this perfectly clear." She arched up and touched her brow to his. "I love you," she whispered before kissing him with the softness of a breeze. "I will always love you."

Graham pressed his lips to hers, sealing that vow with one of his own. Her hands linked behind his neck, pulling him to her, anchoring them together without question.

"*Tha gaol agam oirbh, agus bithidh gu bràth,*" he told her as he took her lips again and again.

I love you, I always will.

Edith clamped both hands hard against his head, her kiss turning positively scorching, dismantling every thought and barrier he'd ever had. This was the end of life as he'd known it, and the beginning of a glorious unknown.

"Yer accent needs work," Edith breathed as she finally released him, her lips grazing his jaw.

Graham chuckled, nuzzling her gently. "All the more reason to marry me. I am sadly losing my Gaelic. And I strongly suspect you are agreeing to marry me just to go back to Scotland."

Edith dusted her lips just below his ear, and his breath caught at the touch. "Well, there is a particular advantage in going to Scotland that tempts me to accept your hand beyond all reason."

"And that is?" he asked, curious, his voice more than a bit rough.

He felt her smile against his skin before she went up on her toes to whisper in his ear, "I am wild to see how you look in a kilt."

He growled a laugh and kissed her, effectively drowning her own laughter.

And there was nothing else to say for quite some time.

Epilogue

One should never make decisions when bored and alone. They will inevitably lead to regret. Especially if they are made with others who are also bored and equally alone.

-The Spinster Chronicles, 25 February 1819

"This meeting of the Spinsters, with a capital S, will now come to order. Is there any business to discuss?"

Charlotte looked around the room but saw no hands go up.

Likely because none of the other Spinsters were in the room.

"Did you expect me to answer? Because I'm not a Spinster, no matter the case of the S, and I don't have any business."

Charlotte glared at her lone companion, who stared back at her without shame. "Shut up, Hensh."

Henshaw chortled a laugh and shook his head, sipping his Madeira. "This is what I get for calling upon you? Abuse?"

"You've had worse," Charlotte muttered, looking away.

The truth of the matter was that she wished Henshaw hadn't called upon her. He was a good sort, in truth, and she was fonder of him than she was of her own brother, but having him here was simply a reminder of her situation.

She was alone. All alone.

"Have you heard from Edith?" Henshaw asked innocently, unaware of her turmoil as he propped his booted feet upon a low stool.

Charlotte nodded once, sitting forward to make herself a cup of tea. "Yes. She and Radcliffe made it to Gretna Green well and whole, as expected, and they married in a church there. Which, in my eyes, defeats the purpose of going to Gretna Green in the first place. Molly is very much enjoying the prospect of Scotland and is apparently being quite entertaining." She shrugged, adding milk and sugar to the tea.

"Well, good for them. And the other Spinsters?"

She heaved a sigh and gave her impertinent friend a look. "Married, Hensh. All married. Prue is entering her confinement, but everyone else is quite simply married."

Henshaw stared at her, eyes wide in surprise. "Heaven help us all."

Charlotte rolled her eyes and sat back, nursing her fresh cup of tea. "I am so bored, Hensh."

"I gathered that."

"I have never been bored during the Season in my entire life," she went on, ignoring his comment. "I don't... I don't know what to do."

His look was clearly an attempt at sympathy, but it failed. "Where is Sandford? He's always been very good at cheering you up, or entertaining you, or whatever you need."

Charlotte sighed at the mention of Michael. "He's away for a few weeks with his family. Besides, I cannot continue to rely upon him as though he were a performing monkey."

"Suppose not."

That made her blink in response, and she glanced over at Henshaw. Was that really all he was going to say? No suggestions, no advice, no offers to help?

Ridiculous. Completely and utterly ridiculous.

Charlotte scowled and brought her tea to her lips. "You need a wife, Hensh."

"Do I?" he replied without concern.

She nodded once as she swallowed. "You're no good to anyone as a bachelor."

Now, he frowned and looked over at her. "Have you been

speaking with my mother?"

"God forbid, I would have so many apologies to offer her for doing so." Charlotte rolled her eyes again, the cynicism not sitting well for perhaps the first time ever. "We're so boring."

"Apologies."

Charlotte shook her head and sipped more tea. "Take a wife, Hensh."

"I intend to," he assured her, making her jerk to look at him in surprise.

"Not me," Charlotte told him firmly.

Henshaw laughed once and grinned at her. "Wasn't asking."

She wasn't sure if that was supposed to make her feel better or worse. She could say, without conceit, that nearly every man in London wanted to marry her. And Henshaw wasn't asking.

But, of course, she knew that.

"People might expect it," Charlotte pointed out. "We do banter like a married couple."

Now, he laughed in earnest. "People might expect it?" he repeated. "When have you ever cared about that?"

She shrugged. "You might."

"I don't," he replied shaking his head. "Besides, I have someone in mind."

Charlotte sat up, smiling with newfound eagerness. "I thought you might."

"If she'll have me," Henshaw added, looking rather uncertain for a man so strong and imposing as he.

There was nothing to do but scoff at that. "She ought to."

He glanced over again. "Why?"

"If I were not me, and you were not you, I'd marry you myself."

Henshaw blinked, then shook his head slowly. "I wish I could make sense of that."

Charlotte waved a hand at him, an idea coming to mind with interesting clarity. "Hush." She wet her lips, then slowly sipped her tea before saying, "Perhaps I will marry, too."

The stool beneath his feet skidded as he sat up in shock. "Will you?"

She nodded, liking the thought more and more the longer it

lingered. "I think so. I refuse to be lonely. Besides, being left out has never appealed to me."

Henshaw was silent for a telling heartbeat before asking, "Whom will you wed?"

She grinned at him. "I haven't the faintest idea."

He quirked his brows, returning the smile. "Shall we wager on it?"

"Can we?" she asked with some doubt. "Hardly seems fair. You already have your intended miss; I have no candidate."

"You have a collection," he reminded her. "Surely, one of them will do."

That was certainly not likely, but she nodded all the same. "I suppose so. Very well, a wager. First one to wed wins?"

Henshaw nodded his acceptance. "I can agree to that. The prize?"

Charlotte considered for just a moment. "A hundred pounds. Or the name of our firstborn child."

"Both?" he suggested on a laugh.

Oh, why not?

"Both," she agreed.

They clinked their drinkware in a solemn vow, and each took a long sip.

Charlotte wasn't particularly settled with it, but she would certainly have much to consider now. She was tired of being alone. She was tired of being entertaining and charming, having a mass of men pretending to care what she said or thought when not a jack of them really knew her.

But she was the only one now, and she had never done all that well standing alone.

Perhaps she would marry, if she could find love as her friends had done.

But she would set aside a hundred pounds for Henshaw on the off chance she failed.

Which she truly might.

Coming Soon

Spinster
EVER
After

The Spinster Chronicles
Book Seven

"Spinster knows best."

by

REBECCA CONNOLLY

Also from Phase Publishing

Emily Daniels:

Devlin's Daughter

Lucia's Lament

A Song for a Soldier

Grace Donovan:

Saint's Ride

Laura Beers:

Saving Shadow

A Peculiar Courtship

To Love a Spy

Tiffany Dominguez:

The Eidolon

Ferrell Hornsby:

If We're Breathing, We're Serving